SIREN

Tricia Rayburn is the author of *Ruby's Slippers* and the *Maggie Bean* trilogy. Despite fearing all creatures of the deep, she's still drawn to the water and makes her home in a seaside town on eastern Long Island in America.

You can visit her online at www.triciarayburn.com

Tricia Rayburn

SIREN

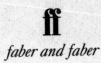

faber and faber

First published in 2011
by Faber and Faber Limited
Bloomsbury House,
74–77 Great Russell Street, London WC1B 3DA

Printed in England by CPI Bookmarque, Croydon

All rights reserved
© Tricia Rayburn, 2011

The right of Tricia Rayburn to be identified as author of this work
has been asserted in accordance with Section 77 of the Copyright,
Designs and Patents Act 1988

*This book is sold subject to the condition that it shall not,
by way of trade or otherwise, be lent, resold, hired out or otherwise circulated
without the publisher's prior consent in any form of binding or cover
other than that in which it is published and without a similar condition
including this condition being imposed on the subsequent purchaser*

A CIP record for this book
is available from the British Library

ISBN 978-0-571-26006-5

2 4 6 8 10 9 7 5 3 1

SIREN

CHAPTER I

My sister Justine always believed that the best way to deal with your fear of the dark is to pretend it's really light.

Years ago, she tried to put the theory into practice as we lay in our beds, surrounded by blackness. Protected by a fortress of pillows, I was convinced evil hid in the shadows, waiting for my breathing to slow before it pounced. And every night, Justine, a year older but decades wiser, would patiently try to distract me.

'Did you see that cute dress Erin Klein wore today?' she might ask, always starting with an easy question to gauge just how bad it was.

On rare occasions, usually when we went to bed late after a busy day, I'd be too tired to be terrified. On those nights, I'd say yes or no, and we'd have a normal conversation until falling asleep.

But on most nights, I'd whisper something along the lines of 'Did you hear that?' or 'When vampires bite, do you think it hurts?' or 'Can monsters smell fear?' At which point Justine would proceed to question two.

'It's *so* bright in here,' she'd declare. 'I can see everything – my backpack, my blue glitter bracelet, our goldfish in his bowl. What can *you* see, Vanessa?'

And then, I'd force myself to picture our room exactly as it had appeared before Mom turned off the light and closed the door. Eventually, I'd manage to forget about the evil waiting in the wings and fall asleep. Every night I thought it would never work, and every night it did.

Justine's theory was useful in combating my many other fears. But several years later, standing on top of a cliff overlooking the Atlantic Ocean, I knew it didn't stand a chance.

'Doesn't Simon look different this summer?' she asked, coming up next to me and wringing out her hair. 'Older? Cuter?'

I agreed without answering. Simon's physical transformation was the first thing I'd noticed when he and his younger brother, Caleb, had knocked on our door earlier. But that was a discussion for another time – like when we were warming up in front of the old stone fireplace at our lake house. First, we had to actually make it back to the lake house.

'Caleb, too,' she tried again. 'The number of broken-hearted girls in Maine must have, like, quadrupled this year.'

I tried to nod, my eyes locked on the swirling water and frothy foam fifty feet below.

Justine wrapped a towel around her torso and took a sideways step toward me. She stood so close I could smell the salt in her hair and pores and feel the coolness of her damp skin as though it were pressing directly against mine. Water droplets fell from the ends of her hair, plopped on the warm grey slate, and sent smaller drops bouncing onto the tops of my feet. A sudden gust of wind lifted the billowing spray up and around us, turning my shiver into a shudder. Somewhere below, Simon and Caleb laughed as they scrambled toward the steep path that would lead them through the woods and back to us.

'It's just a swimming pool,' she said. 'You're standing on a diving board, two feet above it.'

I nodded. This was the moment I'd been thinking about during the entire six-hour drive up from Boston, the moment I'd pictured at least once a day since last summer. I knew it looked scarier than it was; in the two years since we'd discovered the old trail sign marking this secluded spot far from tourists and hikers, Justine, Simon and Caleb had jumped dozens of times, never walking away with so much as a scratch. More important, I knew I'd always feel like a junior member of our little summer group if I never took the plunge.

'The pool's heated,' Justine continued. 'And once you're in it, all you have to do is kick twice, and you're at the steps leading to your comfy lounge chair.'

'Will a cute cabana boy bring me fruity drinks at this comfy lounge chair?'

She looked at me and smiled. That was it. If I was coherent enough to crack a joke, I'd already opted out.

'Sorry to say I forgot the pineapples at home,' Caleb said behind us, 'but the cabana boy's here and ready for service.'

Justine turned toward him. 'It's about time. I'm freezing!'

As she headed away from the cliff's edge, I leaned forward. Whatever relief I felt now was temporary, and my disappointment in not being able to do what I'd vowed all year long would only grow once we left Chione Cliffs. Tonight, I would lie awake, unable to sleep because of the pain I'd feel for being such a chicken, such a baby, yet again.

'Your lips are turning blue,' Caleb said.

I turned to see him shake out his favourite beach towel – the only one I'd ever seen him use, with a cartoon lobster wearing sunglasses and swimming trunks – and wrap it around Justine. He pulled her toward him and rubbed her arms and shoulders.

'Liar.' She smiled at him from under her terrycloth hood.

'You're right. They're more lavender. Or lilac. Because lips like those are just too pretty to be boring old blue. Either way, I should probably warm them up.'

I rolled my eyes and headed for my shorts and T-shirt. Justine had made her own vow for this summer – not to hook up with Caleb again, the way she had last summer and the summer before that. 'He's just a *kid*,' she'd declared. 'I'm done with high school, and he has an entire year to go. Plus, all he does is play that ratty guitar when he's not playing video games. I can't afford to waste another second on what will never amount to anything more than endless hours of making out . . . no matter how good those hours are.'

When I asked why she didn't hang out with Simon, who would be a sophomore at Bates College and was therefore more age- and intellect-appropriate, her face had scrunched.

'Simon?' she'd repeated. 'The walking, talking weather channel? The brainiac who's using college as an excuse to study cloud formations? I don't think so.'

It had taken Justine all of thirty minutes – just long enough for us to unpack the car, have a snack, and hop into Simon's old Subaru wagon – to break her promise to herself. She hadn't jumped on Caleb right away, though it was clear by the way her eyes lit up as soon as she saw him that she wanted to. She'd waited until we were in the car and down the road to throw her arms around his neck and squeeze so tight his face turned pink.

As she nuzzled against his chest now, I pulled on my

clothes and grabbed a towel. Although the sun was out and I hadn't even got wet, I still shook from the cold. This far north in Maine, temperatures in the middle of the summer didn't get much higher than the low twenties, and the biting wind always made it feel at least ten degrees cooler.

'We should get going,' Simon said suddenly, emerging from the trail mouth.

Simon might've been the elder, quieter, more studious Carmichael brother, characteristics previously complemented by a lanky frame and bad posture, but something had happened in the past year. His arms, legs and chest had filled out, and with his shirt off, I could actually see small ridges on his abdomen. He even seemed to stand taller, straighter. He looked more like a guy than a kid.

'The tide's changing, and the clouds are rolling in.'

Justine caught my eye. I knew what she was thinking: different channel, same forecast.

'But we just got here,' Caleb said.

'And what about the sunset?' Justine asked. 'Every year we say we're going to watch it up here, and every year we don't.'

Simon grabbed a shirt from his backpack, throwing it on without bothering to towel off. 'There will be lots of sunsets. Today's is going to be blacked out by that massive storm system hurtling this way.'

I followed his nod toward the horizon. Either I'd been too focused on the water to notice the sky, or the blanket of dark clouds had come out of nowhere.

'I checked before we left – the weather station said that skies would be clear until later tonight. But by the looks of it, we've got about twenty minutes to get back down the mountain before lightning strikes.' Simon shook his head. 'I wish Professor Beakman could see this.'

Before I could ask why, Caleb and Justine started talking in hushed voices and Simon crouched next to where I sat, knees against my chest, to try to warm up. 'You doing okay?' he asked.

I nodded and tried to smile. Over the years, Simon had become a protective big brother not just to Caleb but to Justine and me as well. 'A little cold and now wishing the rubber soles of my sneakers were thicker, but fine other than that.'

He pulled a maroon fleece from his backpack and handed it to me. 'It's no big deal, you know. It's just one day. We have all summer. And next summer, and the summer after that.'

'Thanks.' I looked away, embarrassed. He was sincere, but I didn't need any reminders of my failure so soon after its occurrence.

'Seriously,' he said, his voice soft but firm. 'Whenever you're ready, or never at all is totally fine.'

I pulled on the fleece, happy for the distraction.

'New plan,' Justine announced.

I took Simon's outstretched hand and jumped to my feet. Justine and Caleb had managed to tear themselves away from each other, but only long enough for Justine to drop her towels to the ground. They now stood at the edge of the cliff, holding hands and facing backward.

Justine grinned. 'Just because we're short on time doesn't mean we can't commemorate the first official day of what will surely be the best summer ever.'

'By going back to the house and warming up with hot chocolate?' I suggested.

'Silly Nessa.' Justine blew me a kiss. 'Caleb and I are going to do one more jump.'

'With a twist,' Caleb added.

As they exchanged looks, I glanced at Simon. His mouth was open, as though waiting for his brain to pick the words that would pack the greatest punch in the shortest amount of time. His new, broad back muscles tensed under the thin cotton of his T-shirt. His hands, which had hung at his sides after helping me up, clenched and froze.

'Backflips!' Justine exclaimed.

'No,' Simon said. 'No way.'

I couldn't help but smile. This was exactly what I loved – and envied – most about Justine. While I still

8

slept with a night-light, couldn't read Stephen King, and was physically incapable of making a perfectly safe cliff dive, Justine lived for the same blood-pumping rush I tried my hardest to avoid. Here we were, minutes away from being drenched and fried, and she wanted to guarantee her shot at electrocution by jumping into a whirlpool – backward.

'It'll take two minutes,' Caleb said. 'You can head down as soon as we take off, and we'll meet you on the path.'

'You know the tides get weird in weather like this,' Simon said. 'The water's already much shallower than it was for our last jump.'

Justine looked down behind her. 'It can't be that bad already. We'll be fine.'

I watched her, my beautiful elder sister, her brown hair now dry enough to fly in long wisps around her head. There was nothing I could say – once Justine's mind was made up there was no room for negotiation. As she smiled at me, her eyes shone against the dark clouds that seemed to swallow what remained of the sky.

A jagged shard of neon-white lightning tore suddenly through the air, striking near enough to make the ground rumble. The wind picked up, snatching leaves from branches and dirt from the ground. A long stick flew at me like an arrow from a bow, and I covered my head with both hands and dropped to the ground. The rain started as my legs hit rock, falling softly at first and then harder, until Simon's fleece clung to my back and cold water streamed down my face. I held still for several seconds, hoping the attack would retreat as quickly as it'd struck, but the air only grew colder, the wind stronger, the thunder louder.

Scrambling to my feet but staying close to the ground, I tried to make out the ledge through the darkness and swirling debris. When another jagged bolt ripped the horizon in half, I could see everything as though the sun were shining brightly overhead.

She was gone.

Shielding my face with my arms, I sprinted toward the cliff's edge. A third lightning bolt crashed in front of me, and I saw just how close I was to completing my mission – by running right off the rocks and into thin air.

I tried to stop, but the ground was slick. I fell hard on my back, and one leg shot forward. The silver trim of my sneaker glinted in the light of another bolt, and I saw my foot sticking over the cliff. Crying out, I reached behind me with both hands and clawed at the ground.

One one thousand, two one thousand –

Thunder roared, and the cliff quivered beneath me. Counting the seconds between lightning bolts and their grumbling aftermath usually calmed me during powerful storms – but that's because most storms weren't directly overhead.

'They're okay!'

Simon. He grabbed my waist with both hands, pulling me up and away from the drop. Then he took my hand and stepped toward the edge. After several long seconds, he squeezed my hand and pointed.

The lightning came faster now, making it easier to see the water. The pool spun as small waves pummelled surrounding boulders. Thin trees dotting the base leaned one way then snapped back, their narrow trunks like flexible straws in the wind. I shook my head, certain Simon was seeing things – and then I spotted her, a tiny sliver of white inching through the darkness. Caleb's arm was around her as they half ran, half crawled across the rocks toward the trail.

She was okay. Of *course* she was okay.

Simon looked at me to make sure I'd seen them, and then pulled me back. Somehow, my feet managed to move, and I hurried after him. He grabbed Justine's and Caleb's towels from the ground, then darted across the clearing and into the mouth of the overgrown trail. The branches and roots we'd lifted and stepped over on our way up now slapped and tripped us, but we didn't slow down. My heart slammed against my chest, and I tried to ignore the feeling that, as we ran through the woods, something or someone ran after us even faster.

About a quarter of a mile down, our path merged with another I hadn't noticed on the way up. I wouldn't have noticed it now, except Simon veered suddenly back and to the left.

I stopped short when I saw the reason for the unexpected detour.

Justine. She was in Caleb's arms, and a thick trail of blood trickled from a gash on her knee, wound down her calf, and ended at her foot.

It's just dirt, or seaweed –

'Nessa.' As Simon took her from Caleb, she reached for my hand and kissed it. 'I'm fine, promise. I could've made the trip myself, but someone wanted to play hero.'

'I've got stuff in the car,' Simon said, starting toward the main trail with Justine in his arms.

I looked at Caleb. His face was so tense as he watched them go it was hard to imagine the laughing, cocky boy who'd flirted with Justine only minutes earlier.

'Your sister.' He shook his head and looked at me.

'I know.' We both did. It wasn't his fault. Or mine, or anyone else's. If Justine wanted to run naked through circles of fire, she would. You could wait nearby with a bathrobe and fire extinguisher, but that was the best you were going to do.

We started after them. The longer we ran, the lighter the rain fell. The thunder grew softer, and the seconds between rumbles longer. Even the wind died down from powerful gusts to a normal summer breeze. By the time we reached Simon's old green Subaru parked to the side of the dirt road, the clouds had cleared enough to reveal patches of blue sky.

'See?' Justine called as we ran toward them. She sat on the floor of the open hatchback, swinging both legs back and forth as Simon bandaged the injured one. 'It's just a scratch.'

'It's not just a scratch,' Simon said, 'but it's not going to require a trip to the emergency room.'

Caleb placed one hand on her neck and kissed her forehead. 'Baby . . . you have to be careful.'

She opened her mouth, but then closed it when Caleb's hand moved to her cheek. As his thumb moved gently against her skin, she tilted her head, and her eyes softened.

'You know I'm all for a little adventure, but I'm gone if anything were ever to –'

'I know.' She slid his hand from her cheek and kissed his palm. 'I'm sorry. I know.'

I watched this exchange, a combination of relieved and puzzled. I was glad she was okay and thought it sweet that Caleb was so concerned, but before today, they hadn't seen each other since our last trip north at Christmas. They certainly seemed pretty emotionally connected for two people who occasionally made out.

Which made me think that the making out was exceptionally good, or that exciting near-death experiences just brought people together. I wouldn't know the effects of either possibility.

'You'll need to wash it out,' Simon said, securing Justine's bandage. 'But this will get you home.'

'Thank you so much, Dr Carmichael.' Justine took Caleb's hand and hopped to the ground, landing on her good foot. 'Do I get a lollipop?'

Simon gave her a look which prompted Caleb to lead her around the side of the car and into the back seat.

I helped Simon gather gauze and medical tape. 'We really got things started early this year, huh?'

His hands froze, then pushed down the first-aid kit contents and closed the case. He looked at me, his eyes locking on mine as if there was something he wanted to say, but didn't know if he should. Finally, he reached over to squeeze my shoulder. 'There's an old blanket in the front seat if you want to dry off.'

He closed the hatchback and headed for the driver's seat. I looked once more to the sky, which was now as blue as it had been when we'd arrived, then rounded the other side of the car and climbed in the passenger seat. Inside, I peeled off the fleece while Simon slouched in his seat, and Caleb and Justine did who knew what quietly in the back.

'So . . .' I said when no one had moved or spoken a few minutes later. 'What *was* that?'

Simon looked at me, then out the windscreen, toward the trail. He laughed once and let out a long, deep breath. 'That was Chione Cliffs, welcoming you back.'

I shifted in my seat, knowing what I would find when I looked behind me.

Justine, tucked under Caleb's arm with her injured leg propped up on a folded wool blanket, was grinning from ear to ear.

'What a rush,' she said happily.

'What a ruse.'

'A ruse?' Justine held up her plate as Dad came around with another platter of grilled steak. 'What does that mean?'

Dad speared two slices of meat with a fork, then looked over the deck railing, toward Lake Kanasacka. 'Ruse. An act of shifty deception, usually intended to avoid capture.'

'I know what the word *means*, Daddy. But you really think I scratched my leg climbing rocks on the beach because I wanted to avoid abduction? Are all kidnappers turned off by a little blood? And who's doing the kidnapping? Loony lifeguards? Crazed seashell hunters? The elusive Winter Harbor yeti?'

15

I smiled into my mug of hot tea. There *was* one person who'd probably kidnap Justine if he had the chance, and given earlier observations, she'd probably go willingly. I couldn't joke about this aloud, though, as our parents still thought of Caleb and Simon as the same 'sweet Carmichael boys' they'd known since the boys were babies. They knew we spent a lot of time together during the summer, but they definitely didn't know what one half of our little group had done with much of that time in recent years. And Justine had made it clear that she wanted to keep it that way.

'The elusive Winter Harbor yeti, huh?' Dad dropped a steak onto Justine's plate and replaced the platter on the closed grill. 'Is that what they're calling me now?'

Justine and I looked at each other across the table and laughed. Dad was six feet four and usually stooped forward – something he attributed to dealing with lower door frames 'back in the day', but which was more likely a result of forty years spent at a computer. His slouched yet imposing frame combined with a head of frizzy white hair and a full matching beard did resemble the legendary creature.

'What happened to Happy Papi? Top Pops? Rad Dad?' He sat down and poured himself another glass of red wine. 'And what was the most recent one? Large, something?'

'Big Poppa,' Justine said in mock exasperation, like she couldn't believe he'd forget one of her pet names for him.

'Right. I still don't know whether I should be offended by that one.' He rubbed his round belly. 'But I actually thought of another one on the drive up that I think we should incorporate into our daily conversation as soon as possible.'

'We'll take it into consideration,' Justine said.

Dad took a roll from a basket in the centre of the table, tore off a chunk, and popped it in his mouth. 'King.'

'King?' Justine said. 'King what?'

He shrugged. 'That's it. Just King.'

'Not bad . . . but that would technically make Mom Queen. And I really don't think she's cool being second in command – even just by title.' Justine looked to Mom for confirmation.

Mom, who'd been sawing her steak with a knife like it was made of metal instead of meat, paused. 'I can't believe you're still doing this.'

'The girls are getting older,' Dad admitted, 'but I'll always be their Big Poppa. Until old age catches up with me and I start to shrink. Then I'll be . . . Little Big Poppa? Medium Poppa? Poppa Grande?'

'You can be Grand Master of the Universe for ever. That's not the point.'

Dad raised his eyebrows, considering the title

suggestion instead of the fact that Mom wasn't amused. Not that that fact was out of the ordinary, since Mom was rarely amused. Of the two, she'd always been the more serious one, the disciplinarian. She was president of Franklin Capital, a financial services firm in Boston, and Dad was a writer and professor of American literature at Newton Community College. The characteristics required for their respective professions usually translated to their home life.

'Then what is the point, my sweet?' Leaning across the table, he gently removed the knife and fork from her hands and took over the seemingly strenuous task of cutting her steak.

'That you're eighteen.' Mom frowned at Justine. 'That you're an adult. That mistakes you make now actually matter.'

'So I might have a small scar for the rest of my life,' Justine said. 'Big deal.'

'You're lucky to have walked away with only that.'

Justine glanced at me, the smile she'd worn since climbing into Simon's Subaru fading. 'Mom, we got caught in a rainstorm and slipped on some rocks. Accidents happen.'

'They do. And if you were eight years old and had really been at the beach, I'd kiss your knee and it'd be all better.'

'Wow!' I exclaimed, pointing to the lake. 'The

Beazleys finally got a new canoe. It's so . . . long.'

Finished cutting Mom's steak, Dad replaced the knife and fork on her plate and leaned toward me. 'A for effort, kiddo.'

Justine shook her head. 'I'm confused.'

I tried to catch Mom's eye so that I could silently beg her not to say what she was about to, but it was no use. She was on a mission – and about to get me into serious trouble with the one person I always wanted to keep happy.

'You weren't at the beach, Justine. You were at Chione Cliffs.'

I held my breath. Mom's words were followed by silence.

'That's impossible,' Justine said finally, picking at the napkin in her lap. 'I've never even heard of such a place.'

'Really? Then which dangerous, life-threatening cliff was your sister referring to?'

I closed my eyes and sat back. I didn't have to look at Justine to know she stared at me now, her expression a combination of surprise, doubt and hurt.

'Last summer,' Mom continued, 'you were out and Vanessa was here, upset. I asked what was wrong, and she told me how you had found the cliff, how you go there every year, and how she felt awful for being too scared to jump.'

'Speaking of, maybe we should all take a quick dip in the lake after dinner,' Dad said lightly. 'What do you say?'

'We said we wouldn't tell,' Justine said to me, like we were the only ones at the table. 'We said it was just our thing. That's what made it so special.'

I looked up. 'I know, I –'

'Don't blame Vanessa,' Mom said.

As Justine slouched in her chair, Dad buttered a roll, and Mom drained her wine glass, I frantically searched my brain for the words that would make this better. I wanted to tell Justine that I hadn't meant to say anything, that I was just frustrated with myself after our trip to the cliffs last summer, and that that had made me frustrated with myself for being afraid of everything else in the sixteen years before. I wanted to tell her that Mom was just in the wrong place at the wrong time, and that she promised she wouldn't say anything, so long as I did my best to try to keep Justine from jumping whenever we went again – and that I hadn't done that, because I would never want to stop my sister from doing something that made her happy. And I wanted to tell her that I was sorry, so sorry, for all of it.

But I couldn't. I couldn't tell her anything. Maybe it was because I was scared it would come out all wrong, but the words just weren't there.

'And what are your plans with this Carmichael boy?' Mom asked.

My eyes widened as I looked from Mom to Justine. I definitely hadn't said a word to anyone about Caleb.

Justine's face reddened. 'My *plans*?'

'Between diving off cliffs and doing who knows what with a nice boy who wouldn't know the difference between a video-game system and a laptop, you're risking your entire future. Dartmouth. Medical school. Years of success and happiness.'

'Isn't the steak delicious?' Dad asked. 'Not too rare, not too crispy.'

'I don't think a little fun is going to ruin my life.' Justine pushed back her chair, her blue eyes flashing in the grey dusk. 'And besides, some things are more important than an overrated Ivy League education and a high-paying job.'

'Big Poppa has an idea,' Dad said, licking his fingers. 'How about we call it a draw for now and pick up again tomorrow, after a good night's sleep?'

Justine stood up, her good knee hitting the table and rattling our plates and glasses. She leaned toward me as she passed, and her eyes seemed even brighter than usual, as though lit from behind. She turned her head so Mom and Dad couldn't see her face, and said one word, just loud enough for me to hear.

'*Boo.*'

Warm tears sprang to my eyes. Stunned, I watched her cross the deck and enter the house, letting the screen door slam behind her.

'I just want her to stay on track,' Mom said after a pause.

'And I just want someone to help me paint the front porch,' Dad said. 'I was teasing about her using the scratch as a ruse to get out of it, but now I really might be rolling solo.'

Ignoring them both, I looked toward the lake.

Boo. Not 'Thanks a lot,' or 'You've really done it this time,' or even 'You're on your own now,' all of which probably would've brought tears to my eyes, but wouldn't have made my skin tingle like that one word did.

And there was no way of knowing it then, but that was the very last word Justine would ever say to me. In the days and weeks that followed, I would replay the moment over and over again in my head, seeing her blue eyes, hearing her soft voice, and, for some reason, smelling salt water . . . as though she still stood next to me on top of the cliff, her skin and hair wet with the sea.

CHAPTER 2

When I heard the first siren, I was standing in the sand, watching the water reach for my bare feet. A biting wind whipped my skirt around my calves and carried the sounds of Mom, Dad and Justine laughing down the beach. The soft wail began as soon as the froth wound around my ankles, just as it had nearly every night for two years. Only this time, it didn't fade when I was pulled out and dragged under. It grew louder. Closer. And it was joined by another siren, and another, until I could hear them and see red, white and blue lights flashing like the police cars had driven right into the ocean.

'You should really eat something.'

I blinked. The flashing lights were gone, replaced by green coffee mugs. Next to me, a man in a grey suit leaned against the counter and shoved a pastry into his mouth.

'Good food can be the best medicine,' he said.

Medicine. Like I was just sick. Like this was a hallucination that would fade to normal once my fever dropped.

'Thanks.' Trying to erase the lingering image of the

23

accident, the one I'd been reliving in my sleep since the cops pulled up to tell us they'd found Justine, I grabbed a mug and turned toward the coffeemaker.

It wasn't his fault. He was one of Mom's colleagues. He didn't know me and he hadn't known Justine, but he was obligated to say *something* as he enjoyed Italian pastries with other co-workers. What else was there? It's such a tragedy? She had her whole life before her? What do you make of the Red Sox so far this season?

'The voice of one crying in the wilderness,' I said when I turned around and he was still there. Not knowing what to say was one thing. Hanging around for another shot was a bit much.

'Excuse me?' he said.

I held up my mug. '*Vox clamantis in deserto*. Dartmouth's slogan. Kind of appropriate, don't you think?'

'Vanessa, dear, will you please help me with these muffins?' Mom took me by the elbow and led me across the kitchen. 'Sweetie, I know this is difficult, but we have guests. I would appreciate it if you could be a pleasant hostess.'

'I'm sorry,' I said when we stopped at a counter lined with trays of pastries. 'I just don't know what to say. Part of me wants to lock myself in the bathroom for the rest of the day, and another part wants –'

'Did you eat?' she asked, poking at a scone. 'Here, have a maple walnut.'

I took the scone, not sure what to say. Mom had cried for five days straight – from the moment the police officers had knocked on the lake-house door to the moment we'd pulled up to our brownstone – and had been in dry-eyed, party-planning mode ever since. She hadn't even cried at the funeral, when the collective weeping of Justine's friends and classmates had made birds fly from the trees and the priest shout his prayers. I hadn't cried at the funeral either – or any time before or since – but my reasons were very different.

'Can you check on your father?' Mom lifted a tray from the counter. 'I haven't seen him in an hour, and the guests are starting to wonder.'

I wanted to say that if our 'guests' didn't understand Big Poppa's need for a little downtime, then perhaps they should find another party, but she spun on one heel and disappeared through the kitchen door before I could.

I dropped the scone in the trash and headed back to the coffee-cup cabinet, keeping my eyes lowered to avoid any more helpful healing tips from Mom's co-workers. The Dartmouth mugs still lined the first shelf, where Mom had displayed them as soon as she'd received the shipment of college paraphernalia two weeks before.

'*Vox clamantis in deserto*,' Justine had read aloud then. 'I love how these places try to impress with their love of dead languages. I mean, why bother? Why not just say, "Thanks for shelling out another fifteen dollars for functional proof of the fact that you're important enough to drop two hundred thousand dollars on a chance for your rich kid to get drunk with other rich kids in the middle of nowhere"?'

'Well,' I'd said, 'probably because that wouldn't fit on a keyring.' Of which Mom had ordered two dozen to distribute around the office.

I grabbed the centre Dartmouth mug and filled it with coffee. Still keeping my eyes lowered, I took both cups and hurried across the kitchen toward the back staircase door.

The back staircase had always been Justine's and my escape route – from cocktail parties, dinners and even parental arguments. As I climbed I thought about the last time we'd sought staircase refuge, during Mom's annual Christmas party. While two hundred guests downed champagne, Justine and I sat on the steps, her down comforter draped across our shoulders, sucking on candy canes and getting tipsy on eggnog. That night we'd tried to pretend that we weren't hiding from Mom's drunken co-workers in our brownstone in the middle of Boston, but rather hiding from Mom and Dad in our lake house in Maine, breathless with excitement as we waited to see Santa fall down the old stone chimney.

I climbed the steps slowly now, comforted by the dim light and dark panelling. I blocked the thought as soon as it entered my head, but for a fleeting moment, I was aware of just how strange it was to be there . . . alone. I hadn't been anywhere alone all week, and certainly nowhere I'd only ever been with Justine.

Reaching the landing, I stopped and waited. After a few seconds, I blinked, and waited again. Nothing. Even revisiting one of Justine's and my favourite places couldn't bring on the waterworks.

I continued down the hallway, my heartbeat quickening. I hadn't been inside Justine's room since preparing to leave for Maine the week before, when I'd watched her try on her entire wardrobe as she searched for the perfect thing to wear on the drive north. By the time we'd left, skirts, sundresses and tank tops had blanketed her floor like seaweed on the shore after a receding tide. Now I wasn't sure what I was more afraid of: that the clothes would still be there, exactly as she'd left them . . . or that they wouldn't be.

Closing my eyes, I turned toward the door. I reached one arm forward until my hand found the knob. The brass was cool beneath my fingers, and I waited for my skin to adjust to the temperature before tightening my grip.

It's just Justine. It's just her stuff. Everything will look just as she left it, because she's coming back. Soon, we'll return to the lake house and everything will go back to the way it's supposed to be.

I opened the door. A small sound escaped through my parted lips.

It wasn't my deeply anchored fears floating to the surface. And it wasn't the fact that, compared to the hallway, Justine's room was as hot as an oven.

It was the salt water. The smell was so strong, the air so thick with moisture, if I didn't open my eyes, I'd think I stood at the ocean's edge.

'You get used to it.'

I opened my eyes. Big Poppa sat on the floor in the middle of the room.

'There must be a problem with the pipes. I'll call the plumber tomorrow.' He sounded exhausted and looked it, too. The corners of his mouth drooped toward his chin. His blue eyes were dull, and his shoulders slumped forward. Our strapping yeti had lost his strength.

'Big Poppa,' I said, stepping into the room, 'I know this is difficult, but we have guests. I would really appreciate it if you could be a pleasant host.'

One corner of his mouth lifted as he took the Dartmouth mug. He knew the words weren't mine. 'Your mother's coping, Vanessa. We all are.'

I didn't say anything as I sat down next to him. Until now, the only thing my mother and I had had in common was our adoration for Justine. I didn't understand why Mom worked so much, or shopped so often, or tried so hard to impress strangers. I didn't understand why of the hundred people downstairs, only a dozen or so would be able to tell Justine and me apart in the annual Sands family Christmas card. Most of what Mom did didn't make sense to me. But Dad thought she was the sun and the moon and the stars all in one, and for that reason, I kept quiet.

'She's beautiful,' Dad said after a few minutes.

I followed his gaze to the photo-covered bulletin board hanging over Justine's desk and willed my eyes to water. Because there she was. White-water rafting in the Berkshires. Horseback riding on the Cape. Hanging out in the quad at Hawthorne Prep. Hiking Mount Washington in New Hampshire. And in my favourite picture, the one she'd had blown up to a 5 × 7 that was at the centre of the collage, fishing in our old red rowing boat on the lake in Maine – with me.

'I remember taking that one,' Dad said. 'I wondered what she'd said to make you giggle like that.'

He'd taken the picture from the dock behind the house when our backs were to the camera. Justine's head was turned slightly toward me, and mine was tilted toward the sky. My shoulders were pulled up near my ears, a physical reflex that occurred whenever something made me laugh until tears cascaded down my cheeks.

29

I blinked. Nothing.

'I figured it was girl talk,' he continued. 'Make-up. Boys. Top-secret stuff I was better off not knowing.'

'Probably,' I said. 'Considering her romantic revolving door, the girl talk about boys usually lasted a while.'

'I still don't understand why she needed all that attention,' he said thoughtfully. 'She was so bright, so beautiful and talented. But it was like she didn't believe it unless a different boy was telling her every week.'

I didn't say anything. Justine didn't *need* the attention – she just got it.

We sipped our coffee in silence. After a moment, he released a long sigh. 'I should go and play host for a while,' he said, climbing to his feet. 'You'll be okay?'

I nodded. He rested one hand lightly on my head before leaving the room and closing the door.

I blinked and waited again. When the tears still didn't come, I turned back to the centre photo and thought about what Big Poppa had just said. It didn't make sense. But then, nothing made much sense now.

The police claimed that it had been an accident, that Justine had simply jumped off the cliff at the wrong time. It was dark. The tides were high. Chief Green said the water was so deep and the currents so strong, Triton himself, the Greek god of the sea who could turn the waves up and down with one blow into his conch shell, wouldn't have been able to hold his own. The medical examiner had agreed.

I didn't.

Yes, Justine was a thrill seeker. And that night, she might've wanted to prove a point. But she was too smart to do something so careless.

As my eyes travelled across the bulletin board, I noticed dark thin lines between the photos. It looked as though someone had taken a Magic Marker to the bulletin board padding . . . except the line wasn't drawn on the ivory satin that covered the rest of the board. The background behind the photos was white.

I stood up and went to the desk for a better look, and saw that the lines were actually words.

Name. Email. Phone Number. Caucasian. Parent 1 and Parent 2. Early Decision. Financial Aid. Campus. Degree. Secondary School. ACT. SAT. Extracurricular. Awards/Honours.

I was about to pull out the first purple pushpin when I felt uncomfortable. Guilty, even. Like I'd been snooping through Justine's desk in search of her diary and was now going to read about secret kisses and private conversations she wanted to keep to herself.

'I'm sorry,' I whispered, before pulling out the first pushpin.

Seconds later, the fifty or so versions of Justine's smile were gone. I stepped back to take in the entire board.

There were bumper stickers. Seven of them, collected by Mom on her trips with Justine to Harvard, Yale, Princeton, Brown, Stanford, Cornell and Dartmouth. They formed a wide collegiate circle around a spreadsheet and a printout of the common application.

The spreadsheet listed colleges and had four columns for corresponding deadlines, submission dates and response dates. The deadline column was filled with numbers written in Mom's neat handwriting; the others were empty. The application was blank except for Mom's notes and response suggestions. My eyes quickly fixed on the centre page: the personal essay. A green Post-It was attached to the top, on which Mom had suggested Justine write about the person she was and the person she wanted to become.

Justine's response was brief.

I'm sorry, I don't know.
But neither do you.

I stared at the words. It might've taken me longer than it should've to find them, but I knew instantly what they meant: Justine wouldn't have gone to Dartmouth in the fall. She wouldn't have gone to Harvard, Yale, Princeton, Brown, Stanford or Cornell either. Because before you attended your future alma mater, you had to apply. And apparently Justine hadn't applied anywhere.

Downstairs people were gathered to celebrate Justine's life, to reflect on her lost potential and all the things she would never do, the places she would never go. I was right about one thing: not one of the unfamiliar guests pigging out on pastries had any idea who Justine really was. But I was alarmingly wrong about another.

Neither did I.

A door slammed down the hallway, jolting me back to the present. I took the essay off the board and the photo of Justine and me in the rowing boat from the desk, re-hung the other photos and hurried across the room.

I was about to bolt into the hallway when my hands flew toward my face, covering my nose and mouth.

Salt water. I'd grown used to the smell while in the room, but it was stronger by the door – overpowering, like a tidal wave had already swallowed the rest of the house and was waiting outside Justine's door for an invitation to come inside. It was so strong, I looked down to keep my head from spinning.

'Oh, no.' I lowered my hands from my face. 'Oh, Justine . . .'

A crumpled beach towel was pushed up against the closet door. It was thick and red . . . with a grinning cartoon lobster covered in bits of green and black sea-weed.

33

Caleb's beach towel – the one he'd wrapped Justine in before pulling her to him on top of the cliffs last week. It was now here, dry and stiff with salt, in Boston.

I sank to my knees and picked up the towel. She'd been home. Some time between storming out during dinner on the lake-house deck and late the following morning, when her body was found, Justine had returned to Boston.

It's okay, I told myself, trying not to imagine the crimson terrycloth draped across Justine's shoulders. *Everything's okay.*

Except that it wasn't. It was so far from it, I couldn't even pretend that the beach towel was anything other than what it was: more evidence that, as well as I had thought I knew my sister, someone else had known her better. And that, for whatever reason, she'd wanted it that way.

CHAPTER 3

'Are you insane?'

I lifted my duffle bag from the pavement and shoved it in the trunk of Dad's Volvo. 'Are you sure you're not going to need it?' I asked, as though Mom hadn't just called down from the front stoop where she stood, in bare feet and a cashmere robe, watching us disapprovingly.

'I mean, really,' she tried again. 'Have you both lost your minds?'

Dad rested his bowl of Cheerios on the rusty roof of the car and helped cram in my bag. 'Haven't needed it in months. I'll be fine for another few weeks.'

'Few *weeks*?' Mom's voice shot up an octave.

I placed my hands next to Dad's on top of the trunk and pulled down. When the compartment clanged shut, I rounded the car and stood at the bottom of the steps leading to the front door.

'I'm not sure how long I'll be gone,' I said. 'It could be a few days, a week, or longer.'

'I just don't understand why you're going at all. After everything that's happened –'

'You're going back to work. Dad's going to be writing.

What would I do if I stayed?'

'See your friends,' Mom said. 'Go to movies. Read and relax.'

'Read and relax?' I shook my head. 'I can't.'

'Jacqueline,' Dad said gently, 'Vanessa needs to do what she needs to do. I know it's hard to let our little girl go, but she is seventeen.'

'She's seventeen, but she's a *baby*,' Mom declared, like she was pleased someone besides her had finally raised this very important point. 'Vanessa, sweetie, you've never been anywhere by yourself. And the furthest you've driven is to the Framingham Mall.'

I hurried up the steps, stopping on the one below hers. 'I'll be back soon. Promise.'

As she grabbed me in a tight hug, I felt guilty. And nervous. And sad and scared and confused. Part of me was even tempted to run back into the house, jump into bed and sleep until enough time had passed that I could let it go. Maybe I could even pretend that this was just another of those nightmares I feared every time I turned off the lights.

'The fluids are good,' Dad said before I could change my mind. 'Wipers are on the right of the steering wheel; headlights are on the left. She's old, but she'll get you where you need to go.'

'You rock, Big Poppa.' I jogged down the steps and got in the car.

'Back atcha, kiddo.' He closed the door after me and peered through the open window. 'One more thing. Like any geezer in good health, she gets tired – especially on hills. If she starts to give, ease up on the gas. If you try to gun it, she'll probably roll backward.'

'Well, that's comforting.'

I watched Dad turn to Mom, who now stood next to him. He put one arm around her waist and kissed the tip of her nose.

'You have your cell phone?' she asked. 'And directions?'

I lifted my phone and a stack of Google Map printouts from the passenger seat. 'I also have a full tank of gas, and your Visa, Mobil and Triple A cards. And the key to the house, and instructions for turning on the water and electricity.'

'Please call when you get there,' Mom said as I started the car. 'And maybe along the way, when you get tired, or if there's nothing on the radio, or –'

'I'll call before I get there, and when I get there.'

Mom opened her mouth to make more requests, but then closed it and covered it with one hand.

Her points about my not being anywhere by myself and never driving further than twenty miles from home made me nervous, too. I didn't know how it'd feel to drive on Interstate 95 without Mom, Dad and Justine. Or to pass the sailboat-shaped WELCOME TO WINTER HARBOR sign at the entrance to town, or EDDIE'S

37

ICE CREAM right after that – and not stop for rocky-road waffle cones. Or to drive up to the lake house, all locked and boarded up after our sudden departure only days before.

As I put the Volvo in drive and slowly pulled away from my parents, depriving them of the second of their two daughters in less than two weeks, there was only one thing I did know. And that was that if ever there was a time to grow a thick skin, this was it.

Six hours and four phone calls home later, I sat in the Volvo, staring at the lake house.

By this time each summer, the house was filled with life and noise. Now, it looked strangely abandoned. The front door was closed, as were the windows, their curtains pulled and shades drawn. The ceramic planters lining the front steps that should've held Mom's geraniums were filled with weeds. Dad's favourite flag, the one with the pair of ducks that marked the official arrival of summer, sat on a shelf somewhere in the garage.

Still, despite the sad exterior, I could see her. Throwing open the car door and running down the front path. Dashing from one end of the porch to the other, peeking in windows. And, this last time, pausing at one end of the porch and leaning over the railing toward the Carmichaels' house. Her purple sundress had danced around her ankles in the breeze, and her long, dark hair had fallen over one shoulder and to the side of her face, blocking out the smile I knew was there.

I'd glanced next door then to see if Caleb was outside, waiting for her. I didn't see him but knew he was. He'd probably crouched behind a bush – out of sight, per Justine's wishes – for hours, just waiting for a glimpse of her. I'd thought that that must be a very nice feeling, to know so certainly that someone was waiting for you.

It was one I could've used right then.

I glanced in the rearview mirror when a burst of light flashed behind me. Seeing nothing but our duck-shaped mailbox and a bunch of trees, I turned in my seat to look through the back window.

Silly Nessa. Imagining things before the sun's even set?

I turned back at the sound of Justine's voice darting through my head.

'Time to find Caleb,' I said loudly, opening the door.

I had one sneaker in the dirt when my eyes fell on the folded newspaper lying in the driveway. It was the *Winter Harbor Herald*, a free weekly that mainly served as a guide to restaurants and shops for tourists. The *Herald* tended to break one major news story every summer, when the cover article wasn't about the most romantic sunset spots or the best places to get a true Winter Harbor meal, but about underage drinkers or lobster-cage robbers. Those stories usually came toward the end of the summer, when everyone had already eaten and shopped and could apparently handle a taste of Winter Harbor's underbelly.

This summer, the bad news couldn't wait.

Winter Harbor Tragedy: Girl, 18, Falls to Death at Start of Peak Season.

I stared at the headline, its seriousness emphasised by the large, black font. Directly underneath was Justine's senior portrait. Despite the reason for her picture being on the front page, I was still struck by her beauty. Her dark hair fell in loose waves past her shoulders, her eyes were bright, and her smile was warm and friendly.

I thought of my own senior portrait, which I was supposed to have taken at the end of the summer. It would never be as striking as Justine's, since everything about my appearance fell somewhere in the middle: my long hair wasn't quite brown or black; my eyes weren't quite blue or green; my skin could look creamy or pasty, depending on the light. The only thing that didn't change was my smile, which, though it occurred only rarely, always brightened the rest of my face . . . but with my main source of happiness gone, I might as well pose for the picture with my back to the camera.

I picked up the newspaper as I got out of the car. I didn't want to read about Justine, but I also couldn't leave her in the driveway. I folded the paper and slid it into the back pocket of my jeans.

I walked the short distance to the Carmichaels', jogged up the porch steps and rang the doorbell. As the low notes sounded inside the house, I stepped back and waited.

Caleb didn't answer. Neither did Mrs Carmichael, who usually flung open the door with a smile and arms outstretched. There wasn't even the sound of footsteps moving through the house and toward the door.

I waited a minute and rang again.

Nothing.

Holding one hand to the glass, I peered through a window into the living room. Then I crossed the porch and tried the kitchen window. The counters were clear, the table wasn't littered with comic books and copies of *Scientific American*, and the sink was free of dirty dishes.

The inside of the Carmichaels' house suggested the same thing the outside of ours did: abandonment.

They'll be back, I told myself as I headed back down the porch steps. *They're just at work. Or running errands. They'll return by dinner, at the latest.*

If that was true, I had about five hours to kill. All alone.

I wasn't about to sit in our house by myself for that long, so I took my time going back. I wandered across the Carmichaels' back yard, which had become as familiar as our own over the years. After thousands of games of hide-and-seek, I knew the lawn's every dip and rise, and the best trees to duck behind when you didn't want to be seen. In fact, when I was growing up, hide-and-seek was the only game at which I was ever better than Justine. Mostly because I preferred not to be found, while Justine lived to be seen.

I wandered to the water's edge and onto the dock. When I reached the end, I looked across the lake, then toward our dock a few yards away. My chest ached at the absence of water bottles, sunscreen and open books, all requirements of a lazy summer afternoon. The thick ropes that usually held our red rowing boat in place were still wound around their posts.

Turning away, I slid off my sneakers and socks, rolled up my jeans and sat down. It was warm in the sun; I was tempted to dangle my legs into the cool water but kept them pulled to my chest. For two years, whenever Justine promised that the small fish in Lake Kanasacka were more scared of me than I should be of them, I told her the fish didn't bother me. And what *did* bother me I kept to myself.

'Vanessa?'

He looks different this year, doesn't he?

I looked up. Simon sat in his rowing boat a few feet away, holding the oars still as he drifted toward me.

I smiled, simultaneously surprised and relieved to see him. He looked surprised, too, but didn't return my smile. After a few seconds, he lifted the oars and started rowing again.

I wanted to say hello, to ask how he was. And if I couldn't manage that, I wanted to say something that would break the ice, maybe ask about the notebooks, petri dishes and plastic vials scattered across the bottom of the boat. Justine's and my rowing boat was usually cluttered with Tupperware containers of watermelon and *US Weekly* and *People* magazines; Simon's looked like a floating lab.

When the rowing boat knocked against the dock, he took a rope and wrapped it around one of the boat's metal holds. He gathered the notebooks, dishes and vials and put them in a backpack. He seemed to be stalling, as if a few extra seconds would be enough time to figure out the right thing to say.

My pulse quickened as he stepped out of the boat. He didn't look at me as he wiped his hands on the front of his shorts, then lowered himself to the dock next to me.

'Please don't hate me,' he said after a minute.

'Hate you?'

'I wanted to come,' he said, keeping his eyes on the water below us. 'I can't tell you how much I wanted to be there for . . . your family. I just didn't know if I should. I didn't know if it was appropriate.'

The funeral. I'd been surprised when the Carmichaels didn't show. Our parents often went out to dinner during the summer, and since the Carmichaels were year-round Winter Harbor residents, they kept an eye on our lake house and checked in with my parents periodically throughout the winter. I hadn't asked Mom or Dad about their absence, figuring it was a sensitive topic due to Caleb's involvement that night.

'It's okay,' I said, touched by his concern. 'But thank you.'

His eyes narrowed and his lips turned in, like there was more he wanted to say.

'I thought you were done with school.'

He looked at me, and then at his overstuffed backpack when I nodded to it.

'Summer science project for extra credit?' I tried to keep my voice light.

'Sort of.' He tried to smile. 'I'm helping one of my professors at school with his global-warming research. The weather's been kind of weird lately, so I've been keeping track.'

I nodded and waited for more. Simon could talk about cloud formations and tidal pools and native plant species for hours – and usually did, unprompted. But when he didn't offer anything else, I hugged my knees tighter to my chest and looked out at the lake. Down the shore, happy vacationers swam, rowed and floated on inflatable tyres. My body yearned to join them while my brain scrambled for distractions. Two years ago, I would've given in to the physical urge to leap from the dock and dive underwater. Now, I could only hope it didn't last long.

'I'm looking for Caleb,' I said.

Simon looked away, toward a group of kids diving off rafts in the middle of the lake.

'He was with her that night, and I need to talk to him. I need to find out why she did it.'

'Vanessa . . . Caleb's not here.'

My stomach tightened.

'He came back here after talking to the police, grabbed some food and clothes, and left.'

'Where did he go?'

'We don't know. He didn't say . . . and he hasn't called since.'

I followed his gaze toward the kids. They laughed as they splashed and dunked one another. I wondered if Simon was thinking the same thing I was: that just a year ago, they could've been us.

'When will he be back?' I asked.

He didn't say anything as his eyes met mine. He simply looked at me like he was sorry – and like it was all he could do to keep his arms at his sides instead of reaching forward and pulling me toward him.

CHAPTER 4

'Big Poppa, the lake house is haunted.'

Somewhere in our brownstone three hundred miles away, Dad sipped his coffee.

'I didn't sleep at all last night. I didn't even come close to that fuzzy state where things can still go either way.'

'You were overly tired from travelling. Your body will give in eventually.'

'Doubtful.' I tightened the thick fleece blanket around me. 'At least not while Casper and Beetlejuice and all their fun-loving friends are here, making the floors squeak and ceilings creak all hours of the night.'

I paused, suddenly realising the strangeness of this conversation. If there were ghosts in the lake house, they weren't of the cartoon variety.

'Well,' Dad finally said, 'it's morning. You made it through the night.'

'I did,' I said. 'And I'm fine. You could fit a week's worth of groceries in the bags under my eyes, but besides that, I'm great.'

'Great, huh?'

I nodded, my eyes following the jet skiers on the water below. 'Maybe not great. But okay. I'm definitely, solidly okay.'

'You know you can come home any time. Your mother and I are here for you.'

I looked down at my fleece-wrapped feet. 'How is she?'

'Your mother's your mother, kiddo. She's hanging in there.'

'Working like a machine?'

'With an endless power supply.' He paused. 'You'll call later?'

'Promise.'

After we hung up, I watched happy vacationers play on the water until my stomach started rumbling, reminding me that I hadn't eaten much in almost two days. I went inside, turned on the TV in the living room and the radio in the kitchen, and headed for the shower.

Hurrying down the driveway ten minutes later, I glanced next door. Simon had left yesterday evening and returned at some point late in the night, but the Subaru was gone again. He'd said his parents were so upset by what had happened that they were staying with friends in Vermont for a while, and since no early-morning sounds wafted from the open windows, I assumed they were still gone.

My stomach rumbled all the way into town. In attempts to cater to urbanised tourists who were used to eating good food in a hurry, Winter Harbor offered a variety of convenient, in-and-out breakfast choices. Thankfully, big chains like Starbucks and McDonald's hadn't yet found their way to the secluded town, but there were several places that could give them solid competition if ever they did. You could get coffee and doughnuts at Java Shack, smoothies and Frappuccino knockoffs at Squeezed and egg sandwiches at Harbor Homefries. All made to order and in minutes flat, so you could be on the lake and trails in no time.

I craved a watermelon-guava smoothie and scrambled eggs, cheese and sausage on a fat kaiser roll. That was my requested combo whenever Mom and Dad went into town to pick up breakfast. But I definitely wasn't in the mood for pick-up-and-go today, and I also wanted to avoid as many of the family friends we'd made over the years as possible. So I drove down Main Street, past all the cute, convenient eateries, and kept going until the tarmac ended at a big gravel parking lot.

The lot sat next to Betty's Chowder House, a Winter Harbor institution and popular tourist destination that would give me everything I needed: food, company and anonymity among strangers. Anyone who'd been coming to Winter Harbor longer than a single summer usually avoided Betty's, so as to avoid noisy crowds of newcomers. Chances were slim that anyone here would know my family, so even if people were talking about Justine, at least they wouldn't be talking about her to me.

I slowed down a few feet before the parking-lot entrance. A guy about my age in khaki shorts and a white polo shirt jumped up from a folding chair.

'Morning!' He smiled and stepped toward the driver's-side door. 'Name?'

'Vanessa,' I said as he consulted a clipboard. 'But I don't have a reservation.'

'That's too bad. We're totally booked this morning.'

I looked through the windscreen at the two-storey grey house with Betty's signature dark mermaid silhouette swimming over the top of the front entrance. It didn't look like much from the outside, but I could see through the wide windows that the place was packed.

'You here for the Sea Witch?'

Boo.

I blinked away the image of Justine, dark hair shining and blue eyes glowing. 'Sorry – the Sea what?'

'Witch.' He nodded knowingly. 'Scrambled eggs and lobster patty with hollandaise sauce wrapped up in a buttermilk pancake and topped with cinnamon seaweed. A Chowder House favourite and guaranteed hangover cure.'

The Sea Witch was clearly to this kid what my watermelon smoothie and egg sandwich were to me, so I did my best to hide my disgust. 'You're right.' I returned his nod, then tilted my head toward him through the window and lowered my voice. 'Is it that obvious?'

'Sorry to say. Big night?'

'You have no idea.'

He glanced around. 'Give me a minute, okay?'

I watched him walk away and say something into a walkie-talkie. I could have found another sit-down breakfast place, but on top of wanting to hide out in the Betty's crowd, I was now also curious to see what all the fuss was about. Plus, my stomach felt like it was about ready to start munching on my ribs if I didn't fill it with something *fast*.

'Good news,' the guy said, jogging back. He bent forward, rested his hands on the tops of his thighs and looked at me through the open window. 'My buddy Louis is the chef. He said he'll set you up in the break room and make you whatever you want.'

'Really?' I returned the smile. 'Thanks. That was really nice of you.'

'No problem. Trust me, I've been there.'

It took me a second to remember that I was supposed to be nursing the unfortunate effects of too much night-time fun.

'So just head around the back, near the Dumpster. You'll see the staff cars.'

'Great.' I sat up straight and put the car in drive.

'I'm Garrett, by the way,' he added quickly. 'Let me know when you want to make a reservation – maybe I'll meet you.'

I waited until I was around the back of the house and out of sight before I let my mouth drop open. I was pretty sure that guy had been flirting with me, and the thought made me happier than I'd been in days – and not just because, as bad as I must have looked for him to think I needed the Sea Witch to nurse me back to health, I couldn't have looked *that* bad if he wanted to see me again.

No, what really made me happy was that if he was flirting with me – and not looking sad or uncomfortable, or saying he was sorry, or asking if I was okay – then he had no idea who I was. And that meant I was exactly where I should be.

I parked the car and headed for the back door.

'Can I help you?'

I'd just reached the cement steps and turned toward the voice behind me.

'You look lost.'

I opened my mouth to respond as a girl in a black Betty's apron appeared from behind the Dumpster, but as she walked toward me, a high-pitched note shot sharply through my head. It travelled from the top of my nose to the base of my ponytail and back again. The closer the girl got, the stronger the noise seemed to grow, until my head felt like a small bell being hit with a very large mallet.

'Not lost,' I managed, pressing my fingers against my temples. 'Just hungry. Garrett said his friend was going to help me out?'

A man's voice said, 'There's the cutie in the pony-tail.'

I released my temples. The sound had faded as quickly as it'd hit.

'How bad is it? Headache? Nausea? Is everything around you spinning at a thousand miles an hour even though you're standing still?'

I looked behind me to see a middle-aged guy in a white cooking jacket and black-and-white houndstooth-check pants smiling sympathetically. Garrett's friend. 'All of the above,' I said meekly.

He winked. 'No problem. I'll have you feeling brand new in no time.'

I followed him up the steps, glancing over my shoulder just in time to see the girl toss a bag of garbage into the Dumpster and disappear around the side of the house.

'So, what'll it be? French toast? Eggs? You name it, I'll make it.'

'Anything would be great,' I said as we made our way through the crowded kitchen.

'You should know that, as *New England* magazine's top-rated chef for seven years running, I don't do this for just anyone.' He opened the refrigerator, took out a bottle of water and handed it to me. 'I do this for Garrett.'

'Does Garrett do this often?' I took the water.

'Not before today.' He nodded across the kitchen. 'Paige, darling, will you please escort Miss Vanessa to the rear dining room?'

I turned to see a pretty girl with two long, dark braids smiling and waiting for me near a doorway.

'Welcome to Betty's,' she said over her shoulder as I followed her down a narrow hallway. 'First time here?'

'Yes.' It'd been so long it felt like the first time. 'I've heard so many good things I had to see for myself.'

'You won't be disappointed.' She stopped at a door at the end of the hallway and carefully shifted the plate, juice glass and silverware she was holding.

I lunged forward and grabbed the plate as it started to slip from her grip.

'Thanks,' she said. 'I've been here two hours, and I've already broken three coffee cups and a water jug. Not exactly the way to graduate from busgirl to waitress.'

'Probably not.'

She opened the door with her free hand and headed

up a steep staircase. 'But who knew waiting tables was so complicated? I mean, you carry plates of food and glasses of water every day at home, right? No big deal.'

'Right.'

'Wrong.' She stepped to the side when she reached the landing. 'It's *hard*. Especially when you're supposed to carry five plates at a time, all weighed down by Betty's famous mammoth portions, and your arms are as skinny as shoelaces.'

I smiled when she raised the empty juice glass and flexed.

'Seriously. That's as big as it gets.' She looked wistfully at her flat biceps.

'Maybe you can do push-ups when it's not so busy,' I offered. 'Build up your strength.'

'I wish. Betty's is never not busy.'

I looked around when I joined her on the landing. The break room was a screened-in balcony that jutted out over the pier and offered unobstructed views of the harbour and mountains.

'Best seat in the house,' she said, leading me to a plastic table in the middle of the room. 'The staff inherited it because it's right above the bar and not as romantic when the tourists get rowdy.' She smiled. 'Speaking of, where are you from?'

I started to respond just as a door slammed somewhere below.

'The dirty dishes don't clear themselves!' An annoyed voice carried up the staircase.

'That's for me.' Paige hurried across the balcony. 'Z says my inability to stop talking is even worse than my inability to carry three dishes at once without breaking two of them.'

'Z?'

'Zara,' Paige shot over her shoulder. 'God's gift to hungry diners everywhere. And my elder sister.'

As Zara lectured her from the bottom of the stairs and Paige nodded, I thought again about how nice she seemed. Genuine. In fact, I hadn't noticed it happen while we were talking, but my head felt clearer now, my hunger less painful.

'I'm so sorry, Vanessa,' she called from the landing. 'I'm about a dish away from peeling oranges at Squeezed, so I need to get down there. But enjoy your first Betty's breakfast! I'll try to get back up before you go.'

She flashed me a smile, and I noticed that her eyes were the most interesting shade of light blue; as she talked, they glinted like polished silver.

After she flew down the stairs, I watched the activity in the harbour. Commercial fishermen cast lines from the backs of small motorboats, and a half-dozen yachts bobbed in the water at the far end of the harbour. The yachts were so big, whoever owned them could probably sail from port to port, harbour to harbour, for ever, stepping on land only when they needed to stretch or load up on paper towels and toilet paper.

The thought made me think of Caleb. Where was he calling home now? Why was he hiding – or running? How did no one know where he was? How long could he keep it up without anyone's help?

I wasn't sure why his parents weren't searching the state for him, but since they weren't, then I would. I had to. Not only because he was the only person who had the answers I needed, but also because Justine wouldn't have wanted him wandering around, miserable and alone.

But first . . . breakfast.

'Here you are, my dear,' Louis said, coming onto the balcony with a round tray piled with plates and bowls. 'French toast with triple-berry compote, oatmeal with honey, eggs Florentine, maple bacon and fresh watermelon cubes.'

I followed his finger as he pointed out each dish. 'I don't know what to say.'

'Just enjoy.' He pulled a bud vase with a single daisy from his jacket pocket, placed it on the tray and headed toward the stairs. 'And try not to have quite as much fun tonight.'

Despite wanting to eat slowly so that I could savour every bite while delaying my departure, the food was gone before I was even aware that my hunger pains had started to subside. It wasn't until I was using my finger to wipe up the extra maple syrup pooled in the middle of the bacon plate that I realised I was no longer alone on the balcony. Three guys in black trousers and white T-shirts sat in chairs facing the north side of the harbour, drinking coffee and talking.

'I'm telling you,' said the blond on the end. 'It's just like that girl.'

That girl. They could've been talking about anyone, but I knew immediately who he meant. Just by his tone, and the way he said 'that girl,' like she wasn't a real person but some nameless, faceless character regurgitated in evening news clips.

Justine.

'No way,' said the guy in the middle. 'Totally different situation.'

'How?' demanded the third guy. 'How is it different?'

'For starters, he was an old rich guy, and she was a young, gorgeous model type.'

I stared at the pool of maple syrup, my face growing warm. He *was*. She *was*.

'For another, he suffocated, and she suffered a blunt trauma to the head.'

I swallowed. Blunt trauma to the head was the medical examiner's official cause of Justine's death.

'But most obviously, he washed ashore after his boat capsized, and she jumped off a cliff.'

I held my breath and waited for one of the other

two guys to disagree. *She didn't jump*, I silently begged them to argue. *She fell, or she was pushed. Girls like that don't just jump for no reason.*

'And?' prompted the third guy.

'And, dude, you clearly need more coffee. He was an accident. She was a suicide.'

I dropped the fork I didn't realise I was still holding. It clattered against the porcelain. 'Sorry,' I said, when they all looked at me curiously.

'Anyway,' continued the guy in the middle as they turned back toward the water, 'like I said – totally different.'

'I don't buy it,' said the blond. 'They both die in the water, wash up within half a mile of each other, and are found only eight days apart? It's too coincidental.'

'So what? Some psycho fisherman is using people for bait? Trying something new in preparation for the annual Winter Harbor Shark Tournament?'

The blond shook his head and looked out at the harbour. 'I don't know. But it's messed up – and getting in the way of my surfing, which is really unfortunate.'

'Kind of hard to stand up when you're as stiff as the board you're riding,' agreed the guy in the middle.

It was good that they ended their break then and headed back down the stairs. I didn't know what would've come flying out of my mouth if they hadn't, but I could tell from the burning in the bottom of my stomach that it wouldn't have been pleasant.

After their voices faded completely, I got up and crossed the balcony. I picked up the *Winter Harbor Herald* they'd left on the floor and sank into one of the chairs.

Paul Carsons, 45, Found Dead on Mercury Isle: #23 on Forbes 500 Leaves Behind Wife, Three Daughters.

I scanned the article. Thanks to his discovery of an all-natural caffeine alternative popular in energy drinks, Paul Carsons was very rich. His boat, *Perseverance*, which, judging by the photo of the wreckage once looked a lot like the yachts at the far end of the harbour, had capsized. Most interesting, at least to me, was that his body had been found very close to where Justine's had been. And in the article Chief Green called the weather and water conditions so extreme 'even Triton himself couldn't have held his own'.

I turned the page, and my eyes fell on a picture of Paul Carsons, his wife and their three daughters sitting on a blanket at the beach, and then to the caption underneath:

Carsons and his family bought a vacation home in Winter Harbor last year. This was to have been their first full summer in town.

My eyes lingered on 'was to have been' until a drop of water landed on the words, causing the black print to blur. I thought I might actually be crying – finally pushed over the edge by this new tragedy and physically grieving the way I should have started to days ago – but then the wind shifted. A soft spray blew through the window screens, sending more droplets onto the paper and across my bare arms and legs.

Outside, the sky had grown darker. The harbour, which had been as smooth and still as ice, was choppy. Sails were already being lowered and fishing boats brought in.

'Vanessa!'

'Hi,' I said, folding the paper just as Paige reached the landing. 'How'd it go?'

'You don't want to know,' she said, rolling her silver-blue eyes. 'Like it's *my* fault Charlie ploughed into me like a bulldozer and made me drop the entire bin of plates?'

'No?' I guessed.

'He might've been there first. But, whatever – I'm half his size!' She grinned and dropped into the chair next to mine. 'So how was your first Betty's breakfast?'

'Amazing,' I said. 'Kudos to the chef and his supportive staff.'

'Glad to hear it. Anyway, I can't really chat – I think Z wiretapped me – but I just wanted to say hi and bye.'

'Thanks. It was nice to meet you.'

'You, too.' She hopped back up.

We both jumped as a clap of thunder sounded, making the floor vibrate underneath our feet.

'This weather is *so* not good,' she groaned, looking toward the harbour. 'Everyone's coming off the water now and will be lining up outside, begging to wait it out inside. Countdown to crazy: T minus three minutes.'

'Do you need any help?' I asked, standing quickly.

She looked at me, her eyes flashing against the darkening sky. 'Like, keeping the masses from breaking windows and looting?'

I smiled, hoping she couldn't tell how silly I felt asking what was probably a very ridiculous question. 'Like bussing tables. Or washing dishes. Or whatever you need.'

She seemed to consider the proposition. 'Have you ever bussed before?'

'No . . . but I did make it through my first Betty's meal without breaking a single plate.'

She beamed. 'At least one of us is qualified.'

Later, when the storm had passed and the sun had set, when I was by myself and too scared to close my eyes, there would be plenty of time – there would be nothing *but* time – to think about Justine and Paul Carsons, and whether one had anything to do with the other. And since a few hours of calming distraction were probably about the closest I was going to get to sleep, I would take them when they came.

CHAPTER 5

Vanessa . . . my Nessa . . . come out, come out, wherever you are . . .

I shot up on the couch. My heart beat so fast and so loud, it took a second to hear the Care Bears singing on TV and the DJ chatting in the kitchen. My eyes darted around the room, taking in the thin line of light shining between the drawn shades and the window ledges, the plastic container of wilted salad on the coffee table, and the duck-shaped clock on the shelf above the fireplace: 7:20.

Big Poppa had been right. After receiving the green light from Louis and hauling bins of dishes for ten hours, I'd been so exhausted by the time I got home, my body had finally relented.

I grabbed the remote from the floor, turned off the cartoon and flopped back down. I now saw Justine every time I closed my eyes. And unlike when I was awake, when her smile and blue eyes flashed before me every time I blinked, in the dream she didn't look like the Justine I wanted to remember. She was too thin, too frail. Her skin was grey, not ivory, and mottled

62

with yellow and purple patches. Her dark hair hung in thick tangled ropes down her back, and her blue eyes glowed white. And when she called out for me, a searing pain sliced through my skull.

I reached for the cordless phone on the coffee table, eager to replace Justine's voice with someone else's. I'd just pressed the Boston area code when a loud tapping sounded in the kitchen.

It's just a bad muffler on a passing car . . . or a boat with motor trouble on the lake . . . or Mr Carmichael, back from Vermont and doing yard work . . .

'No more sleep for you,' I said when the tapping sounded again and I realised someone was knocking on the kitchen door. Not sure who'd be visiting so early in the morning, I finished dialling home before answering. 'Hi, Dad,' I said loudly when he picked up.

'Vanessa?'

'Yup, it's me.' I walked through the kitchen, noting the scissors in the ceramic jug by the refrigerator, the fire extinguisher by the stove, the wooden block of knives on the counter. 'Having a great morning. I'm using your extra-sharp Ginsu knives to slice cheese for the omelette I'm making.'

'What Ginsu knives? And why are you yelling? Is everything okay?'

'You're almost here? Turning onto Burton Drive now?' I stopped a foot from the door. Judging by the profile visible through the thin curtain covering the window in the kitchen door, whoever had knocked was definitely male.

'Vanessa, if you're trying to tell me something –'

'Hang on, Big Poppa,' I whispered, grabbing the doorknob. 'Simon?' My potential burglar stood on the stoop in jeans and his maroon Bates fleece.

'Hey. Sorry, I know it's early –'

'You and Caleb always use the back door.'

'I tried the back door,' he said. 'And the front door. And the side door. You didn't answer.'

'Oh.'

'And I was just about to force this door open, because you weren't answering. And because the lights have been on all night, and because I couldn't hear anything out here over all the noise in there. I thought something had happened.'

'Oh,' I said again, feeling ridiculous. 'Sorry . . . I fell asleep.'

'You fell asleep? I'm so glad to hear it!'

Big Poppa. I'd forgotten I was holding the phone. 'Dad, sorry – yes, I finally fell asleep.' I turned, hoping Simon wouldn't notice the light pink travelling from my forehead to the base of my neck. 'But Simon just stopped by. We're going to get something to eat. Call you later?'

'You're okay?' Simon asked as I hung up and turned back.

'Yes. Thank you.' I opened the door wider and stepped aside. 'Want to come in?'

'Actually . . .' He glanced behind him, toward his house. 'I came over to see if you wanted to come out.'

'Out where?'

His jaw clenched. 'To find Caleb.'

My heart thrust against my chest. I'd planned to head back to Betty's, since Louis had said he could use the extra help whenever I wanted to offer it, but finding Caleb came first. 'Give me five minutes.'

He stepped inside as I ran to the bathroom to speed-shower. I didn't know what had made him decide that today was the day to try to find Caleb, but whatever the reason, I was happy he wanted to include me. Not only would it be nice to have company, but a search led by him was guaranteed to take much less time than one conducted only by me; as Caleb's brother, he had to know where to look better than I did.

Pretty Vanessa . . .

I'd finished getting dressed and was drying my hair when I heard Justine's voice. The mirror above the sink was cloudy from the shower, but something behind me had flashed brightly in its reflection – like a lit match, sparking silver instead of gold.

The lake house was seventy-five years old. There was nothing shiny about it, especially not in the bathroom, which hadn't been remodelled since Dad bought the house in the late eighties. The tiles on the walls and floor were moss green, and the cabinets were dark wood with black handles. Anything that was usually shiny in normal, modern bathrooms, like the taps and light fixtures, was dulled bronze.

I wiped the steam away with one hand. 'You're losing it,' I told my reflection. 'About one hallucination shy of certifiable.'

One one thousand, two one thousand, three one thousand . . .

I froze. There was another flash above my right shoulder. Another between my left elbow and torso.

You can look . . . but he has to want to be found . . .

Her voice surrounded me like the cool early-morning mist rising from the lake, covering my arms and legs in the thin, grey film I could never wait to rinse off. I closed my eyes against it, against her voice and the image of her from the dream that still lingered, her skin purple and yellow, her hair falling like clumps of dark seaweed down her back.

'Be right there, Simon!' I yelled in a pathetic attempt to warn away whatever was making me see and hear things.

I knocked hard against the towel rack as I darted toward the door. The impact made me drop the brush I still carried, but I didn't bother opening my eyes to see where it landed. I left it where it was and groped ahead of me until one hand landed on the doorknob.

My eyes snapped open as soon as my feet hit the hallway area rug. Running toward the kitchen, I felt the way I always did whenever I accidentally ended up the last in line while hiking with other people in the woods: like I wasn't *really* the last one in line.

'You okay?' Simon asked when I skidded to a stop in the kitchen.

'Fine,' I said, trying to smile. 'Just excited to get started.' I grabbed my purse from the kitchen counter and headed outside before he could say anything else. When he didn't follow me right away, I peered through the doorway.

'I'm not sure when we'll be back, so I put the TV on,' he said, entering the kitchen from the living room.

I watched him jog down the steps. It hadn't even occurred to me to turn off the radio and lights before walking out the door. And instead of turning them off for me, the way other people might've for someone whose head was clearly somewhere else, he'd turned the TV back on.

'So where are we going?' I asked after locking the door and hurrying after him. 'Where do we start?'

He quickened his step as we approached the Subaru, then pulled ahead of me to open the passenger's-side door. 'The marina.'

As he closed the door and rounded the back of the

car, I glanced around as if sitting there for the first time. Simon had bought the Subaru when he got his licence, and for two summers he'd played chauffeur to our little group, driving us to the movies, Eddie's Ice Cream, the miniature golf course. But this was the first time it'd ever been just the two of us. It felt strange to sit in the front and not feel the car bounce up and down as Justine and Caleb climbed in the back. And, of course, it felt strange to think that this was the first time I'd been in the Subaru since the last time, when the four of us were still together.

'Are you hungry?' he asked, dropping in the driver's seat and starting the car. 'I picked up snacks.'

I was about to say I was fine when I noticed two plastic cups in the holders between us.

'Watermelon guava,' he said, then nodded to the Harbor Homefries bag by my feet. 'And scrambled eggs, sausage and cheese on a kaiser roll.'

I grabbed the bag, surprised that he knew my breakfast of choice. Our foursome never ate the first meal of the day together, which meant I must've mentioned it at some point . . . and he'd remembered. I was so touched by his thoughtfulness and moved by the gesture, I couldn't look at him as I unwrapped the sandwich. 'Thank you.'

In addition to satisfying our hunger, eating gave us something to do instead of talking during our drive into town. It wasn't that I didn't want to talk to Simon; I just didn't know what to say. It felt like we'd fast-forwarded a few decades and suffered from empty-nest syndrome. After all that time, what did parents talk about besides the children who were no longer there?

'So,' Simon finally said as we pulled into the Winter Harbor Marina twenty minutes later. 'I have to ask a huge favour.'

I'd been staring out the passenger's-side window but turned to him when he spoke.

'I don't know where Caleb's been, or what he's been doing. Our parents and I wanted to give him some time and space to deal with things in his own way, but we thought he'd be back by now. Depending on where he's been, if we find him —'

'When we find him.'

He let out a small breath. 'When we find him, I don't know what kind of state he'll be in. Trauma affects people differently, and for Caleb to leave the way he did . . . I just don't know how he'll be after being on his own for so long.'

'Okay . . .'

He glanced through the windscreen as two fishermen passed by, toting rods and reels. 'Would you mind not saying anything?' He turned back to me, and his eyes were sorry. 'At least not right away? I know that he was the last one with Justine, and that you have questions about that night.'

I looked down and fiddled with the straw in my empty smoothie cup. Simon had no idea that what I wanted to ask Caleb went far beyond that night, into the weeks and months leading up to it. He had no idea that I was banking on Caleb having the answers to everything I thought I'd known about Justine in the past two years – and perhaps before that – but didn't.

'I know he'll tell you whatever you want to know,' Simon continued, 'but it would help if we let him go at his own pace. Seeing you will remind him of her . . . and I don't want him to keep running.'

I nodded. 'Of course. I won't say anything until you say it's okay.'

He exhaled. 'Thanks.'

We climbed out of the car, and I was happy to let him take the lead. Going to the marina was a good idea; I didn't think either of us expected to find Caleb there now, but he'd worked there as a dock attendant since he was thirteen, when he'd finally been strong enough to lift the gas nozzle and help pull boats in. We'd heard stories about the marina nearly every day in the summers since then, and we knew some of Caleb's co-workers were also his best friends. Someone there had to know something about where he'd gone.

I followed Simon into the office, which was a one-room shack covered in colourful buoys, like a Christmas tree festooned in ornaments.

'Well, look what the hook dragged in! Wait . . . it *is* you, isn't it?' Captain Monty took off his glasses, wiped them with one corner of his cargo vest and put them back on. 'You look a little big for the elder Carmichael boy, but I wouldn't forget that grin.'

'You're not seeing things,' Simon said, shaking Captain Monty's hand. 'I joined crew at school this year. Turns out rowing for three hours every day is good for more than a suntan.'

That explained it.

'The colour's not half bad either, now that you mention it.' Captain Monty folded his arms on the counter and leaned forward. 'And who do we have here? She's a pretty one.'

I shook my head slightly when Simon glanced at me. I'd met Captain Monty a few times over the years but clearly hadn't left much of an impression. Now wasn't the time to be remembered.

'This is Vanessa. She's a friend from school.'

'Brains *and* beauty, eh? You always were a smart one, my boy.' Captain Monty wiggled his eyebrows in a way that should've annoyed me but didn't, because he was Captain Monty.

'Anyway,' Simon said, 'I was actually hoping you might be able to help us out with something.'

'You name it, it's yours. Except for the mighty *Barbara Ann* out there. She's mine.'

I peered around Captain Monty through the window behind him. *Barbara Ann*, the ancient fishing boat that had been docked in the same spot for thirty years, still bobbed in the water not far from the office.

'Of course.' Simon smiled as he glanced at the boat. 'Captain Monty, we wondered if you knew anything about Caleb.'

Captain Monty's furry white eyebrows dropped. He looked at Simon, like he couldn't believe he'd asked such a thing, then at me, like I had something to do with it. He took a pencil out from its resting place above his ear, slid a yellowing stack of charts on the counter in front of him and examined them.

'I know he hasn't been around the past week or so – that can't be good for business, and I'm sorry he left you in the lurch right at the start of the season. But did he happen to say anything to you about where he was going?'

Captain Monty bent closer to the papers on the counter and made some notes. It seemed like he either coulddn't hear us or was going to ignore us until we gave up and left, but then he started chuckling. Softly at first, and then louder, until the sound spurted through his chapped lips and his shoulders shook.

Simon smiled. 'Did I miss something?'

'I'm sorry – really. I don't mean to laugh.' Captain Monty heaved a big sigh. 'It's just, your brother's something else. I give him a job, decent pay, free gas, all the squid he can fit on a hook, and he just ups and leaves. I felt like a fool when he just stopped showing up without saying a thing to anyone. But, obviously, I wasn't the last one to find out.'

'Find out what?' Simon asked.

Captain Monty looked at Simon over the top of his glasses. 'That he quit. That he left me for a pay rise I couldn't give him ten years from now and a couple of fancy polo shirts.' He frowned. 'Not telling me is one thing – but not to tell your own brother? You'd think that'd be a pretty good sign that something's wrong with the decision you're making.'

'Captain Monty, I'm sorry . . . you're saying Caleb quit? For a few extra bucks?'

'And some fancy polo shirts. You can get one yourself, if you want. I hear they sell them in the gift shop.' He turned from us and pulled a yellow tackle box from the shelf above his small metal desk. 'The fancy Lighthouse has fancy everything – gift shop, restaurant, manicures, massages.'

'Caleb left here for the Lighthouse Marina Resort and Spa?' I asked. The Lighthouse had opened last summer and quickly gained a reputation as the most exclusive, expensive destination within a hundred miles of Winter

Harbor. It had been resisted by locals but pushed by several powerful summer visitors, and it had got approval largely because the project created hundreds of new jobs.

'That doesn't make sense,' Simon said. 'He loved working here. He counted down the days after you wrapped up the last boat for the season after Columbus Day until you unwrapped them again around Memorial Day.'

Captain Monty poked through the tackle-box compartments. 'And I loved having him here. Your brother was a good boy, a hard worker. But, listen, things change. Boys grow up. He did what he did for his own reasons, and I don't fault him for that. I just wish he'd felt he could've told me himself.'

'If you don't mind me asking, if Caleb didn't tell you himself . . . who did?'

Captain Monty raised his eyes to Simon's. 'You know Carsons? That guy they just found washed up on Mercury Isle?'

'Yes,' Simon and I said at once.

Captain Monty nodded. 'It was him. He was one of the main Lighthouse backers, and he came in at the end of last summer, the third day Cal hadn't shown without a single phone call. He wanted to introduce himself and thank me for the great dock hand I'd sent over as a welcome gift from the town. Can you believe that?' He sighed, exasperated. 'Anyway, that's apparently what Cal told them. That's what he wanted them to believe. So . . . I let them believe it.'

'Sorry.'

I held my breath.

'Carsons came in to thank you for Caleb at the end of *last* summer?'

'August twentieth,' Captain Monty said. 'The day of the shark tournament – I remember because your brother always loved measuring the catches.'

Simon was looking at Captain Monty expectantly, as though waiting for the punchline, the 'gotcha'. But none came. And I knew what Simon had to be thinking – *How?* How had he not known? How had Caleb not told him? How had an entire year gone by without someone clueing him in?

They were the kinds of questions I was all too familiar with.

Captain Monty looked at Simon. 'Is everything okay? I mean, outside of the fact that you had no idea what your little brother was doing with his spare time all year?'

I looked down. I knew he now had to be wondering if Caleb was really missing at all, or just off doing something else he hadn't bothered to tell anyone about.

'Everything's fine,' Simon said. 'Just a little miscommunication, I guess.'

'Happens to the best of us. Just wait till things get serious with this one here – then you'll be miscommunicating all the time.'

I smiled politely when he winked at me.

'You take care of yourselves,' Captain Monty called after us as we pushed open the office door. 'And watch out for the sharks!'

I froze at Captain Monty's warning. 'Sharks?'

'They've been busy this summer,' he said. 'Fish carcasses are littering the beaches, and boaters have been reporting sightings. Some folks even think that's what happened to Carsons – he wasn't too banged up, but they think a shark might've dragged him out before losing its grip in the current. If he was in deep enough water, it would've been impossible for him to swim back to shore in that storm.'

I shook my head against the dull alarm sounding inside as we left the building and started across the parking lot. By the time we reached the Subaru, I'd managed to muffle it enough to focus on our current task.

'I don't get it,' Simon said once we were in the car. 'This wasn't just some summer job to Caleb. He never worked here for the money – if that was what mattered, he would've gotten in at one of the restaurants, parking cars or bussing tables.'

'Do you have any idea why he didn't tell you?' I asked gently.

He stared through the windscreen. 'No,' he said finally. 'I don't. I mean, we didn't talk that much while I was at school, but if he quit on August twentieth, I was still here. I didn't leave for orientation until the following week. We did a lot of fishing those last few days . . . he didn't say anything.'

'Maybe he didn't want you to worry? Or think something was wrong when you were about to leave and had enough going on?'

'Maybe,' he said, his voice doubtful.

'Do you want to check around some more? See if any of the other guys know anything else?'

He shook his head and started the car. 'You've seen the shrine to Monty in Caleb's room. All those pictures and charts. He wouldn't have told anyone anything he didn't tell Monty first.'

I paused. 'Except Carsons.'

'Except Carsons.' Sighing, he put the car in drive.

Fifteen minutes later the view through the Subaru's windscreen changed from commercial fishing boats and modest motorboats to two-storey ivory yachts sitting so still on the water they could've been on land. Women sunbathed and men played cards on the sprawling decks, while kids were nowhere to be seen – most likely because they were indoors, holed up with movies or video games in what had to be high-tech screening rooms.

Apparently, members of the Lighthouse Resort Marina and Spa joined not so that they had a place to anchor after a day on the water, but to have a place to anchor *instead* of going on the water.

'This isn't Winter Harbor,' Simon said, watching a Lighthouse employee haul a case of Perrier up a ramp leading to *The Excursion*. 'This isn't Caleb.'

As a silver-haired older man in khaki shorts and a pink polo shirt greeted the kid at the top of the ramp, I pictured Justine's bulletin board. I could see the application, Mom's Post-It notes, the bold college logos as though they were plastered to the windscreen in front of me instead of stuck to the corkboard three hundred miles away. And in the middle of it all – the blank personal essay. I no longer knew who Justine was, so I couldn't guess at who she wasn't.

You can look all you want . . . but he has to want to be found . . .

'Justine wasn't going to Dartmouth,' I said, my voice level. 'For the past year she slept in a Dartmouth sweatshirt, carried a Dartmouth keyring, and used a Dartmouth umbrella when it rained. She convinced everyone who knew her – including me – that that's where she was headed at the end of the summer.' I turned to Simon when I felt his eyes on me. 'But she lied. She didn't even apply. I had to find out by myself because she didn't tell me. And now she's not even

78

here for me to ask why.'

I felt better, lighter, as soon as the words were out. The guilt at not knowing was still there; that wouldn't go away when I said the truth aloud. But at least now there was someone who could understand.

Because Simon's head fell gently against the headrest as he looked at me, and I knew he felt guilty, too. I didn't want him to, nor did I think he should . . . but I also knew he couldn't help it.

'We'll find him, Vanessa,' he said, reaching one hand across the empty Squeezed cups and lifting a few stray strands of hair from my forehead. 'I can't promise much, but I promise you that.'

CHAPTER 6

'When are you coming home?'

'Hi, Mom,' I said, silently cursing caller ID.

'Your father says you're not sleeping.' Her voice was tense; I could picture her in her signature black suit, her laptop open on the kitchen table in front of her.

'I'm sleeping.'

'Your father says you're not.'

'When?' It was pointless to be annoyed, but I wasn't in the mood for a lecture. 'When did Dad say that?'

'This morning.'

'It's seven thirty. Dad rolled over and managed "Vanessa's not sleeping" before you jumped out of bed and on the treadmill?'

Mom paused. 'Vanessa, I will not apologise for being worried.'

'Fine,' I relented. '*I* apologise.'

'Thank you. Now, how are you really?'

'I'm fine, really.'

'Are you about done doing whatever it is you're doing up there? There's a wonderful exhibit opening at the Museum of Fine Arts this weekend, and I've got tickets to the VIP reception. It's a garden party, and I saw a fabulous dress at Saks that would look stunning on you.'

'I don't think I'll be back in time. But thank you for the thought.'

'Sweetie, I know this is difficult, and I don't blame you for wanting to hide out. Do you think I don't need to talk myself out of bed every day?'

I did, actually, but knew better than to say so aloud.

'But people need people. Especially in times like these. That's why I went back to work.'

'I have people here,' I said.

'You do?' Her voice rose on 'do'. 'Like whom?'

Through the windscreen, I looked at the kitchen entrance to Betty's. Probably better to leave that one alone for now. 'Simon. He's home for the summer.'

'Vanessa,' she said, now sounding as concerned as if I'd said that Simon and I had just returned from a shotgun Vegas wedding, 'I don't know that that's such a good idea.'

'Why not? You love Simon. He was the one you guys always left in charge whenever you, Dad and Mr and Mrs Carmichael went out.'

'Yes, I know . . . but things are different now.'

'Things, yes – but not Simon.' I paused. 'He's looking out for me. I thought that would make you happy.'

'What would make me happy is if you came home.

81

The garden party is Saturday night. Why don't you just relax today, think about it, and call me in the morning?'

I wouldn't change my mind, but I told her that sounded like a good idea and hung up.

Mom was right about one thing: being around people helped. That had been confirmed when I returned to the empty lake house last night. I'd left the lights, TV and radio on that morning, but after spending all day with Simon, they'd only served as glaring reminders that I was alone again. I'd considered inviting him over to watch a movie – I'd even picked up the phone and dialled – but eventually decided against it. We'd already spent so much time together, and it had been a tiring day; he'd probably needed a break.

Which was why I was at Betty's Chowder House at seven thirty the next morning.

'Back so soon?'

'Good morning,' I said, getting out of the car. Louis stood on the stairs leading to the kitchen door, smoking a cigarette. Garrett stood next to him, drinking coffee.

'Hon,' Louis said, taking a long drag and letting it out slowly, 'you won't find anyone more supportive of a good time than me – but the summer's barely begun. You might want to pace yourself.'

'Maybe you should look into a chaperone,' Garrett said with a smile. 'I usually work days, so would be happy to help keep you out of trouble at night.'

'Thanks for the offer,' I said, starting up the steps. 'But I'm fine. My Betty's breakfast was not only healing, but preventative. I might never feel sick again.'

Holding the cigarette between his lips, Louis opened the door for me. 'Paige is on silverware duty. She could use your help.'

'I'm off at seven!' Garrett called after me.

I scooted inside and found Paige quickly. She stood over a big red plastic bin at the back of the main dining room, tossing knives and forks into a sorting container.

'Twice in three days?'

I spun toward the voice behind me – and pressed my fingertips against my temples. Maybe I'd spoken too soon when I'd said Louis's breakfast had had preventative powers. Because I didn't feel hungry; rather, that fleeting migraine that had hit two days ago, when I was on my way into Betty's kitchen for the first time, was back.

'There are twenty other restaurants in town.'

My eyes were scrunched against the pain, but the scowl on the waitress in front of me was clear.

'And, let me guess – no reservation?'

'No.' I recognised the waitress as the one who'd spoken to me by the Dumpster two days ago. 'But –'

'Vanessa!'

I smiled as a handful of utensils clattered into the bin.

'Paige, do you see swing sets? Seesaws? A sandbox?'

'Simmer down, Z,' Paige said, coming up behind me. 'Vanessa's not here to play. She's here to work.'

Z. Short for Zara, waitress extraordinaire – the one who'd yelled at Paige from the bottom of the stairs leading to the balcony two days ago. I could see the resemblance – they both had the same dark hair and silver-blue eyes, though Paige's features were softer, plainer – but considering their personalities, it was still hard to believe they were related.

'I'm just here to lend a hand,' I explained, not wanting to get Paige in trouble. 'Temporarily.'

Zara's eyes narrowed. 'Betty's Chowder House is a sixty-year-old institution. People travel here from all over New England for our famous lobster chowder. We have a sterling reputation and won't risk tarnishing it just because my brilliant little sister thought an at-work ally might make sorting silverware more interesting.' She yanked a pad and pen from her apron pocket. 'Have you ever even worked in a restaurant?'

I glanced at Paige. 'Not exactly, but –'

'Z, Louis said it was okay. I guess you were too busy wooing your customers to notice, but he let her help in the kitchen for ten hours the other day, and she didn't break one thing. That's got to be some kind of record.'

I waited, feeling embarrassed, awkward and also impressed. Zara was clearly used to running the show, and Paige was clearly used to putting her in her place when necessary.

'You'll work as a team,' Zara said finally. 'Paige will lead, and Vanessa, you'll be her extra set of hands. As soon as a plate, bowl, glass, ketchup bottle, sugar packet, whatever, leaves her fingers and heads south, grab it.'

'I'm off silverware?' Paige asked.

Zara looked at her. 'You let one thing hit the floor, your friend's gone, and you're back to Spoon Central.'

Paige squealed once Zara left, then took my hand and led me through the kitchen doors.

'Paige,' I said when we reached a closet in the back of the kitchen, 'no offence, but if you're such a physical threat to Betty's, how are you still here? I mean, Zara kind of seems to have it in for you ... and if Betty's is so busy, and the reputation that important, then wouldn't they be a little hesitant to keep someone on who they think needs a lot in the way of –'

'Babysitting?' Smiling, she grabbed an apron from a shelf and held it up for my approval. 'Z's the only one who thinks I need to be monitored like a toddler in a roomful of electrical outlets. And since she's my elder, control-freakish sister, I forgive her for it.'

I took the apron from her. 'But you *do* break a lot of things, don't you?'

'Of course!' She handed me a pad and a pen. 'And

would it be better if my fingers weren't quite so slippery? Maybe . . . we'd save some money, that's for sure, but there'd also be a huge entertainment gap among the staff.'

I tied the apron around my waist and took the pad and pen.

'But what most people – and by most I mean everyone but Z – cares about is that I'm here at all.' She leaned toward me. 'I don't know if you noticed, but my sister is not the easiest person to deal with.'

'Seriously?' I joked.

She tugged on the bottom of my apron until it hung evenly. 'The staff isn't very fond of Zara, but the customers – *male* customers, especially – love her. Thanks to genetics and a certain charm, she can up-sell Coke drinkers to Corona, convince fathers to order something more expensive than grilled cheese for their picky kids, and get husbands to push their weight-conscious wives to take on brownie sundaes. All without making them think they didn't think of any of it themselves.' Her eyes met mine. 'If Zara doesn't bring in at least a thousand dollars in tips one night, then we're closed.'

'And you're never closed.'

'*And* we pool the tips.'

I nodded. 'So the staff has to deal.'

'Through me. I'm the buffer, the filter, the translator, whatever. If Z comes running in here screaming about a slow dish, I come running in after her to calm her down.' She paused with one hand on the swinging door. 'I'm great at my job – that part of it anyway – but even if I wasn't, they'd still have to deal.'

'Why's that?'

She grinned. 'Our family owns the restaurant. Betty's my grandmother.'

Before I could ask any more questions, she was through the kitchen door.

Thankfully, the morning passed quickly. I followed Paige's lead the whole time, noting how efficiently she moved despite her slippery fingers. There were only two near misses: a coffee cup and bread dish, both of which I lunged for and saved from shattering.

'How is it noon already?' I asked four hours later as we stood behind the bar, folding napkins.

'Would you *please* go tend to your old-man friend?'

Zara flew up next to us. My head throbbed instantly, and I wondered if I could be so anxious around a person that my frazzled nerves caused such an immediate, painful physical reaction.

'Um, Z, kind of busy,' Paige said.

'Um, *P* – no one's busier than me. And I don't have time or patience today for that guy's stupid games.'

'You never have patience. And you just have to know how to talk to Oliver.'

I could tell Zara was struggling with which bothered her more – that there was a customer she couldn't win over, or that there was something Paige knew how to do better than her.

Zara frowned. 'I'll try one more time. If he doesn't bite, I'm over it. For good.'

Paige spread the napkin she'd been folding across the counter, rested her elbows on it and grinned. 'Ready for a break?'

I leaned against the counter next to her. 'Who's Oliver?'

'Zara's arch nemesis.' She turned to me. 'Sorry. I sounded pretty happy about that, didn't I?'

'Overjoyed, actually.'

'I can't *help* it,' she said, watching Zara zigzag through the room toward an older man with hair whiter and frizzier than Big Poppa's. She checked her watch. 'Twelve oh two. Right on time.'

Zara stopped a few feet away from the table. She tightened her ponytail and adjusted her apron. Her shoulders lifted and dropped as she took a deep breath.

'Oliver is the *one* customer she can't get,' Paige said. 'He comes in at the same time every day and always sits in her section. She's done everything – offered complimentary meals, discounts, a bigger table even though space is money and he's always by himself. Seriously, she's given it everything she has.'

'Why doesn't he sit in someone else's section?'

She shook her head. 'Don't know. We've offered, and he refuses. But the best part is his reaction. Look at what he does when she tries talking to him – it's classic.'

We were too far away, and it was too noisy to hear – but there was no mistaking his reaction, which was to ignore her completely. She spoke, then waited. Spoke again, and waited again. On the third attempt she seemed to point out breakfast suggestions on the menu lying on the table, and when that didn't inspire conversation, she scowled at Paige over her shoulder.

'It's like she's not even there,' Paige sighed happily.

It was true. Not only did Oliver not say anything, he also stared out the window as if Zara was one of the tall potted plants displayed throughout the dining room.

I grabbed another napkin and resumed folding as Zara stormed toward us.

'Uh-oh,' Paige said.

Zara had stopped in the middle of the room. She leaned down and listened to one of her customers, whose frown and full plate of food indicated a problem.

'This isn't going to be good – she's already fired up.' Paige turned toward me. 'Congratulations, Vanessa! You're being promoted.'

My hands froze mid-fold. I didn't want to be promoted. I didn't even really want to work there. I just wanted not to be me for a few hours.

'I need you to take Oliver's order. He'll want two slices of wholewheat toast with grape jam, a boiled egg, half a grapefruit and a cup of Earl Grey. Super easy. Just smile and let him tell you himself.'

'Louis! Did you wake up this morning, smile at yourself in the mirror and think how glad you were to work at a diner?'

'Paige,' I said as she walked backward toward the kitchen door that still swung back and forth from Zara shooting through. 'I don't think –'

'Gotta go!' she called behind her as the shouting escalated in the kitchen.

My eyes stayed on the swinging door until it slowed to a stop. Knowing I had no choice, mostly because I liked Paige and didn't want to disappoint her, I turned and headed across the room; before long I stood where Zara had moments ago, clutching a notepad and pen.

'Oliver?' I said this so quietly he probably wouldn't have heard me had I leaned down and spoken two inches from his ear. And even that was doubtful, since I could see a small brown hearing aid peeking out from a patch of white fuzz.

It took about ten seconds for his eyes to find me. They landed first on the mermaid logo swimming along my apron and lingered there, expressionless, before travelling slowly up.

He didn't look happy, but at least he was acknowledging me. Bolstered by the progress, I smiled wider.

'Hi,' I tried again, proud when I could actually hear myself.

His eyes narrowed, and he seemed to consider how to respond.

I glanced once more toward the kitchen door. My heart lifted when the door swung open but dropped again when another harried-looking waitress emerged. I turned back to Oliver just as he finished fiddling with his hearing aid. I was about to introduce myself as Paige's friend but refrained when his eyes grew from suspicious slits to stunned discs.

'Wholewheat toast, right? With grape jam? And a hard-boiled egg and a cup of tea?' I ploughed ahead, determined to get out of there. 'What kind was it again – chamomile? Lemon? How about I just bring you every flavour they have, and you can choose?'

He stared at me, and I willed his eyes to blink. When they didn't, I held his gaze and slowly reached down for the menu. My fingers hovered a few centimetres above Betty's lunch specials when he slapped one hand down.

I jumped back. The dining-room buzz softened, and nearby diners watched us curiously.

His eyes were as big as Frisbees as he lifted the menu from the table. He held it toward me and pointed to the small print at the bottom of the page. I hesitated before leaning forward to read what he wanted me to, trying not to notice that his index finger was grey, and peeling at the knuckle, and shaking.

'Earl Grey?'

His finger vibrated sharply, then tapped the menu once.

'Earl Grey,' I repeated, backing away. 'Great. I'll get that order in right away.'

I spun around and bolted for the kitchen door.

'You don't seem to understand what your *mistakes* can *do* to us.'

I grabbed my head as I pushed through the swinging door.

'The woman is allergic to cheese!' Zara yelled. 'Pass-out, fall-to-the-floor, rush-me-by-ambulance-to-the-nearest-ER-before-I-*die* allergic. And what do you do? Fill her omelette with American and pour melted cheddar on top.'

'*That* is today's omelette special,' Louis shouted back. 'If the woman didn't *want* cheese, she shouldn't have ordered it. Or maybe her waitress didn't fully explain to her what was *in* today's omelette special?'

'Okay, people,' Paige yelled above both of them, banging a wooden spoon against an empty pot. 'We have neither the time nor manpower to continue this stimulating debate. The woman saw the cheese before she ate it – no harm, no foul. Louis will whip up the omelette of her choice, and Zara will apologise and comp her meal.'

I hurried behind a counter as Zara charged through the kitchen, her dark ponytail flying behind her.

'I got Oliver's order,' I said when Paige turned to me. 'Where do I –'

'You got Oliver's order?'

I paused. 'Yes?'

'*You* are a rock star.' She grabbed a tray from a table behind her. 'Others have tried, and no one has succeeded but me. And now, you.'

I eyed the tray when she placed it on the counter in front of me. It was Oliver's order, right down to the steaming cup of tea.

'I wasn't positive he'd take to you – which says nothing about you, but loads about him – so I put in the order as soon as I came back here.'

'Great,' I said. 'But are you sure you don't want to take it out?'

'I should stick around until Z comes back. Sometimes the aftershocks do more damage than the main event.' She started after Louis, who was banging pots around the stove top. 'Oh, and you might want to ask how his writing's going, or compliment his drawings.'

I was about to ask what she meant when Zara burst through the door again.

'Okay, let's try this – it's *very* complicated,' Zara yelled across the kitchen. 'She wants a mushroom and spinach omelette. I'm no chef, but I'm pretty sure that means eggs, mushrooms and spinach *without* American, cheddar or Swiss.'

As Louis banged around even louder, I lifted the tray from the counter and moved toward the door. Keeping an eye on the water splashing in the teacup, I somehow made it through the dining room without knocking into anyone or dropping anything. I was so relieved to be almost done with the task I didn't notice the notebook and charcoal pencils spread across Oliver's table until I put down his plate of toast.

'How's the writing going?' I glanced at the open notebook. The pages were filled with small, messy script, but I managed to make out the bigger words across the top. '*A Complete History of Winter Harbor*, Volume Five? I didn't know there was that much to know about such a small town.'

Oliver yanked the notebook toward his chest, revealing a sketch pad underneath. His grey, shaky index finger jabbed the sketch pad, and my arm jerked in surprise, sending a few drops of steaming water over the teacup's edge. When my eyes fell on the drawing, they grew as wide as Oliver's.

Because the drawing clearly depicted a very specific place that was impossible to imagine unless you'd been there.

Chione Cliffs.

CHAPTER 7

'I don't get it,' I said to Simon at the beach the next day. 'I mean, I don't get going in water so deep your feet can't touch the ground without your head going under – but what I *really* don't get is voluntarily going in water that could pull you out and suck you down as soon as it hits your ankles.'

'Does that mean you don't want the surfing lesson I booked for you today?' Simon sounded disappointed.

I looked at him. 'You booked me a surfing lesson?' He didn't know everything about the accident two years ago, but he knew enough not to sign me up for a repeat performance.

He smiled. 'Yes. And after that we're going sky-diving. And bungee jumping. And if there's time, we might try walking through fire.'

'Glad I wore my flame-resistant Nikes.'

He gave me a small smile, then started walking toward a cluster of cars parked down the beach.

I followed him, thinking again how happy I'd been to hear his knock on the back door two hours before. The Subaru hadn't been in the driveway when I returned from Betty's in the early evening yesterday and didn't appear again until almost midnight. As soon as I saw it, I was able to relax enough to lie down on the couch and try to sleep. My eyes had snapped open at five, and by six I'd showered and lowered the volume on the TV and radio so I wouldn't miss Simon if he knocked. He'd come over at eight, bearing more smoothies and egg sandwiches. By eight thirty, we were in the Subaru, heading toward Beacon Beach, Caleb's friends' favourite surfing spot.

And now we were going to try to find out if his friends knew anything we didn't.

'It's messed up,' a guy in a wetsuit was saying as I neared the half circle of beat-up Jeeps and pickups. 'He just took off. Zack went to go pick him up for this barbecue we were having, and he wasn't there.'

'And there's been nothing since then?' Simon asked. 'No calls? Emails?'

The guy – his name was Mark, which I remembered from a picture of Caleb and his friends that Justine had taken last summer – shook his head. 'Nothing. Not a word. We just figured it was too much for him.'

'Too much?' Simon asked.

Noticing me there, Mark nodded toward me. 'This cutie your girlfriend?'

'Actually –' I started, my cheeks warming.

'So you're, like, crazy in love,' he continued before

I could clarify Simon's and my relationship. 'You open your eyes in the morning and your first thought is her. You wonder how she is. What she's doing. When you can see her again. Those thoughts stay with you all day. You share them with whoever will listen – including your best friends, who of course *respect* you but, after a while, out of the kind of concern only real friends have, seriously question your sanity. And you make all sorts of plans – *big* plans, like, post-high school – when the rest of us can barely wrap our heads around the fact that we only have two years left to get a clue.'

'I sound obsessed,' Simon said, reaching over to tug gently on my ponytail.

'You have no idea.' Mark bent down and lifted his board from the sand. 'You live and breathe this girl. You talk about her all the time, you hang out with your friends less and less, you're blind to *other* girls, no matter how hot or into you they are – and some of them are extremely hot and into you – and eventually, you break and actually say you love her.'

Simon looked down, suddenly interested in the multicoloured rocks at his feet.

'Not only that, you tell your *friends* you love her. Which, as you know, is about as major as you can get.'

'I'm obsessed *and* a sap.' Simon nodded. 'Backbone, anyone?'

'Don't be so hard on yourself,' Mark said with a

shrug. 'Your friends aren't. They might think you're a little out there, but they know you wouldn't be for any other girl. It's just because it's her. She's different.'

I felt my face turn pink and silently reminded myself that Simon and I weren't really the couple in question.

'Anyway, this girl is it for you. Food, water, oxygen, sleep – all details. All inconsequential.' Mark sighed and looked toward the water. 'And then she's dead. Done. Gone. Washed up like a fish.'

My knees gave slightly. Of course that's where the sweet story was going, but just like the way it really happened, the tragic twist still seemed to come out of nowhere. 'And then what?' I asked, mostly because Simon was watching me carefully, and I wanted to let him know that I was okay.

Mark turned back to us. 'And then you run. Because the only thing worse than her being gone is that you're still here.'

Simon paused, apparently trying to understand the perspective of someone who had spent much more time with his brother than he had in the past year. 'But why not hang around your – my – friends? And family? And everyone else who cares about me? Why just disappear without saying where I'm going?'

'If she was gone,' he said, nodding at me again, 'would you really want the looks? The questions? The nice but pointless attempts at sympathy? Especially from people who really no longer knew you as you without her?'

I tried to process this. Caleb had loved Justine. Not just liked her. Not just enjoyed having a reliable make-out partner. Had Justine felt the same way? And if he was so important to her, if they were so important to each other, why had she done her best to convince everyone that their relationship was just a casual summer fling? She'd even hung out with several guys from Hawthorne Prep during the school year; if she'd felt that strongly about Caleb, why bother with anyone else?

'No, I guess I wouldn't,' Simon said finally, pulling me back into the conversation.

'Dude, *what* are you waiting for?'

Three guys in wetsuits, looking simultaneously excited and exhausted and dragging their boards in the sand behind them, made their way toward us.

'If you don't get out there soon, it'll be too late,' one of the surfers warned Mark.

Simon looked to the water, his internal weatherman alerted.

'Hey,' the surfer said, noticing Simon and clapping him on the shoulder. 'Bummer about Caleb's girl, man. He'll be back once the fog lifts.'

'It's insane out there,' another surfer continued. 'The waves were about half the size twenty minutes

99

ago, and they just keep coming faster and stronger and higher.'

'Is that normal?' I asked.

'Not even close,' Mark said.

'They're big even for winter waves, when colliding fronts really stir things up.' Simon eyed the water warily.

'Well,' Mark said, attaching the strap at one end of his board to his ankle, 'hats off to global warming. Bad for mankind, great for Maine-kind.'

'Just one more thing,' Simon called after Mark as he started for the water. 'Did you know Caleb quit the marina last year? And was working at the Lighthouse?'

Mark stopped short. 'What?'

'We talked to Monty a few days ago. He said Caleb stopped showing without warning last summer. He found out where he went from one of the Lighthouse backers.'

Mark exchanged looks with the other surfers, who'd all dropped to the sand to recover.

'You didn't know?' Simon prompted when they didn't say anything.

'No,' Mark said, continuing toward the water. 'And I'm surprised to hear it, considering how hard Caleb tried to keep the Lighthouse dark.'

'He went to every town board meeting for a *year*,' one of the surfers explained. 'He made flyers, talked to the papers. He even started a petition and went door to door, collecting hundreds of signatures. He was so against the Lighthouse coming – he thought it would destroy the town and put people like Monty out of business. He even met with the money guys, all by himself. He cornered them at one of the town meetings and wouldn't let them leave until they agreed to a lunch.'

Simon looked like he'd been told that the sky was green and that rain actually shot up from the ground. I understood the feeling. Caleb was a notorious slacker; it was the main reason Mom didn't think he was right for Justine. It was hard to imagine his not only caring that much about the town, but also putting in such effort to preserve it.

'Did they have lunch?' I asked.

'They did. At Betty's, at Caleb's insistence. Which actually turned out to be a bad move – he'd wanted to give them an authentic taste of Winter Harbor so that they'd realise what was already there and leave it alone, but it only made them want in even more.'

I tried to picture Caleb and a couple of suits sitting at one of the tables at Betty's. I wondered if Zara had served them, if her charming way with male customers had pushed the suits over the edge.

'Look at him go,' another surfer said, scrambling to his feet.

We faced the water just as Mark jumped to a low

squat on the board. He tried to stand twice, but placed his hands back by his feet when the wave dropped and lifted, sending him off balance. He tried again, wobbling from side to side as his legs straightened. The wave grew taller, its crest reached forward. I glanced at Simon, who appeared to be mentally recording the wave's height and odd behaviour.

The guys erupted in cheers as Mark rode the wave for three seconds before diving into the water. I held my breath until his head broke the surface; when he beamed in our direction and punched the air with his fist, I finally exhaled.

'Thanks for the info, guys,' Simon said as Mark jogged toward us. 'It was good to see you.'

'Take care, man,' Mark said, shaking Simon's hand. 'If we hear anything, we'll definitely be in touch.'

'Thanks. And you might want to pack it in soon – by the looks of it, you've got about fifteen minutes before all this is underwater.'

They looked at their stuff scattered across the sand, clearly wondering, like me, how that was possible. The water's edge was at least fifty feet away.

'Do you mind if I just grab a few measurements?' Simon asked after a silent walk to the car a few minutes later. 'It won't take long.'

'I don't mind. Do you need help?' I watched him take a backpack and plastic box from the back seat.

He looked to the sky, then toward the water. He scanned the horizon before turning back and looking at my feet. 'You *are* wearing sneakers.'

'Flame resistant,' I reminded him.

'Okay, then.' He gave me a small smile. 'I could use the extra set of hands.'

It became clear almost immediately why my footwear was a concern – the water was rising as fast as Simon had predicted. I looked to the left as we veered right and saw Caleb's friends gathering their boards and gear as the foamy runoff reached for their cars. Given the water's movement, we had to move fast.

Reaching a tall line of boulders a quarter of a mile down the beach, Simon opened his backpack, handed me a measuring tape and pulled out a stack of notebooks. He slid a notebook and three plastic vials in his jacket pocket.

He scaled the smallest boulder, dropped to his knees and held out one hand toward me. He pulled me up easily, as if I were a pillow and not a sixty-kilogram person.

'Hold one end of the measuring tape and keep an eye on the side of the rock,' he said. 'If the water starts reaching further back than where you're standing, follow it. You should be even with the break the whole time. The measuring tape needs to be kept as level as possible. I'll tug when I reach the end of the line, and then we'll both reach over the side so I can get a more accurate measurement.'

'Got it.' I watched him go up and over the rocks like Spiderman in a maroon fleece.

I dropped to my knees and crawled toward the boulder's edge. I peered over and saw a thin layer of foam dissolving across the sand. The water was breaking a few feet away, so I shuffled to the right until a wave struck directly below me. My head snapped back as the spray shot up, coating the rock and my face.

The water rose faster. Simon barely had time to lift up from the last boulder, make notes and reach back down before I was moving with the water and scooting to the left. The waves were so big it was hard to gauge the break, but I judged the movement by where the spray felt most concentrated.

Ten minutes later, as thin, salty streams flowed down my face and my wet hair stuck to my forehead, Simon tugged on the measuring tape. He gave me a quick thumbs-up, and I released my end.

'Awesome,' he said, hopping down to my boulder. 'I mean, crazy and weird and totally unnatural, but . . . awesome. The tide's moving at about two centimetres a minute.' He unzipped his fleece and grabbed at his collar.

'That's not normal?' I guessed, jumping up and helping him pull off the wet fleece when it stuck around his shoulders.

'Not even close.'

I looked away as he straightened his T-shirt. Stressful circumstances were clearly messing with my emotions. I'd seen Simon without his shirt on countless occasions, but now, just catching a glimpse of his bare abdomen had made my face flush.

'Tides move around three metres every six hours – or about thirty centimetres every thirty minutes. Fast enough to notice after a while, but not fast enough to notice while it's happening. At this rate, the tides are rising thirty centimetres every twelve minutes.'

'More than twice as fast,' I calculated quickly.

'Exactly.' He shook his head. 'Crazy.'

'What's also crazy is that you don't seem to notice that you're shaking and your lips are turning blue.' I retrieved his backpack and plastic box from where he'd thrown them. 'We should get back to the car.'

'You're right.' He cupped his hands and blew in them. 'We still have a lot to do.'

He jumped to the sand, and I tossed him his stuff. He shoved the plastic box in the backpack, slid the backpack on his shoulders and stood at the base of the boulder. 'This is the easy part,' he said when I didn't move right away. 'Just pretend you're climbing down a ladder.'

'Ladders don't usually stand at ninety-degree angles,' I said, looking down at the ground.

He waited for me to look at him. When I did, his expression was serious. His concern for me had temporarily managed to replace his excitement for whatever amazing scientific discovery we'd just made. 'Just go slow,' he said. 'I've got you.'

Knowing that the water was creeping along at a couple of centimetres a minute, I didn't have time to debate. I turned around, knelt and lowered one foot, then the other, over the edge. Keeping all of my upper-body weight over the top of the rock, I slid my toes down the side until they fitted in small crevices in the granite. Once my feet were steady, I lifted my torso slightly from the top of the rock and shifted slowly backward.

Boo.

Justine's blue eyes flashed before me. Her grey hands were on my waist, her bruised arms dragging me down, off the rock. Panicked, I let go of the top of the rock, and my feet slipped out from under me. I fell to the ground, my sneakers somehow hitting the wet sand first. I stumbled back before they could sink, before the water could reach me and wrap around my ankles.

'It's okay.'

I looked behind Simon toward the ocean, past his arms that still reached for me, that were still ready to catch me if I needed them to.

'Vanessa,' he said gently, stepping toward me.

A wave hit. I held my breath as it retreated, half expecting Justine to rise up from the sand as it did.

But she wasn't there. Of course she wasn't there. The sand was empty except for clumps of seaweed and a broken crab shell.

My eyes moved to Simon's hands – his tanned, healthy, *living* hands – and I grabbed them with my own. They were cold and wet, but I could finally exhale when they still felt warm against mine.

'It's okay,' he said, now standing less than a few centimetres away. 'You're okay.'

I really didn't want to let go of Simon's hands, but knew I had to, especially if we were going to make it to the car without swimming part of the way.

I let go reluctantly, careful not to look at Simon or behind him, toward the water. As we started back across the beach, I tried to ignore the siren moaning softly somewhere in the distance.

Twenty minutes later we were in the Subaru, driving toward Winter Harbor with the windows down and the heat on. I stared at the passing trees without seeing them, wondering what I was doing there, and why I'd dragged poor Simon into it.

Justine was gone. Done. Washed up like a fish. What difference did it make why, or how? Or what had really happened before then? The bottom line was that she wasn't coming back. As hard as that was to accept, it was the only truth there was – and had to be easier to deal with than trying to dig up what she hadn't wanted me to know. And once I accepted it, everything could go back to normal. Not to the way normal was before, but to the way it was going to be from now on.

'Simon,' I began with a sigh, prepared to apologise and tell him as much. I turned toward him, already sad in anticipating my solo drive back to Boston and the long summer days without him.

But he didn't hear me. He stared straight ahead, eyes wide and mouth set in a thin line.

I followed his gaze as the car slowed and rolled to a stop.

The road was blocked off by three police cars, a fire engine and an ambulance. Flares circled them like sparklers, and flashing lights cast a strange red glow between the surrounding trees. A dozen emergency workers flew about – policemen talked into their radios, firemen wielded axes in the woods and paramedics prepped the ambulance.

Two more paramedics emerged from between the glowing trees, carrying a covered stretcher. They lifted the stretcher to load it into the ambulance, and a grey, heavy hand fell out from under the white sheet.

The purple and yellow marks were visible from six metres away.

Turning, I focused on the red lights illuminating the woods and the firemen hacking at branches. They worked quickly, and before long I had a clear view through the trees.

'Simon,' I said quietly, all thoughts of leaving Winter Harbor and going back to Boston immediately forgotten. 'They're making a path to the beach.'

CHAPTER 8

'The dress is gorgeous, Vanessa. *Gorgeous.* And you will be gorgeous in it.'

'Thanks,' I said, watching the rain stream down the windscreen and wishing I hadn't answered the phone. 'But I might have to be gorgeous in it some time after this weekend.'

'Absolutely! You know I wouldn't buy you some ridiculous one-time-only bridesmaid-type dress. You can definitely wear it past Labor Day. Maybe even all the way till Columbus Day, if the weather holds.'

If the weather holds.

'Sounds great, Mom. Is Dad there, by any chance?'

'Yes, but we still have much to discuss. Make sure you come back to me before hanging up.'

As she instructed Dad to give the phone right back, I leaned forward to look at the sky. Paige and I sat in the car in her driveway, waiting for a break in the rain before dashing to her house. But judging by the thick clouds, a break wasn't coming any time soon.

'Big Poppa,' I said, once Mom relinquished the receiver, 'I need a favour.'

'Name it, it's yours, kiddo.'

'I told Mom I'm not coming home this weekend, but she doesn't seem to hear any voice but hers. And I *really* can't come home.' I pictured the ambulance from yesterday, the stretcher, the disbelief on Simon's face that had stayed there into the night, after we'd finally made it back to Winter Harbor. 'Not yet, anyway. Can you please let her know in a way that only you can?'

'Don't give it another thought,' he said. 'I'll work my Big Poppa magic.'

'Thank you. I have to go. Please tell her I'll call her tomorrow.'

'Parents!' Paige declared as I dropped the cell phone in the cup holder.

'More like parent. Dad's a saint, but Mom's a bit of a handful.'

'I hear you. Wait until you meet Raina – King Kong's hands couldn't contain that.' She leaned forward and wiped the steam clouding the inside of the windscreen with her apron.

'Sorry.' I ducked my head to try to see under the fog, which reappeared the second Paige wiped it away. 'She runs better than she looks. The defroster's the only thing that doesn't work. And the air conditioning. Oh, and the gas cap sticks, and a back window doesn't roll down.'

'Who needs the back window? And, anyway – are

you *kidding*? It was so nice of you to give me a ride.'

'I'm happy to help.'

'I just don't know what Zara's thinking. Look at it out there!' She shook her head. 'They're going to be lined up around the building in no time, and she just drops me off and leaves? My guess is we've got twenty minutes to find her, get her in the car and drive back to town before the insanity starts.'

'Did she say she was going home?' I wasn't about to admit it, since Paige was so determined to find her, but I hoped our search turned up empty. I knew Betty's would suffer without Zara there to wait tables, but I was also wary of witnessing the sparks that were sure to fly between the two of them. Plus, if we didn't find her right away, maybe we could look for her all day. That would definitely help keep me from thinking about Justine.

'She said she had some stuff to take care of, and she'd be back soon. *Soon.* And now it's two hours later. Do you think two hours qualifies as "soon"?'

'No.'

'Me either.' She leaned forward and peered through the cloudy windscreen. 'It's like a monsoon out there.'

I rolled down the driver's-side window for a better look. After driving along miles of narrow, twisty roads, we'd finally reached a large clearing that started level with the tree baseline and rose to a rounded peak. In its centre was a two-storey turquoise house surrounded by rosebushes blooming thousands of blossoms in every colour. There were so many flowers I could smell their sweet fragrance from where we sat, waiting for a break in the rain.

'This is ridiculous. I'm making a run for it.' Paige yanked the hood of her jacket over her head, sending a light shower across the dashboard. She grabbed the door handle and looked at me. 'Do you have any sisters?'

I opened my mouth to say yes . . . and then closed it. Because I wasn't sure. *Did* I have any sisters? Or did I become an only child the second Justine hit the water at the base of Chione Cliffs?

Fortunately, there was a slight lull in the rain then, and Paige ran for the house. I rolled up the window, turned off the car and ran after her, slowing only slightly when I reached the first clump of rosebushes. The flowers were dark purple, with yellow running around the petals' edges. I glanced around as I continued up the hill toward the house, noticing that all of the roses were at least two colours, and sometimes three or four. I would've thought they were fake if my jeans hadn't caught on a thorny stem right before the porch steps.

'Her bark is worse than her bite,' Paige said when I reached her. 'Just hang back and you'll be fine.'

Assuming she was referring to Zara, I was tempted to hang all the way back in the car – but she was in the house before I could offer.

I followed her into the living room, which was done in shades of blue and cream. The couch and armchairs were covered in navy and aqua-blue tapestry. Hanging over the fireplace, which was where our flat screen hung at home, was a wide mirror with an antique ivory frame. The room's decorative touches were turquoise throw pillows, lacy lampshades perched above crystal stands and an ivory shag rug that almost took up the entire room.

'It's my grandmother's stuff,' Paige said, noticing me look around. 'This is her house. Zara, my mom and I have all lived here for ever. Three generations of Marchands all under one roof, which, once you've met Raina, will be really hard to imagine.'

As we headed across the room, I watched the view through the tall windows lining the far wall. It didn't change. The house sat so high up that, at least from the living room, the only thing you could see was sky.

'Vanessa,' Paige said dramatically, spinning toward me just before passing through a wide doorway, 'meet Raina. Queen of the castle, and of my heart.'

I stopped just outside the kitchen. My head throbbed once, the pain so great I grabbed the doorway to keep from doubling over.

'Hello, Vanessa.'

I blinked. The pain was gone.

'I didn't know we were having company today.'

I blinked again, thinking the fleeting attack had affected my vision. Most moms I met resembled my own, who had two looks: professional and preppy. When Mom wasn't wearing black business suits, she was wearing khakis and button-down shirts. When her hair wasn't in a tight bun, it was in a neat ponytail. She was always put together, polished. But standing next to Raina in her best suit and heels, she'd be something else.

Invisible. Which was exactly how I felt now.

'We wouldn't have had company today if Z had shown up to work,' Paige said, standing across the counter from her mother. 'Vanessa gave me a ride.'

'It's nice to meet you,' I said, trying to smile.

Raina held a wooden spoon above a pink plastic mixing bowl and stared at me, her silver-blue eyes flashing. As she sized me up, I tried to get a better look without being obvious. She had to be just under six feet tall, with dark, wavy hair that fell to her waist. She wore a soft, sleeveless white sundress, and a dozen silver bangles that clinked together as she resumed stirring. She wore no make-up, but she didn't need to – her complexion was clear, her skin smooth. She was striking and looked more like Paige's other elder sister than her mother.

'Your sister's upstairs,' Raina said finally. 'But she doesn't feel well.'

Paige nodded toward the kitchen window. 'Have you looked outside today? Do you know what's happening only a few miles away?'

'She'll be back as soon as she's able,' Raina said evenly.

'No one's going to feel well if we're short-staffed,' Paige pointed out. 'Our customers will be hungry. Louis will be cranky. And all because Z's PMS-ing? I don't think so.'

Raina turned on an electric mixer and lowered it into the pink mixing bowl. 'You can try talking to her,' she said over the whirring. 'But don't expect her to be happy about it.'

'I never do.' Paige whirled around. She grabbed me gently by the sleeve when she reached the doorway and pulled me with her out of the kitchen.

'Pleased to meet you, Vanessa,' Raina called after us, sounding indifferent at best.

'See?' Paige said once we crossed the living room and entered a narrow stairwell. 'I'd love it if my biggest issue with my mother was that she bought me a dress I didn't want to wear to go to a party I didn't want to go to.'

'Is that why you call her by her first name?' I asked, ignoring the thudding in my chest. 'Because she's not as warm and fuzzy as other mothers?'

'That – and because she wanted us to. She says she doesn't feel old enough to have two teenage daughters.' She reached the landing and turned to me. 'By the way, I meant to ask – why aren't your parents here? You said your mom wanted you to come home?'

'Right.' I focused on a lit wall sconce. 'Mom's a work-aholic, and Dad's a momaholic, so they went back to Boston for a few days.'

'Awesome,' Paige said, stepping into the hallway. 'I would kill for my own space every now and then. Want to trade?'

I laughed, but the funny thing was, even if the trade included Zara, I kind of did.

I followed her down a long hallway lit by two small crystal chandeliers. 'Are you sure I shouldn't wait down-stairs?' I asked when we stopped in front of a closed door. 'Your sister doesn't seem to like me that much.'

'Z doesn't like anyone that much.' Paige smiled re-assuringly and pounded on the door with her fist. 'You should hear her talk about Jonathan.'

She banged again before I could ask who Jonathan was. I pressed one hand to my forehead when music playing on the other side of the door grew louder. It sounded like jazz, but with drums and a fast, throbbing beat.

'I'm not going anywhere, Z,' Paige yelled. She pounded again, and the pain reverberated between my ears each time her fist connected with the door.

She started knocking and bobbing her head in time to the music. This went on for at least a minute, and I turned away and stood by a tall window, massaging my temples as I watched the rain fall in one heavy grey sheet into the ocean far below. My head started to spin, and feeling like I might pass out, I turned back to Paige to excuse myself and wait in the car.

I was about to tap her shoulder when the jazz stopped and the door flung open. As soon as Zara saw me, her eyes flashed surprise, then confusion, then anger.

'Not feeling well, huh?' Paige asked.

It was a legitimate question. I'd seen Zara only at Betty's, so had only seen her in khaki shorts, a black T-shirt and an apron. The standard uniform was a far cry from her current ensemble: a tight black skirt that ended about six inches higher than the khaki shorts, a fitted black strapless top and sparkly stiletto sandals. Her hair, which I'd only seen in a long ponytail, hung perfectly straight down her back, and her make-up made her silver eyes shine like Christmas ornaments.

'If you're having trouble breathing, you may want to let out a few stitches,' Paige suggested, eyeing Zara's bulging top.

'And unless you want to never breathe again, you'll tell your little friend to leave.' Zara's voice was calm.

Paige nodded. 'Okay, then.' She looked at me. 'Meet you downstairs?'

I was grateful for the out and started down the hallway before Paige had even closed the door behind her. I hoped whatever issues they had could be worked out quickly, because I now wanted nothing more than to make it out of there before the winding roads leading down the mountain and back to town flooded.

Vanessa . . .

I quickened my step.

My dear, sweet, Nessa . . .

She was outside my head again, calling to me from the crystal chandeliers above, the pictures lining the walls, the rug beneath my feet.

You've come so far . . . Please don't go . . .

I walked faster, shaking my head sharply against wailing sirens and flashing red lights, purple and yellow bruises, and Justine standing in the water, her skeletal arms reaching for me.

I had one foot on the first step leading downstairs when the house fell silent. I stopped and held my breath. Nothing. No funky jazz. No shouting from the end of the hallway. Not even the rain pounding the roof overhead.

'Vanessa?'

In the mirror hanging on the wall across from me, my eyes widened and my face went white. The voice didn't belong to Paige or Zara. And there was no one behind me. The hallway was empty.

'You've lost it,' I said to my reflection before starting downstairs. 'Officially.'

'Vanessa?' the voice asked again.

I froze, my heart hammering in my ears.

'Is that you . . . ?'

It was coming from the opposite end of the hallway, nowhere near Zara's room. I stared at the landing at the base of the stairs and willed my feet to move.

And they did move, finally – upstairs and down the hallway.

My pulse threatened to break through veins, and my fingers and toes tingled. My timid inner voice warned me, begged me to turn around and get out of there. But I ignored it. Every muscle and nerve fought to pull me in the other direction, but I had to see who was there.

Because, what if? What if it was her? What if, somehow, despite all logic – and the medical examiner's report, the wake, the funeral – Justine was still here? I knew it was crazy . . . but how was it any harder to believe than everything that had already happened?

The door was open slightly, revealing a thin, vertical line of light. Not breathing, I placed one palm on the door and pushed it in.

It took me a second to see her. When I did, I was a combination of disappointed and relieved that she wasn't Justine.

A woman sat in front of a fireplace on a lilac-coloured chaise longue, wearing a purple robe and weaving a needle and thread through a thin piece of fabric. Her hair was long and wavy like Raina's; it had probably once been as black as liquorice, too, though time had turned it a powdery charcoal, like the ash under the logs burning in her fireplace. When she smiled at me, her eyes were more grey than silver, and cloudy. They focused not on mine, but above my head.

Somehow, the woman had known I was there without seeing me. Because she couldn't see anything.

I wanted to turn around and tiptoe back down the hallway. But I didn't. I couldn't. Maybe because it didn't feel right to ignore her and make her think the senses she had left were starting to fail. Maybe it was because her purple walls were covered in dozens of needlepoint tapestries depicting different views of Chione Cliffs in winter, spring, summer and fall.

Or maybe it was because I stood there waiting for Justine to say something, anything, inside my head or around it . . . and she didn't.

'I'm Bettina,' the woman said quietly, her voice as smooth as ice. 'But you may call me Betty.'

CHAPTER 9

'Your grandmother's blind,' I said when the Betty's crowd finally thinned several hours later.

'Yes,' Paige said, drying a wine glass.

'She can't see,' I said. 'At all.'

'Right.'

'Okay . . . then how did she know who I was?'

Paige glanced around, then pulled me to an empty corner behind the bar. 'Grandma Betty was in a very bad accident two years ago,' she whispered. 'She hasn't been the same since.'

'What kind of accident?' I asked.

'Good news,' a male voice said before she could respond.

We looked across the bar to where Garrett stood, holding up two tickets.

'Dave Matthews. Portland. Tonight.'

'I thought that show sold out months ago?' I said, since he was looking at me.

'I pulled some strings – and gave an online broker next year's tuition.' He started backing away. 'I know you're busy, so don't say no yet. Think about it first.'

'Aw, someone has a summer crush,' Paige said once he was outside. 'He's a sweetie. You should go.'

The idea of going out and having fun was too strange to consider. 'You were saying? About your grandmother?'

'Right.' Paige resumed drying. 'She kind of went swimming in a lightning storm.'

'Ouch.'

'No kidding.' Paige shook her head. 'Before the accident, Grandma Betty spent more time in the water than out of it. It didn't matter what time of year or how cold the water was – as long as it wasn't frozen, she was swimming. That's actually how she ended up here, in Winter Harbor. She grew up in Canada and came down the coast on a road trip with some friends. She was so excited that the water here wasn't iced over, the way every other body of water this far north is in the middle of winter, that she never went back.'

'That's dedication to your sport.'

'Or the kind of dependency that can get you in trouble.' She looked at me. 'You know when you were little and counted the seconds between thunderclaps and bursts of lightning? And the longer the time between them, the further away the storm was?'

I nodded without sharing that I'd actually done that quite recently.

'Well, on the day Grandma decided to jump from our back yard into the ocean below, the thunderclaps

123

and bursts of lightning were happening *simultaneously*. The storm was right over us. She said it was just something she needed to do, which, of course, doesn't explain squat. And she hasn't talked about it since.'

Paige looked up when a table of four men across the room burst into laughter. It had taken the promise of the next weekend off to get Zara out of the miniskirt and back into her Betty's uniform, but she had eventually conceded. By the time she did, I was waiting in the car. I'd shaken Betty's hand and complimented her needlepoint, and then I'd hightailed it out of there. Paige and Zara had emerged ten minutes later and driven together in Zara's red Mini Cooper so that Paige could make sure Zara didn't embark on an unexpected detour. Now, it was back to business as usual.

'Grandma wasn't the same after that,' Paige continued. 'She lost her vision, and her other senses were also affected. She thought she was dying when she was still in the water because she couldn't see anything, but she could hear the rain, waves, crabs crawling, whales singing. In the hospital, she couldn't see the shock on the doctor's face – but she heard him say that she was going to live . . . and also heard a patient breathing on the respirator in the next room, and another patient's heart stop on the floor below.'

'Wow.'

'I know. We thought the insane claims would end

once she was home and the trauma was behind her, but she kept insisting that she could hear the fish bubbling in the ocean, the roses blooming in the front yard, the mailman coming from miles away. Then she started smelling things, and sensing things, like some kind of super senior citizen. We joked that we might see her shooting across the sky one day, wearing her purple bathing suit and a beach towel tied around her neck like a cape.'

'Is that how she knew who I was without seeing me?' I asked. 'Did her super senses clue her in?'

'Your guess is as good as mine.' She put a glass down and leaned toward me. 'No one outside our family knows that Grandma Betty went off the deep end and never fully returned after the accident. Raina tells anyone who asks that she's just suffering from normal old-age issues and is too weak to leave the house. She thinks that's easier than dealing with questions we don't know how to answer . . . and I know she'd appreciate it if our little family secret stayed a secret.'

'You got it.' I nodded. 'No problem.'

'Thanks.' Paige smiled, then looked at the TV perched above the bar. 'Hello, daily depressing update.'

I followed her gaze and hoped she didn't notice the colour leave my face. The news anchor was easy to hear, since everyone with a clear view of her stopped talking to listen to what she said.

'Winter Harbor police are having a busier summer than usual,' the woman said into the camera. 'Instead of dealing with the usual seasonal issues of underage drinking and unapproved late-night beach parties, local authorities are contending with a series of seemingly unrelated deaths.'

Next to me, Paige shook her head.

'The first victim, eighteen-year-old Justine Sands, who would have been a freshman at Dartmouth College in September, leapt to her death from a cliff. Paul Carsons, an entrepreneur and father of three, died when his boat capsized in a severe thunderstorm. Charles Spinnaker, a corporate attorney and father of five, drowned while fishing fifty feet from shore.'

As their pictures flashed across the screen, I focused on breathing.

'The fourth victim, Aaron Newberg, president and CEO of pharmaceutical company ImEx, Inc., was discovered earlier this morning at the base of the Winter Harbor Lighthouse. It is believed that he also drowned, though authorities are still investigating.'

The news clip ended abruptly with a list of phone numbers for witnesses to call with more information. It seemed as routine as a traffic and weather report.

'Hey,' Paige said, lifting a crate of water glasses to the counter and snapping my attention from the television. 'What time is it?'

I checked the clock hanging over the sink behind me. 'Almost ten.'

She folded her arms and rested them on the edge of the crate. 'Well, that's strange.'

I followed her gaze across the dining room. My heart skipped once, then seemed to stop.

It skipped when I saw Oliver sitting in Zara's section – two hours ahead of schedule – and looking around the room instead of out the window. That was what had obviously caught Paige's interest.

And it seemed to stop when I saw Simon standing in the lobby, also looking around the room.

'Hello, cutie,' Paige said when he waved to me. She squinted. 'Is that Simon Carmichael?'

'Yes.' I was glad Grandma Betty's supersensory powers weren't hereditary so Paige couldn't hear my sudden arrhythmia.

'Wow. And they say college is good for the mind. He looks totally different.'

'Would you mind helping Oliver?' I asked. 'I'll just be a second.'

'Take your time.' She took a pad and pen from her apron and smiled. 'The day Jonathan shows up here for me will probably be the last day you see me for a week.'

I made a mental to note to ask about Jonathan later. My list of questions for Paige was growing long, and included others, like, What had happened to Paige's grandfather? What did Paige's dad think of all this? What was with all the Chione Cliffs arts and crafts? How did Grandma Betty know my name? And why did Justine seem to want me to meet her?

The answers would have to wait.

'What's wrong?' I asked when I reached Simon. He'd smiled when he first saw me, but now he looked serious.

'Hey,' he said. 'Sorry to just show up, but I couldn't wait to see you.'

It was obvious by his expression that he didn't mean that in the romantic sitting-at-home-pining-for-me sense, and I was surprised when the words still made my arms tingle, like someone had lightly trailed a feather across my skin. 'It's okay. What's going on?'

He glanced around, as if someone might actually hear us over the hundred other people in the room, and stepped toward me. He stood so close I could see the smudges on his glasses and the tiny bristles of hair along his jaw. 'Caleb called.'

The buzz around us seemed to grow softer. 'Where is he? Is he okay?'

'I don't know – he didn't say anything. I didn't recognise the number, and when I answered, there were a few seconds of light, bumpy breathing, like he was moving around. And then just as it sounded like he was going to speak, there was another voice. A female voice. She said Caleb's name, and then the line went dead.'

A family of five entered the restaurant, gently pushing us backward. As we moved, my eyes fell on the mirror behind the hostess stand. I held my breath, sure I would see Justine looking back at me, surrounded by a sparkling spray of silver.

'I checked the number online.'

I looked away from the empty mirror.

'There was no listing, so I tried calling. No one answered the first few times, but a park ranger finally picked up.'

'A park ranger? Where?'

His eyes held mine. 'Camp Heroine.'

I could no longer hear the customers talking and laughing in the dining room. It was as if Simon and I were the only people in the entire restaurant.

'I wouldn't think of going under any other circumstances,' he said. 'And he might be long gone by now. But this is the first lead we've got. I can't just let it go.'

I managed to nod. He stood so close now I could smell the spearmint toothpaste on his breath.

'Will you come with me?' he asked quietly.

My pulse quickened. Besides Chione Cliffs, Camp Heroine was the last place I wanted to go. But if it meant possibly finding Caleb – and spending the day with Simon – then there was nowhere else I should be. 'Be right back,' I said, untying my apron.

I flew from the lobby and headed for the bar. Paige was gone; a quick scan of the dining room showed her talking to Oliver. I couldn't disappear without telling her, but I also couldn't go over and endure another strange senior moment. I waited for her to turn from him before waving.

'Is everything okay?' she asked when she reached me.

'Yes,' I said. 'Or it will be, as long as you don't hate me.'

'Impossible.'

'Even if I leave now? For the day?'

She looked over her shoulder, toward the lobby. When she turned back to me, her eyes glittered. 'You're leaving with Simon?'

I paused, then nodded.

'Lucky girl.' She grabbed my arms and squeezed. 'If only the Lighthouse ever gave Jonathan the time to think of such romantic gestures.'

'You're sure you don't mind?' I asked, noting the Jonathan–Lighthouse connection for my ever-growing list of questions.

'I'd mind if you *didn't* go. Of course, there is one person who might care a bit more . . .'

I peered behind her to see Oliver staring at us.

'He almost pulled his signature Zara move on me when he saw that I wasn't you.'

That made no sense. I'd said all of ten words to him, and he'd seemed to grow crankier with every one.

'But if you don't go now, I'll fire you.'

I smiled. 'I'll be back as soon as I can.'

'We've been here more than fifty years,' she said lightly, hurrying toward the kitchen. 'We'll be here when you get back.'

I kept my eyes lowered as I crossed the room and headed for the lobby, and was only a few feet away from Simon when I had to stop. I grabbed the edge of the closest table and closed my eyes. The pain had hit so sharply, so intensely, it was like someone had doused my hair in kerosene before dropping a match to it.

'Are you okay? Do you need to sit down?'

I opened one eye enough to see a young father in a blue baseball hat looking at me. His eyebrows were wrinkled with worry – which was quite nice of him, I thought, considering that my thumb had missed his plate of blueberry pancakes by an inch.

'She's fine.'

I let go of the table to grab my head with both hands.

'Aren't you, Vanessa?'

To everyone else within hearing distance, Zara's voice probably sounded perfectly normal – even sweet. Like we were the kind of friends who knew each other so well she knew my headaches were fleeting and didn't warrant concern. But to me, it sounded like long metal nails being drilled through my ears and into the centre of my skull.

'Hey,' Simon said gently, and I could feel his warm breath on my face as he put one arm around my waist. 'I've got you.'

My head throbbed less with every step we took. By the time we reached the front door, I could open my eyes all the way, and I turned to see Zara watching us. Her arms were crossed over her chest, and her eyes were narrowed into long silver slits.

'Do you know her?' I asked Simon. He'd never mentioned her, but they'd both grown up in Winter Harbor – they'd probably even gone to school together.

He glanced behind us and sighed. 'It's kind of hard *not* to know Zara Marchand.'

CHAPTER 10

I spent ten minutes of the drive to Camp Heroine wondering what it was about Zara that made it hard not to know her. It was hard for *me* not to know her, since she'd seemed to dislike me as soon as she saw me, and my resulting anxiety caused blinding migraines every time she was near. But she clearly didn't have that effect on men – or teenage boys. So what was it? Her looks? The charm she switched on like a light when she wanted to? Or was it some special love potion she slipped in their drinks when they weren't looking? Because there had to be more to it than just her silver eyes and fleeting charisma.

I spent five minutes of the drive wondering why it bothered me so much that her effects weren't lost on Simon.

Thankfully, the drive was only fifteen minutes long. We pulled up to the rusty, crooked gate of Camp Heroine before I could do anything I'd regret later – like ask Simon what exactly he meant when he'd said what he had before leaving Betty's.

'Why?' he asked as we sat before the gate. 'Why was he here?'

I forced Zara from my mind as we got out of the car. As far as I could tell, there was no reason for Caleb to be there. There was no reason for *anyone* to be there. In the 1940s, Camp Heroine had been a top-secret military base disguised as a quaint New England fishing village to fool approaching enemy ships and planes. Over the years it had evolved from a military base to a park to a place for thrill-seeking kids to play truth or dare. In the 1990s, after several bodies were found on the camp's beach and trails, state officials decided the area's elemental conditions – dense fog, heavy surf, rocky outcroppings – were too dangerous for hikers and swimmers, and closed Camp Heroine for good. Now you heard about it only when the latest group of curious young tourists tried to see for themselves if the place was as bad as its reputation suggested, and the *Herald* reported on their illegal antics.

'We'll have to climb it,' Simon said after tugging on the gate's padlock and chains. He turned to me. 'Unless you want to wait in the car?'

I shook my head. There was no way I was waiting by myself in the Subaru – or letting him wander through Camp Heroine alone.

He hoisted himself up the tall iron gates. When he got to the top and jumped to the ground on the other side, I took the rusty iron slats in both hands and wedged my sneakers between them. I moved up by pulling with my arms and sliding my feet in the narrow spaces between the slats.

'This isn't like climbing down a ladder,' I said when I reached the top. The iron slats ended in sharp points, so unless I wanted to wander Camp Heroine with a punctured abdomen, I couldn't turn around and use the same pull-and-slide method down the other side. Not helping was that it had started to rain, making the iron slippery in my hands.

'It's not that big a drop,' Simon promised. 'I'll catch you.'

Two metres seemed like a pretty sizeable drop to me, but I didn't really have a choice. Using all my strength to keep my body a few centimetres above the sharp ends, I brought my feet over, and then pushed off.

'You're tough for a city girl,' Simon said when I landed on the other side.

I tried to smile, but was too aware of his arms under mine, his hands on my waist, our chests pressing together – and the fact that he didn't automatically let go, even though my feet were firmly on the ground.

'There's the pay phone,' I said finally.

He released my waist and turned around. The phone was next to what had once been an information hut during the camp's state park days. It was hard to imagine visitors stopping at the dilapidated, roofless building for brochures and hiking maps. Even harder to imagine was Caleb standing there just hours before.

'It's dead,' Simon said after jogging to the hut and picking up the phone. He hung up and tried again. 'No dial tone. No buzzing. Nothing.'

'It looks like someone wanted it that way.' Joining him, I lifted the jagged ends of the phone's severed cord.

'That's strange. I checked online. The park only had one phone, which the state kept in service just in case the weather messed with radio signals during rangers' monthly visits.'

'Apparently whoever Caleb was with wanted his undivided attention.'

Simon's lips set in a straight line as he replaced the receiver. He circled the small building and then forced open the door.

I stepped toward him as he disappeared through the doorway. What if whoever had wanted Caleb's undivided attention was still there? Hiding in the hut, just waiting for his next victim? Shouldn't we call for backup? Or grab the small medical scissors from Simon's first-aid kit? Or –

'Empty.'

I exhaled as he reappeared in the doorway.

'Nothing but leaves and old newspapers.'

He hurried down a dirt path, and I jogged to keep up, my eyes darting from one side to the other. Visible reminders of Camp Heroine's divided past were every-where. Concrete artillery bunkers covered in crawling vines sat a few feet off the path. Sagging picnic tables and metal wastebaskets were scattered throughout the overgrown brush. Black graffiti decorated the sides of long, rectangular buildings. If Caleb was trying to hide, this was a good place to do it.

'The main buildings are on the bluff,' Simon called over his shoulder as he veered right, onto another dirt path leading up and away from the one we'd been following.

I struggled to hear him over the rain. It was falling faster now, harder. The sky had been clear during our drive but had since grown dark. Peering through the leafy canopy overhead, I could see thick grey clouds rolling in off the ocean. When we reached the path's end at the top of the bluff ten minutes later, the clouds had dropped lower, the rain was falling in a cold, solid sheet and the first bolts of lightning were shooting at the ground.

'How did we not know this was coming?' I yelled, joining Simon at the edge of the bluff. The rain fell so heavily it was hard to tell where sky ended and ocean began. I couldn't even see the beach below us.

'I checked the weather before we left,' Simon yelled back. 'It said *chance* of thunderstorms.'

I followed him to a building tucked in the woods

several yards from the edge of the bluff. From the outside the building looked like a small church, complete with fake stained-glass windows and a fake steeple. Simon took a flashlight from his fleece pocket and shone it around the room. The bright beam illuminated wooden bunk beds attached to the walls, empty except for leaves, branches and a forgotten sleeping bag.

'It's not the Lighthouse Resort,' Simon said, looking out at the rain, 'but it'll keep us dry.'

My heart raced as I stood next to him, and I wasn't sure if it was because we were temporarily stranded in Camp Heroine in the middle of a thunderstorm, or because simply being near him felt different now.

'This wasn't in the forecast,' Simon said, his eyes meeting mine. 'The radar didn't show any sign of this system – here, or anywhere close to here.'

'Storms don't move that fast, do they?'

'Not usually.' He turned his gaze back to the rain. 'But the frequency of these storms is increasing, and so is their strength. And the meteorologists are dumbfounded every time, because there's nothing to indicate their approach.'

'Like when we went to Chione Cliffs? You checked the weather, and it said it was supposed to be clear?'

'Like then. And today, and every other time the sky has gone from blue to black without warning, like

Mother Nature just hit the switch so no one can see the damage she's about to do. It's what I've been researching. Because the meteorologists don't get it. The National Weather Centre doesn't get it. My professors don't get it. And by the time they do, there could be millions of dollars' worth of damage done. Towns could be devastated. More lives could be lost.'

More lives.

'And it's not just an off summer?' I asked. 'Another example of global warming throwing the planet out of whack?'

'I wish it was that easily explained. But these storms, as big as they are, are confined to a very specific area. The Pacific Northwest sits at about the same latitude as the upper Northeast, and their weather patterns are totally normal compared to other summers.' He looked at me. 'Remember how crazy the waves were when we saw Mark and his friends surfing? And the way the tides moved?'

I nodded.

'I think they're related – the hyperactive ocean and the storm systems. I don't know how or why, but I'm trying to find out. I've been travelling up and down the Maine coast, recording high and low tides, salt content, pH, hourly weather conditions – anything that might help piece together why this is happening where and when it is.'

'That's a big project for one person.'

He looked down. 'Except I'm not just one person. Not any more.'

My cheeks warmed, as if the summer sun had broken through the blanket of clouds.

'And besides, I have to do it. I can't *not* do it.' He paused, and when he spoke again, his voice was softer. 'If this were any other summer, Justine would still be alive. If this were any other summer, Caleb wouldn't be running.'

This clearly wasn't any other summer. And as the thin wooden walls shook and the rain roared even louder overhead, I began to think that Simon might be right.

'Do you hear that?' he asked a moment later.

I held my breath and listened. Outside, the wind and rain slowed, and the air grew still.

The wind resumed first. As it whistled through the walls and shook what was left of the door, it felt colder, like the temperature outside had instantly plummeted thirty degrees.

The rain followed a few seconds later. At first, it was hard to hear over my throbbing heart, but then it fell faster, harder, shaking the ceiling like a herd of moose galloping across the roof. Soon, the noise was so overpowering, I braced for the church to rip from its foundation and spiral up and away with us inside.

'Is that hail?' I shouted as Simon grabbed my hand and led me away from the door.

He didn't answer. Reaching the back-left corner of the room, he dropped to the floor and pulled me with him. The air grew so cold I could see my breath, and Simon took off his fleece, wrapped it around me and held me close. It was the kind of protection any caring big brother would've offered in the same situation . . . but I didn't feel like Simon's little sister. In fact, I thought that if he moved his face just an inch closer to mine, and if our lips accidentally brushed together, I probably wouldn't even notice the church flying from its foundation.

'I think that was the worst of it,' he whispered a few minutes later.

I opened my eyes and lifted my head from his chest. The church was still standing. Through the shredded door I could see water dripping from the trees instead of the sky. The air grew brighter and warmer as the sun shone through thinning clouds.

'Are you okay?'

'I don't know,' I said truthfully. Because we'd just survived a freak assault by Mother Nature, we still had to find Caleb . . . and all I could think was that I didn't want to move.

'Are you cold? Hurt? Did anything fall on you?'

'No.' I made myself pull away and climb to my feet. 'Just a little rattled.'

'Well,' Simon said, standing, 'that enormous cloud had a silver lining. If Caleb was here before the storm, he's still here now; he couldn't have got far with that going on.'

I followed him outside. The military had apparently done something right when they built Camp Heroine. There was no physical evidence of what had just transpired besides a fresh layer of leaves and twigs blanketing the dirt path. The fake steeple still stood atop the fake church, and the rest of the buildings had survived just as well.

'Do you mind if I get a few measurements before we keep looking?' Simon asked. 'It'll take three minutes, tops.'

'Of course. Go ahead.'

He looked like he was going to say something else, but then turned and started down the bluff. I stayed close behind. The bluff was steep, but sandy instead of rocky, which made the trek fairly easy. When we made it to the beach, he pulled a small notebook and plastic case from his backpack and jogged to the water. The ocean hadn't recovered from the storm as quickly as the sky, and waves still pummelled the shore. Keeping an eye on Simon, I stayed near the bluff to avoid the spray.

He took several samples and scribbled in his notebook. Three minutes turned into five, and then seven and then nine. After ten minutes, I walked a few yards down the beach, turning every few feet to make sure he was still there and okay. Reaching a low group of rocks that would give me perfect views of him and the water, I stepped carefully across them and sat down.

I closed my eyes and tilted my head toward the sun. I had to get it together. A lot had happened and continued to happen, but that didn't mean I could just let it drag me out and pull me under. Whatever I was feeling for Simon was natural, considering how much time we were spending together in strange circumstances. I would feel the same way about a fireman who pulled me from a burning house, or a policeman who recovered my purse from a thief. The feelings would return to normal eventually.

I opened my eyes when the cool ocean water reached the toes of my sneakers – and keeping it together was no longer an option.

'Simon,' I whispered.

I wanted to yell, to scream his name at the top of my lungs. I wanted to jump off the rocks, charge up the bluff and get as far from Camp Heroine as possible. And if I couldn't manage any of those things, I wanted to close my eyes and open them again later – hours later, if necessary – after the tide had retreated and taken with it everything that now slid around the sand I sat only twenty centimetres above.

But I couldn't do it. I couldn't do any of it. My entire body was frozen, as if encased by a thick block of hail.

'Simon,' I tried again, my lips barely moving. '*Simon*.'

I don't know how he heard me, but he was by my side in seconds.

'Vanessa? What –'

And then he froze, too.

A lifeless arm, attached to a lifeless body, stretched from the water toward the rocks. The body was face down, but it was clear from the build that it was a man.

'Simon . . .' I breathed, my eyes filling with tears. 'It's not . . . ?'

'No,' he said, his voice grim. 'It's too big. And Caleb doesn't wear a watch.'

My eyes managed to move from the purple hand to the swollen wrist, where a thick, silver band glinted in the sun like beach glass. A second later, a tall wave crashed onshore, sending the runoff streaming past the rocks – and the victim turning on his back.

I turned away, and Simon's arms were around me, pulling me off the rock and away from the man. 'What's wrong with him?' I whispered into his shoulder as tears ran down my cheeks. 'What's wrong with his face?'

He tightened his arms around me and rested one hand on the back of my head to keep me from turning again and seeing anything more. 'Let's go. We'll call the police from the car.'

Simon didn't have to worry about my seeing anything more. I'd already seen too much. As police and ambulance sirens howled toward Camp Heroine, I slid down the passenger seat of the Subaru, closed my eyes and thought of Mom, Dad, Justine, Paige, Zara, Betty's, the lake house – anyone and anything that would keep me from seeing it again.

The man, whoever he was, was dead. Done. Gone. Washed up like a fish.

And when he turned over, his eyes were wide open and his mouth was stretched in a wide smile, like he was happy about it.

CHAPTER II

'I can't believe you can just lie there like that.'

I lifted my head to see Paige jogging toward me across the rocky shore. 'It's twenty-eight degrees. *Twenty-eight.* That's ten degrees warmer than the last warmest day we had.'

'Which is why you should be *swimming.*' She spread a towel next to mine and dropped to the ground. 'You can actually dry off outside without freezing.'

I let my head fall back and closed my eyes. 'I don't swim.'

'What do you mean? Your family has a house in one of the East Coast's most beautiful waterfront vacation destinations. How could you not take advantage of Winter Harbor's greatest natural asset? The one thing – besides Betty's Chowder House, of course – that has drawn visitors here for decades?'

My right cheek grew warmer as I turned toward her. 'Truthfully?'

'Please,' she said, wringing out her hair. 'On a day like today, the reason is going to be hard to believe no matter what.'

I paused. Today, as in recent days, the truth included a lot of things I didn't feel like talking about. And not that I would've anyway, but after my Camp Heroine discovery three days before, I definitely wasn't jumping in the ocean any time soon. It was probably better to tell her *something* than to let her come to her own conclusions.

Plus, she was Paige. I trusted her.

'I'm scared of the water,' I said finally. 'I wasn't always – up until a few years ago, the only thing I *wasn't* afraid of was the water. It didn't matter if I was in the ocean, Lake Kanasacka, the school pool, wherever. I always felt comfortable . . . safe even.'

She stretched out on her towel and turned her head toward me. 'So what happened?'

'On a cold June day two years ago, my family and I decided to have a picnic on Beacon Beach. There'd been a bad storm the day before, and the waves were huge.' I closed my eyes briefly, picturing the blue sky, the green water, Big Poppa's hair growing frizzier in the salty spray. 'And after lunch, my sister dared me to go in the water.'

'I didn't know you had a sister,' Paige said.

I looked away. In my moment of partial honesty, I'd almost forgotten which things I wanted to keep private. 'Later,' I continued, hoping Paige wouldn't press, 'she said she was kidding. But at the time, I thought she was serious. And there weren't – aren't – many things I hate more than disappointing her.'

'I know what you mean,' Paige said with a sigh.

'So since my parents would've flipped, I said I was going for a walk. I headed down about half a mile – close enough that they could see me, but far enough that they could mistake me for someone else if they weren't really looking.' I shot up and scooted back when the cool runoff reached my feet. 'It was a bad idea. As soon as the water hit my ankles, I knew it was a bad idea. But I did it anyway.'

'*Sisters*,' Paige groaned. 'A blessing and a curse at the same time.'

'Seriously,' I said after a pause. I trusted Paige, but she didn't really need to know that pleasing Justine wasn't the main reason I let the water pull me in.

'There are no lifeguards at Beacon Beach,' she said a minute later. 'Did you make it out on your own?'

I focused on the water as my cheeks burned. 'Paramedics are pretty strong swimmers.'

She shuddered. 'Oh, Vanessa. I'm so sorry you had to go through that.'

I offered her a small smile. 'Anyway, I haven't been swimming since. I still love the ocean, but it's just so *big*, you know? And it can change direction, gain momentum and drag you toward the horizon without warning.'

'Plus there's the issue of all the scary creatures lurking below.' She tilted her face to the sun. 'Before the accident Grandma always said that she was more comfortable in the water than on land, and that if she didn't go in for at least an hour a day she felt mentally and physically off. Raina and Z aren't quite that dependent, but they swim at least a few times a week, and Z's gotten even more into it since graduating. I like swimming – but I also like dancing. And going to the movies. And eating cereal for dinner. It's a fun thing to do every now and then, but it's not something I *need* to do.'

'Does being in the ocean ever make you nervous?'

'Not really . . . maybe because I've spent so much time around it if not in it? But I can see why it might make other people nervous. Especially here, especially now, with bodies washing on shore every other day.'

My breath caught.

'But on to happier topics,' she said after a moment, her voice brighter. 'Like your sister. Where is she? When can I meet her? Can she give Zara any tips?'

I opened my mouth, prepared to say that Justine was in a summer-school programme in Switzerland, or working as a nanny in Paris, or some other harmless white lie that could explain her absence for the rest of the summer. Before I could pick one, I spotted Raina standing with one arm around a young, good-looking guy on the top of the stairs leading down to the beach.

'Wow. Your mom is Maine's very own Demi Moore.'

Paige followed my gaze, then jumped up and waved. 'That's not Ashton – that's Jonathan.'

As she flew across the sand, up the steep stair-case, and into Jonathan's arms, I jogged after her and thought of Simon. He'd left the day after our trip to Camp Heroine to do more research, and I hadn't heard from him since. I didn't know when he'd be back so was doing my best not to think about him, but that just made me wonder why not thinking about him had become so hard. *That*, however, was better than think-ing that I missed him. Which I did. A lot.

'Hi, Mrs Marchand,' I said, feeling increasingly see-through as I neared the top of the stairs. Raina was wearing a short red sundress that showed off her long legs and golden skin, and her dark hair hung in a loose braid down her back. If Jonathan *had* been her boy-friend, I wouldn't have been surprised.

'Vanessa,' she said coolly, 'please call me *Miss* Marchand. "Mrs" is for the poor woman who believes marriage is a good idea.'

'Like me,' Paige said, hanging from Jonathan's neck. 'Vanessa, please meet the best boyfriend ever.'

I smiled and held out my hand to shake his but quickly retracted it when the happy couple kissed like they were alone in a darkened room. I glanced at

Raina, expecting to see a disapproving frown – and then grabbed the other railing with my other hand when she beamed with pride.

'And Jonathan,' Paige said, coming up for air, 'I'd like you to meet Vanessa, my new best friend and soul sister. She's giving Zara a run for her money.'

'It's great to meet you.' He smiled at me as he put his arms around Paige's waist and lifted her off the ground. 'I've heard a lot about you.'

Given their current mutual obsession, I didn't know how there was time left to talk about anything else, but the thought made me smile anyway. We didn't know everything about each other, but Paige and I were still pretty close for having met only a few weeks before. And I was glad she seemed to feel the same way.

'Jonathan,' Raina said, hooking her arm through his and gently pulling him away from Paige, 'I hear you're training for a marathon in the fall? Tell me more. It's obvious that you're quite the athlete . . .'

'Isn't he the best?' Paige sighed as they continued walking and we followed several feet behind. 'And how cute is it that he and Raina are, like, BFFs?'

'Very,' I said, watching Raina put one arm around his waist.

'Speaking of boyfriends,' Paige said when we reached the porch and Raina and Jonathan disappeared inside, 'Z's got another one. Unlike me, who's only dated one guy ever, she goes through guys like a tornado through a cornfield.'

'Who's the latest?' Given Zara's temperament, I wasn't sure whether to imagine a clean-cut tourist type or a tattooed, leather-clad biker.

'I'll show you, but we have to hurry. Z worked the lunch shift today.'

I followed her inside. As we headed for the stairs, I caught a glimpse of Raina and Jonathan in the kitchen. She poured him a glass of orange juice, then leaned across the counter and tilted her head toward him like whatever he said was the most fascinating thing she'd ever heard. She laughed lightly, and my head pulsated in response. The feeling eased as I hurried after Paige upstairs.

'She would totally kill us if she knew what we were doing right now.'

I stopped short outside Zara's open bedroom door. 'Then maybe we shouldn't do it.'

But Paige was already inside the room and opening Zara's desk drawers. 'She'll go for me first, so you'll get a good head start.'

'Um, Paige?' I watched her rifle through papers and pull out folders. 'I don't really want a head start. I do my best to avoid all potentially life-threatening situations.'

She glanced at her watch. 'If she left right away, we still have at least seven minutes.'

Nessa . . .

My head snapped to the left. Justine had sounded like she stood right next to me, but the hallway was empty.

Dear, sweet Nessa . . .

I hadn't heard her in a few days and couldn't tell if I was scared or relieved to hear her now.

It's okay . . .

'Got it!'

I forced myself to look away from the hallway and into Zara's room. Paige sat on the bed, triumphantly holding up two books.

You'll be okay . . .

I knew it was crazy to be reassured by her words, but I was anyway and walked slowly through the doorway, my heart beating faster with each step. I braced myself for the instant, excruciating headache that always seemed to hit whenever Zara was near, but it didn't come. When my head remained clear, I looked around the room hesitantly, taking in the white comforter, the sheer white fabric cascading from the top of the four-poster bed, the dresser lined with crystal perfume bottles. A white table sat in front of the wall of windows facing the ocean and held a glass vase filled with roses.

Paige patted the bed for me join her. 'So Z likes to think of herself as this beautiful, sophisticated, mysterious person . . . but, really? Total dork. Exhibit A.'

I sat down and took the smaller of the two books. '*La Vie en rose*?' I rubbed my thumb over the script pressed into the white leather cover.

'Life in pink,' Paige said. 'Open it.'

Something flashed suddenly in the dresser mirror across from us. 'I don't think so,' I said, handing it back.

'You know we're on dry land,' she said, taking the book. 'There are no creatures of the deep to be afraid of here.'

'You just said Zara would totally kill us.'

'Fine.' She held the book out so I could see and flipped through the pages.

'It looks like a diary.'

'Exactly. Except . . .' She pointed to the top-right corner of a page in the middle of the book.

'*Avril*?'

'April,' she said, her silver eyes glittering. 'The whole thing's written in French.'

She seemed excited by this, but I didn't get it. 'And?'

'*And* Z took Spanish in school. We both did.'

I still didn't get it, and we were running out of time. 'So she picked up another language. Maybe she got some books on CD, or took an online course.'

'Sure. But the point is, she writes all of her inner-most thoughts in the most beautiful, sophisticated, romantic language in the world. Because that's her, or

154

who she wants to be – beautiful, sophisticated, desired by all.'

'Okay,' I said, even though I thought that maybe the real reason she wrote all of her innermost thoughts in the most beautiful, sophisticated, romantic language in the world was so that her little sister wouldn't be able to read them when she went snooping for secrets.

'Unfortunately, I haven't been able to hold on to this long enough to translate any of the entries, but when I found *this*, I didn't need to.'

The second book was bigger than the first, and its quilted pink cover was trimmed in delicate white lace. In the cover's centre was a small pocket with a window, and in the pocket was a photo of Zara standing on the cliff behind their house with the ocean in the background. She wore a long white sundress, and her dark hair floated around her in the wind.

'She *is* beautiful,' I said. Even if she was mean and cranky and hated me for no reason, there was no denying that.

'Look,' Paige said eagerly, turning the cover.

'A scrapbook?'

'Do you have one?'

I shook my head. Mom had been trying to get me to start one for years, but I didn't think I'd done or experienced anything worth remembering. Unlike Justine – her scrapbook was actually two thick albums, and they were filled with ski-lift tickets, boarding passes, certificates and blue ribbons.

'They're kind of lame, but also kind of fun,' Paige continued. 'Mine has the usual stuff – movie tickets, birthday cards, notes from my friends. But Z's got a totally different approach.'

The first page of Zara's scrapbook was a collage of photos of herself. Justine's had something similar, though her photos also included other people. But the second page was where Zara's approach to scrapbooking took a different turn.

'That's a *lot* of hair.'

'Xavier Cooper,' Paige said. 'And he didn't really have that much hair in person. It just looks like a lot because the picture's enormous.'

'Why so big?' The head shot took up the whole page and almost made me uncomfortable, like Xavier was really there, his head in Paige's lap.

'*Because*, Vanessa . . . when you date Zara Marchand, when you get that close to greatness and maybe even call it your own for a little while, your mug deserves a full page.'

'Wow.'

'Yes. Xavier and Zara dated two years ago, for what I and everyone else thought was about three weeks. He started following her around between shifts at Betty's, and just when it looked like they might actually be a couple, she cut him off. Totally ignored him. The poor guy would actually walk behind her, asking how she was and if she wanted to hang out after work, and she wouldn't say a word. Thankfully, his family only came that summer. A quick, permanent exit is the best you can hope for when you get your heart smashed into a zillion pieces.'

'And the guy still got a full page? Obviously she didn't think whatever they had going on was a very big deal.'

'That's what we thought.' She turned the page. 'But we were wrong.'

'Eddie's Ice Cream?' It was yellowing with age, but I recognised the wafer-cone wrapper immediately.

'"Where it all began,"' Paige read from the hand-written note underneath. '"May twentieth. Saw Xavier today. He was working. I ordered a chocolate milk-shake and decided he was the one."'

'The one?'

'Cheesy, right? But May twentieth was almost two months before anyone noticed something going on. And look – a blade of grass from when they walked in the park. A receipt from the cafe where they first held hands. The empty Tic Tac box from when she ate a mint before kissing him for the first time. There's some weird artefact from almost every single day between May twentieth and when we first realised they were

157

hanging out.' She flipped forward a few pages. 'And look at this. A greeting card turned to the inside where he wrote –'

'"I love you always . . ."'

'*I love you*. He loved her. Always. And then a week after he tells her so, she can't bother to give him the time of day.'

'Harsh.'

'And topping off this amazing display of dorkdom . . .' She pointed to the small script under the card.

'"Start: May twentieth. End: August twelfth. Total Time: eighty-four days."'

'She counted the number of days between the ice-cream-cone wrapper and the greeting card, and recorded it like some sort of tombstone inscription. Who *does* that?' She flipped forward a few pages. 'And it's the same kind of thing with every guy. Head shot, weird mementoes, some declaration of love, and – bam. End date. Game over.'

It really was like a game and seemed pretty mean, even for Zara.

'The only things that change are the guy and relationship length. And her boyfriend choices don't make any sense after a while. Xavier was a somewhat logical pick because he was older than her, very popular with the summer crowd, and adorable. But this guy?' She turned to Max Hawkins, toward the back of the book.

He looked several years older than Xavier, had three hoops in his bottom lip, and his eyelids hung so low he looked half asleep. 'Not only is he not Z's type, but he's the kind of guy who usually makes fun of girls like her. He eventually said he loved her in permanent marker on a CD case, but their relationship – or whatever you want to call it – started on August twenty-fifth and ended September twelfth. It lasted nineteen days.'

I was thinking that that was nineteen days longer than any relationship I'd ever had when a dull pressure began to build near my left temple. 'I think Zara might be home.'

'Really?' She checked her watch.

'I think I heard a car door slam.' Resisting the urge to press my fingers against the growing pressure, I was relieved when Paige closed the book and dashed to a hallway window.

'Game over!' she squealed. She flew back into the room, her silver eyes shining at having come so close to being caught. She replaced the journal in the desk and the quilted scrapbook on top of a tall white bookshelf. 'She was just getting out of the car.'

She grabbed my hand and pulled me with her, toward the door. I couldn't get out of the bedroom fast enough, but stopped abruptly when Paige ran into the hallway.

'What?' She looked at me. 'What is it?'

I still stood in Zara's room. I held my breath and looked slowly over one shoulder. The three walls that weren't lined by floor-to-ceiling windows overlooking the ocean were lined with floor-to-ceiling mirrors. I hadn't noticed before because their reflections were muted by sheer white curtains. The windows were closed, but the curtains, which had hung motionless while Paige and I sat on the bed, moved now, floating away from the mirrors. They revealed bursts of silver light, like a thousand paparazzi stood in front of each mirrored wall, their camera flashes all going off at the same time.

'Paige!'

The pressure exploded in my head at the sound of Zara's voice downstairs, but I hardly felt it.

'When you see Louis tonight, I have a few choice words I want you to share!'

Paige squeezed my hand before releasing it. If she saw the lights, she didn't say so. 'I'll go tame the beast. Meet me in my room.'

I followed her as she ran for the stairs, but when she was halfway down, I turned around. Paige had closed Zara's door behind us, and the lavender carpet glowed white in the light shining out from under the door.

He has to want to be found . . .

I stood in front of the closed door, my heart slamming against my chest. The last thing I wanted was to go back inside Zara's room, but my body seemed to be moving without checking with my brain first. Something was pulling me back. Something strong, something that didn't care whether Zara discovered me there.

'It's just a disco ball,' I whispered, placing one hand on the doorknob. 'It's just a disco ball reflecting the afternoon sun.'

I shielded my closed eyes with both arms and turned away as soon as I opened the door. The whole room was engulfed in a blinding silver cloud. I waited, my heart threatening to fly through my chest. The cloud thinned after a few seconds, and I opened my eyes slowly. When I could see into the room without cringing, I stepped through the doorway.

The curtains reached toward me as I moved in the glittery haze. The bursts of light still danced across the mirrors, but they were smaller now, softer. Like a million tiny lightning bugs had pushed out the paparazzi.

One pocket of light didn't fade. It shone strong, a beacon cutting through the fog, from the top of the white bookshelf.

It's okay, Nessa . . . you're okay . . . I'm here . . .

'I don't know what I'm doing,' I whispered again, my voice cracking. 'I don't know what you want me to do.'

I neared the bookshelf, and my brain screamed to

turn back, to leave it alone and run out of the room, out of the house. But my feet kept moving. They didn't stop until I stood in front of the bookshelf, engulfed in silver.

He wants to be found . . . he just can't see past the light . . .

My hands shook as my arms stretched up. I braced for something as my fingers touched lace -- searing pain, my palms burning, my entire body melting into a liquid pool – but my hands actually grew steadier. I slid the scrapbook from the shelf, cradled it in one arm and turned the pages. I turned past Xavier Cooper. Alex Smith. John Martinson. Trevor Klemp. Zach Holbrook. Eric Parks. Max Hawkins. And at least a dozen others Zara had led into loving her, then left behind. I turned until I reached the very last head shot, and then I sank, with the light, to my knees.

'Caleb Carmichael,' I said softly.

He looked younger than the last time I'd seen him, on top of the cliffs, so I assumed the school picture was from the year before. He was smiling. He seemed happy. My stomach turned for him, for this younger, happier Caleb who had no idea what he was going to have to endure several months later.

Keep going, Nessa . . . you must keep going . . .

I forced myself to turn the page, not wanting to see what came next. In this collection of romantic targets, Zara had eventually hit the bull's-eye every time. If she'd zeroed in on Caleb, even if she'd done so before things had developed with Justine, I didn't want to know. I didn't want to know what they'd done together, or how long it had taken for her to win him over. I didn't want to know that he'd cared for anyone else the way he'd cared for Justine.

'"May first,"' I read aloud. The starting date was written in pink ink under a paper napkin with a navy-blue anchor in its centre and 'The Lighthouse Marina Resort and Spa' across its top edge. Underneath the date was only one other word.

Bingo.

'I don't care how you do it, just *do* it!'

Zara's voice was closer. I flipped through the remaining pages, relieved and confused when they were blank. Caleb was the scrapbook's last target, and the napkin was the only memento marking his connection to Zara.

Go, Nessa . . . now . . .

I snapped the scrapbook shut, jumped to my feet and replaced it on top of the bookshelf. The silver light was gone, the sheer white curtains hanging straight and still against the empty mirrored walls. Every part of my body seemed to be working together again, and when my brain screamed to run, my feet listened. I flew from the room, closed the door behind me and was at the other end of the hallway just as Zara started stomping up the stairs.

I wasn't sure which was Paige's room. Not wanting to guess wrong, I froze behind a small potted tree. I didn't breathe as Zara reached the top of the stairs and a fresh jolt of pain shot between my ears. She stopped suddenly and cocked her head to one side, as though listening. Her back was to me, but when she stepped to the right instead of in front of her, toward her room, I ducked into the nearest room and gently closed the door behind me.

'Do you hear that?'

I turned slowly. Grandma Betty sat in her chaise, facing me. She held a needle in one hand and a half-finished project in the other, but both hands were still. She smiled as her eyes rested on the empty space above my head.

'She's talking to you.'

I swallowed. 'Who?' I asked this so quietly, I almost wasn't sure I'd said the word aloud. I stepped away from the door, as though Zara wouldn't be able to hurt me if I stood closer to her grandmother. Because Grandma Betty's supersonic, supersensory senior powers were obviously picking up Zara saying my name as she moved down the hallway. She heard Zara breathing, her muffled footsteps coming this way. She could sense Zara's unprompted anger at my presence and knew something very, very bad was about to happen.

Grandma Betty's cloudy eyes travelled slowly from the space above my head, stopping when they were level with mine.

'She's talking to you, Vanessa,' she said. 'Your sister. Justine.'

CHAPTER 12

'"William O'Dell and Donald Jeffries were found late last night on top of the boulders at Beacon Beach, a popular surfing spot ten miles north of Winter Harbor. It is believed their bodies had been there several days before Winter Harbor officials discovered them."'

I sat in the parked Volvo, watching two little girls hurry toward an SUV with their mother.

'This is in the *Globe*, Vanessa. The *Globe*! People are dying practically every day there, and I had to wait for a Boston paper to pick up the story? Why didn't you tell me?'

The girls wore matching yellow sundresses and carried picture books. Ten years ago, they could've been Justine and me. My stomach turned at the thought.

'I hope you're not spending so much time with Simon that you're oblivious to the world around you. I will *not* let another Carmichael boy put one of my daughters in harm's way, do you understand?'

'Mom, I'm fine.' I looked away from the girls and grabbed the door handle. 'They were all water-related accidents. You know I don't go in the water.'

'Your sister never jumped off cliffs before she started hanging around Caleb.'

'Sorry . . . is Dad there? I wanted to ask him about the kitchen tap.'

'The last time I handed the phone to your father, you used him to do your dirty work. You can talk to him when we're done.'

I frowned. I really wanted to talk to Big Poppa, to tell him everything that was going on, to confess that I was more scared than I'd ever been, because there was no one else to tell . . . but I didn't think I could make it through twenty more minutes of Mom. Plus, Simon was waiting.

'Never mind, I have to go. I'll call you later.' I hung up before she could argue, turned off the cell-phone ringer and hurried into the Winter Harbor Library.

'Vanessa, I'm *so* sorry,' Simon said when I reached the basement. He stood and gave me a quick hug. 'I didn't intend to be gone that long. How are you? Is everything okay?'

'I'm fine,' I said, aware that my arms kept tingling even after he'd let go. 'And things are better now.'

Something flashed across his face as he looked down, but I couldn't decipher the expression in the basement's dim lighting.

'How was the research?' I asked. 'Did you get any answers?'

'Yes, actually.' He pulled out a metal folding chair for me before sitting himself. 'How many storms hit here while I was gone?'

'Four.' I didn't have to think about it. The sky now turned as dark as night at least once a day.

'Know how many hit Ashville? And Gouldsboro, and Corea?'

'Four?' I guessed.

He looked at me. 'None.'

'But those towns are only a few miles from here.'

'It was seventy degrees and sunny every day in every town within a hundred miles of Winter Harbor.'

My eyes travelled over the dozens of temperatures and weather conditions listed in the notebook he held toward me. 'I don't understand. The storms don't always last long, but they're huge. How can they not be hitting anywhere else?'

'I don't know.' He closed the notebook. 'What I *do* know is that they originate and dissipate right over Winter Harbor – and *only* over Winter Harbor.'

'Isn't that, like, scientifically impossible?'

'Not impossible – but highly improbable. And unfortunately, the weather isn't the only thing we need to figure out.' He dragged a fat black binder across the table, opened it and flipped toward the back. 'I didn't mention it because I thought we'd already been through enough for one day, but when the police were inspecting the beach at Camp Heroine, they referred to "the other ones".'

I frowned. Not wanting me to have to revisit the scene of the accident, Simon had insisted I stay in the Subaru while he led police to the beach. Whatever he'd heard, he'd been processing on his own for four days.

'At first, I assumed they were talking about the other victims from the past few weeks,' Simon continued, 'but then they started throwing dates around. June 1970. August 1975. September 1983. May 1987. August 1989. When I asked what they were talking about, all they said was that they've never had a situation of this same magnitude, but they have had similar incidents over the years.'

'I don't remember hearing about anything like this before.'

'Me either. And there's nothing about weather-related deaths in those back issues of the *Winter Harbor Herald*.' He turned the binder around and slid it toward me. 'But there is this.'

'"Orin Wilkinson, twenty-five, beloved son and brother, passed away in his rowing boat, near the Winter Harbor Marina. His parents said he was never happier than when he was fishing, and that he was still smiling on the water, even in death."'

'That's from May 1987.' He swung another binder around to face me. 'This one's from June 1992. "Jack

Fleischman, twenty-nine, was found on Long Wharf, lying motionless on his surfboard, grinning from ear to ear."

'May 1998.

'"Vincent Crew, twenty-two, was discovered near Beacon Beach, his water skis still strapped to his feet, a smile frozen on his face."

'July 2003.

'"Lucas Fink, thirty-one, had been scuba diving off Ashawagh Pier the day Coast Guard officials found him floating face up, reportedly still smiling from whatever he'd seen on his last trip below the surface."'

I looked at Simon to find him already looking at me.

'All of these victims were found smiling.'

'Just like Tom Connelly,' I said, recalling the name of the man we'd found. I hadn't read the article in the *Herald*, but couldn't miss his name blown up on the front page.

Simon pulled another binder from a stack on the floor. 'This one just happened last year, and probably bothers me the most.'

I recognised the three hoops through the bottom lip immediately.

'"Max Hawkins, twenty-three, loved music, movies and mountain biking. He was found on the docks near Betty's Chowder House, smiling as though he'd just finished a bowl of the restaurant's famous fare."'

He looked at me. 'Caleb and I met him when we were fishing on the pier and ended up talking to him quite a bit. He wasn't a particularly happy guy, and he *never* smiled. Ever.'

'Simon . . .' My heart hammered in my ears as I stared at the same photo I'd seen for the first time only two days before. 'The other day, when you said it was hard to not know Zara Marchand . . . what did you mean?'

He sat back, apparently surprised by the question. 'I guess I meant that she doesn't really let you forget her.'

'How?' I asked. 'How doesn't she let you forget her?'

He looked at me, clearly wondering why I wanted to know, especially now. 'Well, she's gorgeous, for one thing.'

Grateful for the basement's dim light so he couldn't see my face burn, I lowered my eyes back to Max's picture.

'But she's the kind of gorgeous that throws you off, makes you uncomfortable. Like when you go to an art museum and feel guilty for even looking because the security guards are watching your every move. And she knows it and isn't shy about using it to get what she wants.'

'What does she want?'

'Attention, mainly.'

I looked down, and my eyes landed on Max's death date.

13 September. The day after Zara broke up with him.

'Do you know a guy named Xavier Cooper?' I asked hesitantly. 'Or Trevor Klemp? Or Eric Parks?'

'The names don't ring any bells.' He leaned forward. 'What is it, Vanessa?'

'Nothing,' I said. 'I'm sure it's nothing.'

'You're talking to me,' he said, his eyes locking on mine. 'Mr Science Guy. Everything is something worth considering – even if it's eventually ruled out.'

Was that true? Or would he think the connection completely ridiculous? A case of jealousy gone very bad? 'Zara keeps a scrapbook,' I said before I could change my mind. 'Of her dating conquests. She records start and end dates of every relationship she has and keeps small mementoes of every date – blades of grass, napkins, breath-mint boxes, whatever.'

'I wouldn't have thought her the sentimental type.'

'She's not,' I said. 'She stays with each guy long enough to get him to say he loves her, and then breaks up with him.'

'A never-ending game of catch and release?'

'Sort of.'

'Okay, well . . . this is new insight, but not entirely surprising. What does it have to do with them?' He nodded to the newspapers.

'Xavier Cooper was her first boyfriend. They started

hanging out in May and stopped in August. On day eighty-three of their relationship, he gave her a card that said he loved her. On day eighty-four, she stopped talking to him. Trevor Klemp and Eric Parks followed.' I paused. 'So did Max Hawkins.'

His eyes fell to Max's faded picture in the *Herald*.

'They dated for nineteen days. On September twelfth he told her he loved her.'

He followed my gaze to the dates by Max's picture. 'And on September thirteenth his body was found by Betty's Chowder House.'

'I'm not saying that she drove them to their deaths, to take their own lives . . .' I shook my head. 'Or maybe I am. I don't know. But Max is gone. Xavier, Trevor and Eric may or may not be gone. And Max was found smiling . . .'

'Just like Tom Connelly.'

'And maybe the others, too?'

'But what about Orin Wilkinson?' he said. 'Vincent Crew? All the people who died in the seventies and early eighties, before Zara was even born?'

'I'm not sure.'

He reached across the table with one hand. He raised his just above mine, then lowered it so that it rested an inch away. 'What about Justine?' he asked, his voice soft. 'She was the first one found.'

I focused on his hand, his neat nails, the way his

fingers widened slightly at the knuckles.

'You were there, weren't you? You saw her?'

'She wasn't smiling.' I answered his next question before he could ask it.

He sat back in the chair. 'I'm not saying Zara doesn't have something to do with it. The scrapbook is an interesting piece of evidence, and I don't doubt her ability to do whatever she sets her mind to. But there's also all the storms, the tides, the crazy atmospheric activity –'

'Caleb was in it.'

He paused. 'What?'

'Caleb was in the scrapbook. He was her last entry, and the only one without an end date.'

'But Caleb can't stand Zara. Not to mention he was out-of-his-mind crazy about Justine.'

I didn't want to say it because I really didn't want there to be any truth to a relationship between Caleb and Zara, but it did no good denying that we didn't know everything about our siblings that we once thought we did. 'Justine didn't apply to Dartmouth,' I finally reminded him.

He stared at me, his eyes flicking back and forth as his brain tried to process the latest bit of illogical information. The room was so quiet I could hear the single bare lightbulb buzzing overhead.

We both jumped when his cell phone rang and

vibrated at the same time, sending the phone skipping across the metal table.

'Hey,' he said, answering the phone. He got up and stood under the narrow window at the top of the far wall. 'Caleb?'

I looked up from Max's obituary.

'Caleb, if this is you – don't hang up. I'm finding better reception.' He motioned for me to follow before disappearing upstairs.

Never more anxious to get out of a dark basement, I closed the binders, grabbed Simon's backpack and ran upstairs. I was halfway across the main floor when I realised the librarian sat at the circulation desk and slowed from sprint to speed walk.

'I'm sorry,' she said to the man before her, 'but you've already borrowed five books from the library. As soon as you bring one back, you may borrow another.'

'But . . . you don't understand . . . I need these books. I need these books *and* the five I already have.'

'Again, I'm sorry. But you know library policy, Oliver.'

I stopped short. I hadn't recognised the voice because I'd never heard it – Oliver never spoke at Betty's. Everyone attributed his silence to crankiness and the kind of hearing difficulty that can accompany ageing – but now he seemed to hear himself and the librarian perfectly.

Through the front door I could see Simon in the

parking lot, still on the phone. Thinking it wouldn't hurt to give him a few minutes to talk to his brother alone, I darted behind a tall shelf and hurried down the aisle. When I stopped at the other end, Oliver stood only a few feet away. Peering through spaces between books, I could see he wasn't wearing his hearing aid.

'Of course I know library policy,' he said. 'It hasn't changed in the eighty years I've lived here. But I'm asking you to make an exception. Just once, just for me.'

'Your record is impeccable. But if I made an exception for you, I'd have to make an exception for everyone.'

I ducked slightly when Oliver glanced over both shoulders. 'No offence, Miss Mary,' he said, turning back to the librarian, 'but just like most days, it seems I'm the only one here. I don't think anyone else would have to know.'

'Oliver, please. There are rules –'

'Have you noticed what's been happening?' he asked sharply.

My eyes widened as Mary's mouth snapped shut.

'The heavens are attacking.' Oliver rested both hands on the counter and leaned toward her. 'People are dying. Those who are still here are panicking. No one knows what's going on – not the police, not the reporters and certainly not the weathermen. And *no* one is looking in the right places.'

Mary's expression went from annoyed to nervous to sorry as Oliver placed one shaky hand on top of the small stack of books between them.

'History repeats itself,' he said. 'And in order to find out what's going on now, someone has to find out what happened in the past. When was the last time you saw the chief of police in the library?'

'Oliver,' Mary said gently, 'the authorities are doing everything they can. It's very nice of you to want to help –'

'Not nice,' he snapped. 'Necessary.'

I shook my head. Mary was patient, but he'd just pushed her too far.

'Bring back the other books, Oliver,' she said, turning her attention to the computer before her, 'and I'll be happy to sign these out for you.'

He stared at her. When she continued to type without another word, he hobbled away from the front desk as fast as his cane would carry him.

I squatted down and shuffled backward, out of sight. I didn't want him to see me and know I'd heard any of the exchange. But his bizarre outburst had me curious, so I peered over the top of a row of books to watch him leave.

He stopped short by the entrance. He looked up, toward the ceiling, and slowly tilted his head from one side to the other, like he was listening to something . . .

but the library was silent.

'Be careful,' he finally said. His voice was so low, I almost didn't hear him. 'Be very careful.'

I held my breath until the door closed behind him and waited for his car to pass in front of the building before hurrying from the aisle.

'Welcome to the Winter Harbor Library!' Mary beamed as I approached the circulation desk. 'Is there anything I can help you with? Are you in the market for new releases? Literary classics?'

'Actually,' I said, trying to smile. 'I kind of know that guy who was just here.'

'Oliver?' Mary's megawatt smile dimmed. 'I swear, the man writes a few local history books and thinks he's for ever entitled to every book in the library.'

'Oliver published books about Winter Harbor?' I pictured the illegible scrawls in his notebook at Betty's. Apparently, his writing wasn't simply a hobby.

She opened a drawer, took out four fat books and handed them to me. 'I started keeping them up here so he'd stop asking why no one borrowed them.'

I ran my fingers over the worn brown cover of *The Complete History of Winter Harbor* . . . by Oliver Savage. I looked at the stack of books on the counter, wondering why they were so important to Oliver, and whether I really wanted to get involved. 'I know you have a five-book policy, but since I don't have any books out, I thought maybe I could borrow these and share them with him.'

She blinked. 'Why would you want to do that?'

'I don't know. He seems kind of lonely, and books seem to make him happy.'

'Well, letting one person borrow for someone else isn't exactly library policy either . . . but it would be nice to have a break from him for a few days.' She looked at me. 'You do realise you'll be completely responsible for these books. If anything should happen to them, you will incur all related fees.'

'I do. And nothing will happen to them. I promise.'

'Vanessa Sands,' she read from my card when I found it in the back of my wallet and gave it to her. 'Why is that familiar? You're not a full-timer, are you?'

'No.' I hoped she wouldn't try to place me.

Thankfully, she scanned my card and the books without further question, placed the books in a canvas tote and slid the tote across the counter. 'You can hang on to those for as long as you want,' she said, nodding to *The Complete History* set I still held.

I thanked her, took the bag and dashed out of the library.

'He's in Springfield.' Simon was sitting in the front seat of the Subaru with the door open, inspecting a map. 'At the Bad Moose Cafe.'

'What's he doing there?'

He folded the map and slid it between the dashboard and windscreen. 'I don't know. It was the same weird call – breathing, then a girl saying Caleb's name and laughing, then nothing. I called the number back as soon as he hung up. He was already gone, but maybe we can catch up with him.'

'Great. Your car or mine?'

He looked at me. 'Are you sure you want to come?'

Was I sure? Did that mean he wasn't sure? Had he decided he had enough to worry about without worrying about me, too?

'Don't get me wrong – I'm thrilled if you do. But the last time didn't exactly go well.' He glanced toward the harbour, a small sliver of which was visible from the parking lot, and then turned back to me. 'And I won't let anything happen to you.'

For the first time in I wasn't sure how long, my heart raced from something besides fear. 'Let's go.'

CHAPTER 13

'Sorry, folks. I haven't seen anyone who matches that description.'

'That's impossible,' Simon said, opening and holding out his cell phone. 'He called from this number less than an hour ago.'

Ernie, the stout owner of the Bad Moose Cafe, breathed heavily and wiped his hands on a stained dish towel as he leaned forward. 'That's us.'

'And you don't recall anyone asking to use your phone today?'

'Kid,' Ernie grunted, 'look around. Do you think I'd actually *forget* someone asking to use the phone? That kind of thing makes for a big occasion around here.'

Simon and I glanced around the tiny restaurant. It was empty except for an elderly couple in a corner booth.

'Be nice, Ernie,' a waitress said, coming out of the kitchen with a tray of half-empty ketchup bottles. 'Remember what we talked about? About how one little smile can mean the different between returners and one-timers?'

Ernie flashed us a quick, fake smile before throwing the dish towel over one shoulder and disappearing into the kitchen.

'Pardon him. Ernie still believes that *food* is the only thing people care about when they go out to eat.' The waitress put down the tray and smiled. 'Let's try that again. Welcome to the Bad Moose Cafe. I'm Melanie. What can we do for you today?'

'Melanie,' Simon said, 'we're looking for my brother. He called from here about an hour ago. Do you recall anyone asking to use your phone?'

She squinted as she considered this. 'Nope . . . but that might be because we weren't around for him to ask. Ernie's been engrossed in *The Martha Stewart Show* all morning, and my pesky nicotine addiction takes me outside a few times every hour.'

Hurry, Vanessa . . .

'Did you happen to see him?' I asked. 'He's sixteen, just under six feet tall, with dark blond hair and brown eyes.'

'There's only been one boy in here today besides Ernie and Mr Mortimer.' She winked at the elderly man in the corner. 'Couldn't say how old he was, but his hair was dark brown – definitely not blond – and kind of messy. At least from what I could see of it, since he wore the hood of his sweatshirt up the whole time.'

'Did you notice anything else?' I asked.

'Just that his girlfriend made me feel as pretty as a rock,' she said, heading for the couple with a pot of coffee. 'I swear, once my shift's over I'm going on a diet, dyeing my hair black and ordering coloured contact lenses.'

My breath caught. I couldn't even look at Simon. 'What colour contact lenses?'

She gasped and brought one hand to her chest. 'Silver.'

Simon and I stood so close I could feel his entire body tense.

'And not just, like, dull silverware silver.' She held up a fork from the table. 'Pretty silver. Magical silver. The silver of Christmas tinsel.'

'Did they happen to say where they were going?' Simon asked.

'They didn't say a word. He ate, she didn't, and they were gone when I came back from my second cigarette.'

'Thank you for your help,' I said, before hurrying after Simon.

As we got in the car and sped out of the parking lot, I tried to stay calm and keep my head clear. I didn't know how I was hearing her, and whether I should listen . . . but Justine had told us to hurry. If I could just stay open, maybe she would tell us which direction to hurry *in*.

'She's not *saying* anything,' I groaned softly after a few minutes.

Simon glanced at me. 'Who?'

I stared out the passenger's-side window, wishing the dark-green blur of pine trees flying by would re-wind and reverse. I hadn't meant to refer to Justine out loud; the words were out of my mouth before my brain had even registered them. Would he think I was crazy if I told him? Would he think I was as scientifically im-possible as the Winter Harbor storms, or the smiling victims? And wouldn't he be right if he did?

'She talks to me,' I said reluctantly.

He glanced through the windscreen, then back at me. 'Who?'

'Justine.' My voice sounded normal, but I knew what I said sounded crazy. 'Not all the time. Not even every day. But it started after she died, as soon as I got back to Winter Harbor.'

The Subaru slowed. 'What does she say?'

I felt like crying when he didn't automatically make the judgements he would've been justified to make. 'My name.' Now that it was out there, there was no point in holding back. 'And she talks about Caleb.'

His fingers tightened around the steering wheel.

'She hasn't said much, but it's like she's trying to guide us to him.'

'How?'

'So far she's said that he has to want to be found, that he *does* want to be found but can't see past the light . . . and that's he's getting tired.'

'Tired of what?'

'I don't know. She's not always forthcoming. Like now – she said we had to hurry, but she left out why, or where.'

Simon was silent as he stared straight ahead. I looked out the window, thinking that I'd better make the most of this trip just in case it was the last we took together.

'Vanessa –'

'I know it's crazy,' I said before he could. 'I know it sounds like I've lost it, and maybe I have. I mean, most normal people aren't terrified of the dark, and the ocean, and heights, and flying, and being alone. Some people might be afraid of one thing, but I'm afraid of *everything*. It's not normal. *I'm* not normal. So this – hearing my dead sister talk to me from somewhere above – is probably par for the course. It's like I've maxed out on everything in the world there is to fear and have started making up my own. So now I can start fearing that, too – whatever else my twisted imagination is capable of.'

These words, like the ones I'd initially spoken about not hearing Justine say anything, were out before I could consider the damage they'd do.

'Vanessa . . .' he said again, his voice softer. 'I was

185

going to say that it must be very difficult. To hear her like that, when you miss her so much.'

Outside, the long line of trees was broken by a gas station, a coffee shop, a post office.

'And you're not crazy.'

We passed the school, a market, a dentist's office. The buildings grew closer together as we entered downtown Springfield.

'In fact, I think you're –'

'Simon.' I twisted in my seat and craned my neck to look behind us. 'Turn around.'

'What?' A sharp edge replaced the softness in his voice. 'Did you see him?'

'No.' I turned to him and could already feel the headache starting. 'But we just passed a red Mini Cooper.'

He swerved onto the shoulder and made a wide U-turn so fast the tyres squealed across the road.

'There.' I pointed to the car. It sat on the side of the road, nowhere near any of the surrounding businesses.

He slammed on the brakes, skidded onto the shoulder and threw the car into park.

'Are you sure it's hers?' he asked as we sprinted across the street. 'It looks abandoned.'

He was right; the car was parked haphazardly, its nose tucked in the woods and its back end sticking out on the small strip of grass between the trees and the road. If I hadn't been staring out the window, we would've driven right by.

'I'm sure.' The pain in my head grew stronger with each step.

We stopped by the car and peered in the windows. The interior was immaculate, except for the passenger seat, which was filled with clothes, make-up and empty water bottles. A crystal perfume bottle hung from the rearview mirror. An atlas opened to the state of Maine sat on the dashboard.

I lingered by the passenger's-side door as Simon started into the woods. I closed my eyes and pictured Justine. I saw her blue eyes, her smile, her hair. I tried to hear her voice, willed it to sound from somewhere outside my head so that we could either follow its instructions or the direction it seemed to come from.

But she was silent. The only sounds were of birds singing, cars passing, Simon crunching through leaves and sticks . . . and the drumming in my head. It banged louder, faster, as I headed into the woods.

'This is ridiculous,' Simon said ten minutes later. 'There's no trail. How do we even know they're in here? We're walking in circles, and they could already be gone.'

I stopped. 'Simon.'

He looked at me, then followed my gaze to the dead tree standing a few yards away. A victim of age, disease,

fire or some combination, the tree looked like a skele-
ton rising from the leaves. And hanging from one long,
grey, leafless limb was a hooded maroon sweatshirt.

Reaching the tree, Simon lifted one sleeve and
turned it toward me so that I could see the Bates logo.

'The leaves are flattened,' he said, looking down and
away from the tree's narrow trunk. 'They kept going.'

He started jogging, and I hurried after him, terrified
and relieved when I had to press both hands to my
forehead against the searing pain. As we ran, Simon
glanced behind him every now and then to make sure I
was okay. Soon the pain was so powerful I could barely
see past the bright white dots distorting my vision, but
I assured him I was fine.

But then she laughed.

I dropped to my knees, my chest pressing against the
tops of my legs. I closed my eyes and grabbed at the
ground, my fingers digging through leaves and into the
cold dirt. I'd never heard Zara laugh, and the sound was
like nothing I'd heard before. It was like one long high
note hitting a glass prism and shattering into a million
high notes – some short, some long, some loud, some
soft – that shot out into the atmosphere at different
angles until they completely drowned out all other noise.

It was also like a grenade had been detonated in
my skull.

I kept my head lowered and focused on breathing.

She didn't laugh again, and after a few minutes the pain dulled enough that I was able to open my eyes.

'Simon,' I whispered. He stood a few feet away, staring into a cluster of trees. When he didn't hear me, I lifted my torso and crawled toward him. '*Simon.*'

My nervousness gave way to alarm. Whatever he saw through the trees was so bad he hadn't noticed I was no longer behind him. I climbed to my feet and shuffled as quickly and quietly as I could. He didn't turn around once – not even when I stood next to him.

I stepped closer and peered through the trees.

Zara. She wore a short white skirt that lifted away from her legs in the breeze and a fitted white tank top. Her feet were bare. The outfit was so unlike the tight black skirt, black tube top and stilettos I'd seen her in that day at her house, I was almost relieved. Serial killers didn't wear all white the day they decided to off their next victim, did they?

'Beautiful.'

My head snapped toward Simon. He was still staring, transfixed, like Zara was a flawless, translucent pendulum swinging in front of him.

'She's beautiful . . . isn't she?'

I turned back, my face burning. How could he think that at a time like this? He wasn't some random teenage guy whose every thought careened around the same track. He was *Simon*. Mr Weatherman. Mr Science Guy.

How could he of all people get caught up in hormones, emotions or whatever, when Caleb sat only a few yards away?

And how could I suddenly wish I'd put more thought into my appearance that morning so that I had the same hypnotising effect?

I watched her sit near Caleb at the top of a group of large rocks surrounded by trees. She leaned back on her palms with her legs stretched out before her. She faced him while he faced forward, his back to us. I couldn't see his expression, but it was clear by the way he sat – perfectly straight and still – that he was uncomfortable.

She leaned forward and shifted to her knees. She crawled toward him, the white skirt flitting around her tanned legs, her dark hair falling over one shoulder. She watched him as she moved, her silver eyes like stars, and smiled, apparently anticipating the reaction she knew would come.

Reaching him, she stayed on her hands and knees and stretched forward until her mouth was next to his ear. She said something that made his entire body tremble, and then brushed her lips against his earlobe, his cheek, his neck. His head tilted toward hers, and she moved even closer, lifting up so that her chest pressed against his arm.

I wanted to yell, to scream at her to stop. I wanted to

sprint through the trees, shove her off the rock and grab Caleb. I wanted her to stop doing what she was doing, and I wanted him to stop liking what she was doing. But I couldn't speak, and I couldn't move.

I inhaled sharply when Caleb stood. He walked across the top of the rocks, away from her. He reached one end of the rocks and looked like he was about to jump to the ground when she flew up next to him. She placed one hand on his arm, stood on her tiptoes and reached her mouth to his ear again. This time when she whispered, he tried to push her away – but she used the movement as an opportunity to stand between him and the edge of the rock, blocking his escape route.

He looked away but didn't move, and she stretched her arms overhead and wrapped them around his neck. She looked at him the way I'd seen Justine look at him so many times.

Caleb's arms stayed tense by his sides. He endured her lips trailing down his neck and her fingers tracing the lines of his face. His expression was blank as she dipped her head to one side and her hair fell against his hand. He didn't flinch when she moved closer, making the whole lengths of their bodies touch.

What got him was when she tried to kiss him.

Even I had to look away. I felt guilty, like I'd stumbled upon any young couple about to do what I'd never even come close to doing. I'd never stood before a guy, tilted my head up and held my lips centimetres from his, daring him to refuse me. I'd never kept my eyes open and locked on his as I waited for his response. I'd never pressed my mouth against a guy's at all, let alone taken his bottom lip gently between my teeth. And I'd definitely never had a guy put his arms around my waist and yank me to him, as though finally giving in to an urge he was tired of fighting. And I wanted to run as much as I wanted to know what happened next.

Because the longer I looked, the less the two people on the rocks looked like Zara and Caleb.

And the more they looked like Simon and me.

When I peered through the trees again, they still weren't kissing – she kept trying, though his lips wouldn't move – but her arms were around his neck and her legs were around his waist. His hands slid along her back. When the tips of his fingers slipped under the bottom of her tank top, she beamed.

He lowered himself to his knees. She pressed on his chest with one hand until he was lying on his back, and continued to smile as she lowered her face, slowly, inch by inch, toward his.

'*No . . .*' I moaned softly when her hair fell to one side, blocking our view of their lips. Simon and I vanished, and I was jolted back to what was really happening. The idea of their kissing, of Caleb's kissing Zara instead of Justine, was just too much.

'Caleb!'

I jumped at the sound of Simon's voice.

'Are you okay?' he asked, turning to me.

I nodded. My head still throbbed, but I was too startled to speak.

'Stay here.'

I watched him dart through the trees, the hammering in my chest overpowering the one in my head.

'It's okay, Caleb!' Simon yelled as he ran. 'Stay away from him!'

Zara shot up, unsure of who deserved her attention more: Caleb, who was emerging from the trance she'd worked so hard to put him in, or Simon, who ran at her like a bullet from a gun. The decision was made for her when Caleb fully snapped out of it, threw her off him and scrambled to his feet.

'Don't move, Simon!' Zara shouted, following Caleb as he backed across the rocks. 'It's okay, baby. Don't worry. Everything's fine.'

Caleb's eyes shifted from Zara to Simon. He seemed scared of them both; when Simon climbed onto the other end of the rocks, Caleb looked at him, shook his head and jumped into the leaves below.

'Caleb! Where are you –'

Simon froze when Zara spun around. She walked toward him slowly, deliberately, like he would wait for her for ever if that was how long it took her to reach him.

'Run,' he called out without looking away from her.

I knew that was for me, but I stood there, my feet planted as though they'd grown from seeds in the ground.

The road, Nessa . . . he's heading for the road . . .

I took one more look through the trees, cringing at the sight of her standing only a few feet away from him, and then bolted in the opposite direction.

I ran faster than I'd ever run. Branches scratched my face and my ankles twisted as my feet flew across uneven terrain. I slowed down only once, to grab Caleb's hooded sweatshirt from the tree. When I shot out of the woods and onto the shoulder of the road, I was sweating and gasping for breath.

'Which way?' I whispered, resting my hands on the tops of my legs. I glanced to the right and the left. Both the Mini Cooper and Subaru were still where we'd left them. 'Which way did he go?'

Back . . . back the way you came . . .

I sprinted down the road, past the dentist's office, the market, the school. Past the post office, coffee shop and gas station. I ran until the buildings grew further apart and the trees lined the road uninterrupted. I ran until I felt as if my lungs would explode and my legs break off, and then I kept running. I didn't stop until Justine told me I'd gone too far.

Across the street . . .

I stopped. The gas station was tucked back in the woods. I darted across the street and down the long driveway. Reaching the building, I hurried around the perimeter and then inside. The place was empty except for the driver of an old blue pickup truck and the gas attendant.

But Justine offered no other instructions. Caleb had to be there.

I waited until the driver went inside to pay for his gas, and then headed for the truck. I crouched down and followed the side not facing the building. When I reached the driver's-side door, I stood up, just enough to see into the cab. It was empty.

I was about to try a nearby shed when the truck bobbed. Not much and just once, but it was definite movement. And the driver was still inside the building.

'Caleb?' I peered over the edge of the pickup bed. It was filled with wrinkled tarps and old blankets, which were vibrating, like the truck was still running. 'It's okay, Caleb. It's Vanessa.'

I waited a second and then lifted the edge of one blanket. He was curled into a ball and lying on his side, shaking like it was winter instead of summer, and the blankets and tarps were sheets of ice. His dirty blond hair was dyed dark brown, just as Melanie the waitress had described. His eyes were wide open, his lips trembled, and when he realised who I was, his face crumpled.

'Vanessa . . .' he said, his voice thin. 'No. Not you.'

'Caleb, you have to get out of there.' I looked up as the driver laughed inside the building. He was giving the gas attendant cash and would be on his way out soon.

'I can't.' He shook his head, and tears ran down his cheeks. 'I can't do it without her.'

'Caleb.' I reached into the truck and took his hand. 'Justine's here. She helped us find you. She wants you to come with us.'

He looked at me, wanting to believe me, and then toward the sky, sending a fresh stream of tears from his eyes. 'So tired . . . I'm just so tired.'

He let me help him out, and I was startled to see how thin he'd got. It had only been a few weeks, but his jeans and T-shirt hung loose around his body. He could still move, though, and we were jogging down the road before the pickup driver could realise he'd picked up a hitchhiker.

'What if she's still there?' he asked as we neared the Subaru, sounding like a scared little boy. 'What if she's still in there, waiting for me?'

Chances were good that she still waited for him somewhere, but my head no longer throbbed. I'd been so focused on finding him I wasn't sure when it had stopped, but it had. She was gone. And as we reached the car, I could see the Mini Cooper was gone, too.

'She's not,' I said.

'What about Simon?' Caleb looked at the Subaru's empty driver's seat. 'What if she took him with her?'

I didn't know what to say. I wanted to tell him that Simon was fine, that he wouldn't have let us go unless he was sure he could make it on his own, but the truth was I had no idea what Zara was capable of.

'Are you okay?'

'Oh, thank God,' I whispered before turning around.

Simon came out of the woods and crossed the street toward us. He moved slowly, awkwardly, like he'd just woken up, but besides that, he appeared fine.

I waited by the back of the Subaru as Caleb met him in the middle of the road. They hugged without speaking.

Simon's eyes found mine as he released Caleb. Before he could say anything to me, I threw my arms around his neck and squeezed like I would hold on for ever if he let me.

CHAPTER 14

'It started in the spring. I even remember the exact day, because before all the days that followed, it was the strangest of my life.'

I handed a cup of hot tea to Caleb, who was wrapped in a fleece blanket on the couch, and one to Simon, who sat across from him. There was room on the love-seat next to Simon, but embarrassed by the vice grip I'd put him in earlier in the day, I sat on the floor near the fireplace instead.

'I mean – this is *Zara*. Zara Marchand. Before May first, the girl couldn't be bothered to *look* at me, let alone talk to me. And then she just showed up at the Lighthouse.' Caleb winced as he looked at Simon. 'By the way – I left the marina.'

'I heard.' Simon said.

'I had to. I needed the money. I didn't tell you – or anyone – because everyone who knows me knows how I feel about Monty and the marina, and I didn't want to be talked out of it.'

I frowned into my mug. He'd needed money? What had been so important – and expensive?

'It's okay,' Simon said when Caleb's voice wavered. 'We'll get to that later.'

'So she just shows up one day,' Caleb continued. 'I'm hauling boxes to the supply shop, and she stops me on the dock to say that she had a note from her mother for one of the owners, Carsons.'

Paul Carsons. The first victim to die after Justine.

'And honestly? I wanted to ignore her. I wanted to walk right by and not say a word – treat her the same way I'd seen her treat so many people at school.' He looked out the window behind the couch. 'And I really wish I had.'

I glanced at Simon. He watched Caleb intently.

'But you talked to her?' Simon asked.

'Yes. The Lighthouse is all about money. Its investors want it to grow, expand and be the best waterfront resort in the country.'

'Which means keeping its customers happy?' Simon guessed.

'Exactly. Employees are required to be polite and helpful so guests feel wanted and important. That's why I couldn't just brush past Zara. If word somehow got out that I wasn't helpful – even to someone who wasn't a resort member but could one day become a resort member – I would've lost the job. And I *needed* the job.'

I caught Simon's eye and knew we both wondered the same thing: Why?

'Anyway, I tried to find Carsons for her. I went through the entire property and told Zara about all of its features, just like we do for anyone visiting the Lighthouse for the first time.'

'Sounds painful,' Simon said.

'Not as much as you'd think. She was impatient at first, but she lightened up the longer we walked and the more I talked. She asked questions and listened. She even laughed when I made the same stupid jokes no guests ever laugh at.' He sipped the tea. 'We never found Carsons, but after looking for him, she seemed to forget he was why she was there. And then . . .' He stared at the mug, which twitched in his hands.

'And then?' Simon said.

'And then she asked if I'd have a drink with her.' Caleb closed his eyes and shook his head. 'On the pier at the end of the property.'

'A drink? Like, right then?'

Caleb nodded. 'I don't know why I said yes. I was working, and she was still Zara. The experience wasn't completely miserable, but I hadn't forgotten who she was.'

'You were just caught off guard,' Simon said. 'Who wouldn't be?'

'It was the stupidest thing I've ever done.'

'It was just a drink, Caleb.'

'But it *wasn't*. We sat at the end of the pier and shared

a bottle of champagne that probably cost a week's pay
. . . and I actually had *fun*. She was funny. I liked talking to her. We sat there for three hours.'

Justine had been silent since I'd found Caleb in
the back of the pickup truck in Springfield. My heart
lurched as he spoke of Zara now, and I wondered if
Justine could hear him.

'Before she left, she said she was sorry that it had
taken us so long to have a real conversation. She said
she wished we hadn't wasted so much time, but that
she was glad we still had so much time to look forward
to.' Caleb shook his head. 'And I didn't tell her about
Justine. I didn't even think to mention that I had a girlfriend until hours after she'd left. And Justine was all
I ever thought about. She's still . . . all I think about.'

I'd been watching him but had to look away when
the first tear slid down his face.

'But I didn't *know*, you know? I didn't know what
would happen after that. If I had, if there was any way
I could've . . .'

Simon waited for Caleb's jagged breathing to return
to normal before speaking. 'What happened after that?'

'She was everywhere,' he said softly. 'Waiting for
me before school. After school. Before work. After
work. She'd bring me things – video games and comic
books. She showed up at the beach when I was there
with my friends. And she started stalking them, too,

to find out where I was, what I liked, if I ever talked about her. They thought it was funny at first, that Zara Marchand, the most gorgeous girl in Winter Harbor, had picked *me* of all people to pursue. But then she wouldn't stop. I asked her to stop – I begged her to. But she wouldn't.'

'And you told her about Justine?' Simon asked.

'Every day. It was the first thing I said the next time I saw her. I told her I'd already met the girl I was going to spend the rest of my life with.' The mug shook harder in one hand as he wiped his eyes with the other. 'But it was like she didn't hear me. Or if she did, she didn't care. Because it went on like that for weeks.'

I pictured Zara's scrapbook, the blank pages following the Lighthouse napkin. There were no other mementoes of time spent together because, unlike the rest of her targets, Caleb had resisted her.

When he spoke again, his voice was almost a whisper. 'I thought it would stop once Justine got here for the summer. I thought she couldn't pretend Justine didn't exist if she was right there in front of her.'

I focused on my tea, feeling Simon's eyes on me.

'And I was right. For about fifteen amazing hours, Zara was gone.'

Fifteen hours. They hadn't even been reunited a whole day before Justine was gone, too.

As we fell into a long silence, I noticed a light rain had started to fall.

'She was here that night,' Caleb said a moment later. 'Waiting for me after I got back from the cliffs. She was in my room, on my bed, wearing a long white dress. She didn't say anything, but I knew that somehow, she knew what had happened. And I knew that in her crazy, twisted mind, she thought we were going to be together.' He looked at Simon. 'So I ran. I hated leaving Mom and Dad. I hated leaving *you* . . . but I couldn't handle it.'

'I know,' Simon said.

'I dyed my hair. I hitchhiked. I did everything I could to get as far away as I could, but she always found me. And every time she did, something happened – I was drawn to her. I wanted to be near her. I wanted to scream and push her away, too, but those instincts were overpowered by the others.' The tears started again, falling faster. 'I began hearing things whenever she was around, and it was like my brain just shut off – I couldn't see or hear anything else. I didn't know where I was, or what was going on. All I knew was that Zara was there, trying to take me with her.'

I jumped up when the fleece blanket around him began to vibrate like the blankets and tarps in the back of the pickup truck earlier. I took the tea from his shaking hands and put it on the coffee table, then sat next to him on the edge of the couch.

'There's something wrong with her,' he said, shaking even harder as he looked at me, then Simon. 'Beyond the obvious. That's why I didn't tell you where I was going, or call along the way – I didn't want her to use you to get to me.'

Outside, the rain fell faster, louder.

'I think she had something to do with it,' Caleb whispered, his eyes flicking around the room like someone besides us might hear him. 'With Justine. I think Zara did something to her.'

My knee hit the coffee table as a lightning bolt tore through the sky and shook the ground. The force sent Caleb's mug crashing to the floor. 'Sorry,' I said, scrambling to pick up the ceramic pieces. 'I'm sorry.'

Simon stood to help me, but I gathered as much as my hands could hold and hurried into the kitchen. I stopped at the kitchen table, no longer feeling the broken pieces in my hands as my heart pounded and Caleb's words spiralled in my head.

As soon as he'd said it I realised it was something I'd begun to suspect myself – that in addition to the men who had died that summer, Zara was somehow responsible for Justine's death. But hearing Caleb say it out loud made it real, and I didn't know how that was possible.

I stared at the small mirror hanging over the kitchen table, cupping the broken ceramic pieces as tea dripped through my fingers. I didn't know if Simon and Caleb continued talking after I left the living room. I didn't know if I kept breathing, or if my heart kept beating. All I knew was that at some point, Simon was behind me.

'I'm sorry,' I whispered. My fingers relaxed, and the ceramic pieces fell from my hands. They clattered against the table and tile floor, shattering into even smaller bits. I looked down at the mess and reached forward to gather them. 'I can fix it,' I said, my voice cracking.

But I couldn't see them – there were too many, and my eyes were too watery. Soon, the tears pooling in my eyes spilled onto my cheeks, and I sank to the floor and cried.

Simon didn't try to comfort me; he just sat near me and let me cry. Eventually, when my eyes were dry and my body exhausted, I slid back and joined him against the wall. I hugged my knees to my chest and leaned my head on his shoulder. I listened for the question I knew had to be coming and watched the second hand move around the kitchen clock; when it made five rounds and Simon still hadn't asked if I was okay, I turned my head.

His shoulder tensed under my cheek. I lifted my chin, until my mouth was only inches from his neck. I held my breath when his chest rose and fell faster.

We were friends. Really good friends. And maybe

I should've been concerned about how that might change if I did what I now had the overwhelming urge to do. Maybe now wasn't the best time or place for it. Maybe he would think my emotional collapse had sent me over the edge – because I, scared-of-her-own-shadow Vanessa Sands, simply didn't *do* things like this.

But in spite of that – or perhaps because of it – I did it anyway.

I closed my eyes and pressed my lips to his neck.

I pulled back when he trembled. I waited for him to ask what I was doing, or to move away. When he did neither, I kissed the same spot, then the soft hollow under his jaw.

He turned his head and pressed his face in my hair.

I kissed his neck again, feeling his pulse quicken each time my mouth grazed his Adam's apple. I kissed him faster, stronger. I kept my eyes closed and focused on his breathing, the warmth of his skin, the way my heart raced like I was being chased through the woods even though I wasn't scared at all.

After several minutes, he pulled me onto his lap. It was my turn to tremble when he touched my face, and his fingers brushed my forehead, my cheeks, my chin.

'Vanessa . . .'

I opened my eyes. His face was so close to mine I could feel his breath warm against my mouth. He looked like he wanted to say something else, maybe to ask finally if I was okay, if I was sure I wanted to be doing what we were doing.

I answered by pressing my lips to his.

The jolt shot from the top of my head to my toes. His hands travelled from my face to my back, grabbing at my hair along the way. I put my arms around his neck and pulled my body closer, until I could feel his heart beating against my chest.

Eventually, that wasn't close enough.

'Is Caleb . . . ?'

'Probably sleeping,' Simon whispered. 'Probably for days.'

I held my eyes to his, then took his hands and stood. Catching our reflection in the mirror hanging over the kitchen table, I hesitated. It wasn't that I didn't look like me that threw me off – it was that I looked like some-one I didn't know I could be. My skin was flushed, my eyes were bright. My hair hung down my back in loose waves. I even seemed to stand up taller, straighter. I didn't look like a nervous little girl; I looked confident. Excited. Alive. And standing behind me, watching me like he almost didn't know what I'd do next, Simon saw it, too.

I led him out of the kitchen and upstairs. I knew every corner of the Carmichael house almost as well as I knew the lake house, but it felt different – still warm and comfortable, but also like I'd never been there before. When we were in Simon's room with the door closed, I was happy to see the familiar periodic table of elements and world map hanging on the walls, but also felt like I was seeing them for the first time.

It was the same when I turned to him. He was still Simon, the same boy I used to race down the Slip 'n' Slide. The one who always lagged behind with me when Justine and Caleb ran ahead on hiking trails, who made sure whatever movies we watched didn't exceed my quota of blood, guts and gore. He was still the one looking out for me and making sure I was okay. Even standing before me now, he was watching, waiting, not wanting to do anything that would make me uncomfortable.

But now, for the first time, he didn't look entirely calm. He didn't look like he believed that there was nothing to be scared of, and that he could assure me of the same.

'Are you okay?' I asked, stepping closer.

'Vanessa . . .'

Even my name sounded different.

'I just . . . I don't know . . . are you . . .' He closed his eyes, as if he was trying to piece together his fragmented thoughts.

I stepped as close as I could without our bodies touching. 'Is this okay?' I kissed his cheek.

He nodded, his eyes still closed.

'And this?' I kissed his other cheek.

He nodded again.

'And this?' My lips pressed against his chin, his jaw.

He closed his eyes tighter and nodded again.

'And –'

My mouth hadn't yet touched his when he took me by the waist and pulled me to him. He kissed me like his heart might stop if he didn't, and he kept his arms around me as I moved back, toward the other side of the room. I turned when we reached the bed so that he lay down first, then crawled on top of him. His hands were stronger, more sure, as they travelled down my back and pulled me closer. My skin felt like it was burning through my clothes as our bodies pressed together.

'It's okay,' I whispered as his hands slid, then paused, under the back of my T-shirt. When he still didn't seem sure, I pulled it over my head and tossed it to the floor, then helped him take off his sweatshirt.

His lingering uncertainty seemed to disappear when I lay back down. He kissed me harder and grabbed every part of me he could reach – my face, my hair, my shoulders, my waist, my hips. It felt so good, so natural, as if for seventeen years my body had just been hanging on in anticipation of this very moment. When he slipped his fingers between my bare skin and the button of my jeans, I nodded without hesitating and kept kissing him.

He paused only once more, when lightning struck the ground nearby and his desk lamp went out.

'I can get candles . . .' He lifted my face away from his until our eyes met.

The dark. It was night, a storm raged outside, and the only light in the room came in fleeting flashes though the window. This was normally when I would've grabbed a flashlight and hidden under the blankets until the power came back on. But it didn't bother me now.

'It's fine. But thank you.' I went to kiss him again, but he pressed his head back, into the pillow. 'What? What's wrong?'

He lifted a loose strand of hair away from my face and behind my shoulder. 'Nothing . . .' he said, looking at me thoughtfully. 'It's just that, right now . . . in this light . . . your eyes look almost silver.'

CHAPTER 15

I shot up in bed the next morning, my heart hammering and my head spiralling. I closed my eyes and braced for the usual image of me standing by the ocean's edge, or the more recent one of Justine reaching for me with bruised arms. They were always the first things I saw each morning, since they were all I saw each time I managed to sleep.

'Hey.'

I opened my eyes.

'You okay?'

I registered the globe in the corner of the room, the periodic table of elements hanging on the opposite wall . . . and Simon, pressing his lips to my bare shoulder. 'What time is it?'

'Nine,' he said gently. 'And I could stay here all day, but we should probably clean the kitchen before Caleb wakes up.'

I nodded as he slid out of bed, and I tried to process what had happened. Surprisingly, I wasn't thrown by the fact that we'd leapt across the formerly solid, unwavering line between friends and more-than-friends, or that I had no idea where that left us now. I wasn't paralysed with shock or regret that I'd done something so forward, so unlike me, with anyone, let alone the one person I didn't want to lose.

What made me focus silently on the lake through the window instead of making small talk was that it was nine o'clock. It was nine o'clock, and I wasn't blinking away visual remnants of last night's nightmares. Which meant that for the first time in a long time, I'd slept eight uninterrupted hours.

'I think we're too late.'

My head snapped toward Simon. 'Too late?'

He stood next to the closed bedroom door, tilted his head and listened. I heard it then, too: dishes clanking downstairs.

I jumped out of bed and threw my clothes on, wondering what Caleb would think of our entering the kitchen together. I figured it'd be a shock, since the idea of Simon and me together like that definitely wouldn't have occurred to anyone, but I hoped it wouldn't be hurtful, too. What if seeing us together triggered fresh, painful memories of Justine? What if he felt betrayed and ran off again? What if –

'Eggs?'

I froze in the kitchen doorway. If Caleb was shocked, hurt or betrayed, he didn't show it. He sat at the table, which was now clear of the broken ceramic pieces

Simon and I had left there the night before, eating breakfast and reading.

'They're on the stove,' Caleb said without looking up from his book. 'OJ's in the fridge.'

Taking a glass of juice from Simon, I sat across from Caleb. He'd washed the brown dye out of his hair and, after eating and sleeping, already appeared stronger, healthier.

'It's pretty early,' Simon said. 'You must still be tired. Don't you want to get some more sleep?'

'Nope,' Caleb said, closing the book.

I slid *The Complete History of Winter Harbor* toward me when Caleb pushed it aside. Flipping through, I searched for passages about strange Winter Harbor weather patterns, unexplained deaths and smiling victims.

'So after we call the cops, I think we should confront her directly.'

Simon sat next to me. 'We can't call the cops yet. We only have suspicions, not proof. And how can we confront her? What are we going to say? "Hey, Zara, I know what you did this summer"?'

'Pretty much,' Caleb said. 'Vanessa can hang back and pretend to be a tourist with a digital camcorder so we can record the guilt on her face.'

'Cal,' Simon said patiently, 'I understand you're angry, but we have to give this a little more thought. If we're too rash, we could scare her off before we get any answers. Plus, you said you can't be near her without her messing with your head. What makes you think you'll even be able to talk to her?'

They continued to debate the issue as I scanned the history books. Oliver certainly knew a lot about Winter Harbor – his research went back centuries – but there was no mention of bodies washing mysteriously onshore. I also looked for passages about the Marchands, but found only one small paragraph about the founding of Betty's Chowder House.

'Why don't I talk to Paige?' I said several minutes later. My face grew warm when they turned to me. Despite the current topic, I couldn't help but wonder if Simon thought of last night when he looked at me now, and whether Caleb could sense what had happened.

'Aren't those two really tight?' Caleb asked.

'That's exactly why I want to talk to her,' I said. 'And don't worry – I wouldn't say anything about yesterday, or about Justine. Paige is pretty open, so I don't think I'd have to push too hard to find out if Zara's been acting stranger than normal lately.'

'Sounds like a plan to me.'

'Hang on,' Simon said, shooting Caleb a look. 'I don't – *we* don't – want to do anything that could pull her attention to you.'

I didn't really want her focused on me either, but for

some reason, I thought I could handle it better today than I could've even twenty-four hours before. 'I'll be fine. I'll do it this morning, when they're both at work. What's the worst Zara can do in a public place, surrounded by tons of people?'

'Okay,' Simon said after a pause. 'But we're going with you. We're staying together until this is resolved.'

'Fair enough,' I said.

'I'm going to charge my iPod.' Caleb stood from the table and shot Simon a look. 'You should bring yours, too.'

After Caleb left the room, Simon and I silently cleared the table. I wondered if he was mad at me for wanting to talk to Paige – or, worse, if he regretted what had happened last night. I tried to summon the same nerve that had enabled me to do everything I'd done the night before. I would just ask what was going on. I'd ask if he regretted it, and when he said that he did, I would promise that I was totally fine with just being friends. It could be like nothing happened, if that was what he wanted.

After starting the dishwasher, I looked at him. He leaned against the counter, watching me. I grabbed the counter to keep from running to him and held on tight until he reached out one hand.

'Vanessa,' he said, pulling me to him, 'last night was . . .'

'I know,' I said, relieved. 'I mean, I'm glad you think so, too.'

He put his arms around me and rested his chin on the top of my head. When he spoke again, his voice was soft. 'I think, though . . . that maybe we shouldn't let it happen again. At least not now.'

I froze, then pulled back.

'It's not that I don't want it to,' he said quickly, his face flashing concern. 'Believe me. It's just that it might be too much, too soon for Caleb. I'd hate for him to feel worse than he already does.'

I tried to come up with an argument but couldn't. Because it wasn't fair. Regardless of what I wanted, Caleb had been through enough, and we would only remind him of what he'd lost.

'I should go,' I said finally. 'I'll come back after I shower.'

He opened his mouth to say something else, but I was out the door before he could.

I hurried across the Carmichaels' back yard, and then ours, barely noticing the early-morning lake activity or feeling my stomach turn. Maybe the timing wasn't right . . . but that didn't mean that what we'd done was a mistake. It didn't mean it shouldn't have happened. Simon and I shouldn't feel guilty, or regretful, or –

I stopped short. I'd just crossed the deck and entered

our house, and it was too quiet. I didn't remember turning off the TV and radio . . . but maybe that was just because I'd been too excited to meet Simon at the library the day before. Deciding that was it, I headed for the kitchen.

'Sleep well?'

I froze in the doorway. 'Mom?'

She sat at the kitchen table, her laptop open in front of her. A cup of coffee sat next to her BlackBerry and car keys. She stared at the computer screen and pretended to read without looking at me. 'I heard there was quite a storm last night. I know how you hate storms, so I'm sure you didn't sleep a wink.'

'What are you doing here?'

She took the coffee from the table, sat back and looked at me.

'I told you I was fine. I hope you didn't cancel any important meetings to drive up here and take me back to Boston, because I'm not going.'

Her perfectly glossed lips turned up. 'You did tell me you were fine. You also told me you were sleeping well. So you can imagine how surprised I was to get here before dawn this morning and find your father's car not in our driveway, but in the driveway next door.'

'We got back late,' I said, my face burning. 'They invited me over for dinner, and since it was already raining, it was just easier to park there than here.'

217

'They?' Mom's face relaxed. 'Mr and Mrs Carmichael are back from Vermont?'

I looked down.

'Vanessa?'

'No . . . but it's not what you think.' Even though it was probably *exactly* what she thought. 'We just fell asleep watching movies.'

'Forgive me, Vanessa – I didn't sleep last night and have only had one cup of coffee this morning. I want to make sure I'm getting this right.' She raised her eyes to the ceiling. 'You're telling me that after *weeks* of making me worry about your being here all by yourself, and not calling me back or answering your phone all day yesterday, that you're completely fine? That you were fine enough last night to watch movies with Simon Carmichael, even if his brother is responsible –'

'Don't say it.' I stepped into the kitchen. 'Caleb isn't responsible for what happened to Justine. He loved her more than anyone. He wouldn't have done anything to hurt her.'

'Vanessa, please. Too much time alone in the wilderness has obviously taken a toll. If he and your sister had any kind of relationship, it was a meaningless mutual crush. It meant nothing. If you think whatever you have going on with Simon is any different, I'm sorry to say you're a very confused little girl.'

I stared at her. 'Where's Dad?'

She pressed one manicured hand to her forehead. 'Your father is in Boston.'

I strode across the kitchen and grabbed the phone from the wall.

'What are you doing? This conversation isn't over.'

'Dad understands,' I said, dialling quickly. '*He* didn't come because he knows I needed time. He knows this was what I needed to do. And since you obviously don't get it, maybe he can try explaining it to you again.'

I turned away from her as the phone rang on the other end. It rang once, twice, three times. After six rings, I hung up and tried again.

'No answer.' It wasn't a question.

I hung up and walked past her, out of the kitchen.

'I'm not going anywhere, Vanessa,' she called after me. 'If you want to stay here all summer, that's fine by me. The deck will make a lovely home office.'

I grabbed my duffel bag from the downstairs bedroom and dragged it into the bathroom. I showered quickly but took longer than usual getting dressed. Even if nothing happened between Simon and me again, I still wanted to look nice for him.

Of course, I'd had no idea before leaving Boston that I'd have reason to wear anything other than jeans, shorts, T-shirts and sweatshirts in Maine. My options limited, I finally decided on a clean pair of jeans, a white tank top and a fitted purple cardigan. My footwear selection was also limited, so the best I could do was switch from sneakers to flip-flops. I left my hair loose to air-dry and put on mascara and lip gloss – which I happened to have only because Justine had insisted I always carry them in my purse, just in case.

When I was done, I looked in the mirror above the sink. I almost expected to see flashes of silver surround my reflection, just as I had the morning Simon had shown up before we went to the Winter Harbor Marina. When they weren't there, I was almost disappointed.

Back in the kitchen, Mom was still at the table. She didn't look up from her laptop as I passed. 'I'm not going to chain you to the couch to get you to stay. But you can at least tell me where you're going.'

I paused at the door. That was it? Even Dad put up a bigger fight when he was unhappy with me. 'Betty's,' I said without turning around.

She sipped her coffee. 'Dinner's at six. Call if you're going to be late.'

I opened my mouth to tell her that I would be back when I was back, and that I'd been managing to eat all on my own . . . but then closed it. There were several other people whose company I would've preferred to Mom's, but the thought of her being there – of *someone* being there – when I got back wasn't entirely terrible.

Simon and Caleb were ready and waiting for me on the front porch by the time I reached their yard.

'Sorry it took so long,' I said, quickening my pace. 'I had a surprise visitor.'

Simon looked toward our driveway. His eyes grew wide when he spotted the BMW.

'Don't worry. I'm not going anywhere – at least not yet. I think she just needed to see me in person to believe that I hadn't fallen off the planet.' I peered behind Simon, at Caleb. He sat in a wicker chair, eyes closed and head bobbing. 'Is he okay?'

'I think so. And he seems to think that Green Day will help keep him that way.'

We were quiet on the drive to town. Caleb listened to his iPod and stared out the window in the back seat. Simon focused on the road ahead. And I thought about what I would ask Paige, feeling less sure about everything the closer we got to Betty's. It was one thing to imagine talking to Paige with Zara nearby while safe in the Carmichaels' kitchen, but it was definitely another actually to do so.

'Wow,' I said as we turned onto Main Street. I almost didn't recognise it – the pavements were too quiet for such a sunny day, and yellow banners announcing the first annual Lighthouse Resort and Spa Northern Lights Festival stretched overhead, across the road.

'What does that mean, "first annual"?' I asked. 'My family and I go – went – to the Northern Lights Festival every year.'

'This is the first time it's sponsored by the Lighthouse.' Caleb sounded resigned. 'There was an article about it in the *Herald* this morning. It said this year's festival will attract thousands of guests from across New England and promises to be the best ever by combining old traditions with exciting new rides, games and activities.'

'It's in a week,' Simon said quietly as we passed underneath.

He didn't elaborate, but I knew what he was thinking. A lot could happen in a week: between bodies washing onshore and families fleeing for safety, there might not be anyone left in town by the time the first festival lights were lit.

'Park in the main lot,' I said as we neared Betty's and the mermaid logo above the front door grew larger. 'Staff parks in the back.'

Simon did as I instructed, slowing down and opening his window as we approached the lot entrance.

'Reservation?'

'Hey, Garrett.' I leaned across the middle console.

'Vanessa.' He lowered his clipboard and smiled. 'Hey. You missed a great concert the other day. Are you working?'

'I'm just picking up a cheque, actually. Is it okay if we park here while I run in?'

His smile faltered at 'we'. He looked at his clipboard

and then behind him, at the lot. 'I guess so.'

'Thanks. You're the best.'

'Oh, by the way.' He leaned down to look at me through Simon's open window just as we were about to pull away. 'A bunch of people are going out tonight. Do you want to come? We could grab dinner first?'

I tried to smile as Simon looked down at his lap. 'That sounds great . . . but I don't think I can tonight.'

His eyes shifted to Simon as he stood back up. 'Right. Maybe another time.'

We pulled into a space toward the end of the lot, away from the main dining room's windows. I turned to Simon, not sure whether I should explain the dinner Garrett referred to, or if he even cared.

'Okay,' he said before I could decide. 'Do what you need to, but do it quickly. And the second you feel uncomfortable, get out of there.'

'I will,' I said. 'I promise.'

Caleb's arm shot between the seats. 'Aerosmith,' he said, shaking a portable CD player at Simon. 'Old-school, but effective.'

I climbed out of the car and hurried across the parking lot. I tried to focus on what I wanted to find out from Paige, like if Zara had said where she was yesterday, if she was acting weird, or if she'd mentioned anything about her latest boyfriend recently, but my head spun too fast to think straight.

Seeing Zara first didn't help. She stood in the dining room near the lobby, taking orders from a young couple. She talked and smiled like nothing out of the ordinary had happened, like she hadn't just tried to brainwash and seduce her next victim less than twenty-four hours before. The headache started as soon as I spotted her, but this time my stomach turned too.

I ducked behind the hostess station until she turned away from me to help another table, then scanned the dining room. No Paige. I grabbed a stack of menus and held them to the side of my face as I scurried along the dining room's back wall and shot through the kitchen door.

'Louis, where's Paige?' I dashed toward the counter where he stood.

'Good morning to you, too, my dear.' His knife sliced through carrots, sending fat orange discs flying across the counter. 'Actually, I take that back. It's *not* good. It's quite the opposite. Pretty Miss Paige decided to call in sick for the first time ever.'

'Sick?' My heart skipped. 'What's wrong?'

'I'm a chef, not a doctor. All I know is that she's not here, and Satan's offspring has already threatened to fire me three times.'

'Louis! You call this *poached*?'

My head snapped toward the swinging door, then back to Louis. 'Hang in there.'

I ran out the back door and behind the staff cars. The red Mini Cooper was parked next to the Dumpster. I glanced in the driver's-side window, encouraged when the atlas and pile of clothes were gone. It looked like Zara was taking a day off from her pursuit.

'What happened?' Simon said when I threw open the passenger's-side door. 'Was she there?'

'Yes,' Caleb said.

I looked at Simon then turned toward the back seat. Caleb was still listening to his iPod, but he'd slid down the seat. His eyes were wide and his breathing fast.

'She's there.' He looked at me. 'I can hear her.'

His bottom lip trembled and a thin stream of perspiration ran from his temple to the back of his neck. They were separated by a hundred yards, by walls made of wood and concrete, but he was transforming into the scared Caleb we'd found the day before. It was as if Zara stood right outside the car, smiling down at him.

Vanessa . . .

My eyes grew as wide as his.

She's not done . . . she won't stop until she has him . . . or until you stop her . . .

I turned back to Simon. 'We have to go.'

'Where?'

'To their house.' I waited for Caleb to protest from the back seat, but only heard him inhale a sharp, shaky breath. 'Now.'

CHAPTER 16

Twenty minutes later I stood on the Marchands' front porch. I glanced over my shoulder, happy when I couldn't see the Subaru hidden in a cluster of trees at the end of the driveway.

'Hello, Vanessa.'

My head snapped back. Raina stood in the open doorway, wearing a sheer white kaftan over a black bikini. Her face, still striking without a touch of make-up, was blank. Her dark hair was wet, and she smelled like salt, like she'd just come in from a swim.

'Hi.' I forced a smile and resisted the urge to look behind me again.

'May I help you with something?'

'Nope,' I said quickly. Too quickly. 'I mean, I was just looking for Paige.'

'I'm afraid you'll have to look at Betty's. Paige is at work.'

If she were just Paige's mother, I would've explained that I'd already been to Betty's, which was where I'd learned Paige wasn't well. But because she was Zara's mother, too, I thought the more left unsaid, the better.

'Silly me.' I waved one hand. 'I thought she was off today.'

Her expression didn't change as she moved to close the door. 'Tell her hello for me when you see her.'

'Actually,' I said, bringing one hand to the door, 'I don't know if I'll make it all the way to town today. Would it be okay if I left a note?'

She paused. 'I'm happy to pass along a message. What would you like me to tell her?'

'It's private.'

She looked as surprised as I was by my boldness. I probably should've let her close the door in my face and sprinted as fast as my flip-flops would carry me back to the car. But I knew she was lying. And that just made me even more determined to get inside.

'It's girl stuff,' I said, lowering my voice. 'I'm completely hung up on this guy who doesn't know I exist – but I just have to tell Paige about my latest lame attempt to get him to notice me.'

She pursed her lips, clearly trying to decide whether I was really that clueless.

'See?' I pointed to my face, which had turned fuchsia the second she opened the door. 'This happens when I *talk* about him. Can you imagine how ridiculous I look when I'm actually *near* him? Total disaster.'

Her face relaxed slightly. 'You might want to start with those clothes.'

I looked down, thrown by the suggestion – and that she seemed to believe me.

'You're seventeen, yes?'

I looked up and nodded.

'That figure is the best it's going to be. Take advantage of it. Show it off. Trust me – he'll notice.'

'Okay . . . thanks.'

Apparently deciding I needed more help than that, she opened the door wider. My heart raced as I stepped inside. It took a second for my eyes to adjust to the soft living-room light, but I thought I saw two women retreat to the kitchen after seeing who was at the door.

'A woman's power over a man is her strongest weapon.' Raina crossed the living room and motioned to the couch. 'Used correctly, it can get her anything she wants.'

'Oh.' I sat down. 'Well, all I want is for him to see me when I'm standing in front of him.'

She tilted her head and smiled, like she found my innocence cute. 'Stay there. I have just the thing.'

I watched her leave the room. I was curious to see what she returned with, but knew this was my chance. Hearing drawers open and close, I jumped up and flew toward the stairs.

Hurry, Nessa . . .

I took the stairs two at a time, then sprinted down the hall toward Paige's room.

The other way . . . go the other way . . .

I shook my head against Justine's voice. The only room in the other direction was Betty's.

'Paige?' I knocked on her door and opened it at the same time. 'Sorry to barge in, but Louis said you were sick, and Raina said you were at work, and I just had to see you because I have to talk to you about –'

I stopped once the door was closed behind me. She was stretched out on a daybed, propped up by pillows and covered in white blankets. She wore a white turtle-neck that she'd pulled up to her chin. She was bundled up like it was winter, yet the sun still shone outside and all the windows were open, letting in a salty breeze.

'Are you okay?' I asked, walking toward her. 'Do you have a fever? I can close the windows –'

'Don't,' she said. 'The air's nice.'

I sat on the bed next to her. Besides the winter attire, she didn't look sick at all; her hair fell past her shoulders in loose tendrils, her cheeks were flushed pink, and her silver eyes glittered. 'Paige . . . why do you look like you just came in from making snow angels?'

'Vanessa,' she said, leaning toward me. 'We're close, right?'

I glanced at the door. 'Right.'

'They told me I shouldn't tell anyone,' she said, her eyes shining brighter. 'They said it wasn't the kind of thing people really wanted to hear, considering we're

229

so young and our backgrounds are so different . . . but it's not like everyone won't find out eventually. And I know you won't tell anyone.'

'Won't tell anyone what?' I asked carefully. I cared about Paige, but didn't know how embedded in the Marchand inner circle I wanted to be.

She leaned closer. 'My secret.'

'I won't tell,' I said, since she seemed to be waiting for me to say so, and I wanted to move this along so I could get out of there. 'Promise.'

Her smile grew. 'I'm pregnant.'

You have to go, Nessa . . .

'Isn't it amazing?' she squealed softly, her nose scrunching. 'I mean, I know I'm young. And Jonathan's young. And I'm staying here and he's going to school, but I really think it's going to be fine. It wouldn't have happened if it wasn't meant to be, and we'll just make it work. No matter what, we'll make it work.'

My brain strained to process this. 'What did your mom say?' I finally asked, thinking of my own.

She brought one hand to her flushed forehead. 'Oh my goodness, I was *so* scared to tell her.' She lowered her hand and shook her head. 'But she was so great. She actually knew what was going on before I did. I hadn't been feeling well for a little while – I was nauseous, hot and thirsty all the time. I'd take cold showers and drink gallons of ice water and still feel like I was baking in the desert. And then two days ago, she noticed me sweating after my third cold shower and asked what was going on. I told her how I was feeling, and she immediately put it together. She said she felt the same way during her pregnancies.'

'And she was really okay with it?' I asked, blinking away images of Simon and me in his room only a few hours before.

'She really was. Zara was shocked at first and didn't talk to me for a few days, but she eventually came around, too. They both said a new life is a beautiful gift whenever it comes, and that we should always welcome it. What I *don't* welcome?' She made a face and held up a glass jug filled with murky green liquid. 'Salt water – from the ocean, complete with seaweed – is Mom's magical cure. It works, but I have to drink it nonstop . . . and it tastes as good as it looks.'

My stomach turned as my eyes followed the brown and green clumps floating through the water.

'The salt baths help, too. I have to take one of those every hour. Which is why, getting back to your original question, I look like I just came in from making snow angels.' She reached for my hand. 'Do you want to feel?'

'I don't think so, I really should –'

She moved aside the blankets, slid her sweater above her belly button and placed my hand against her stomach. When I felt the movement swimming below the surface of her skin, I yanked my hand back.

'Crazy, right? I swear, the kid's going to be an Olympian.'

'You know, I should probably get going,' I said, standing. 'My mom's in town, and I told her I wouldn't be gone long.'

'Wasn't there something you wanted to talk to me about?' Her face was concerned as she lowered her sweater.

I'd been walking backward but stopped just in front of the door. Every bone in my body wanted to bolt for the nearest exit – but I'd already come this far, and given Paige's strange medical quarantining, I didn't know when I'd see her again. By the time I did, it could be too late.

'Actually, yes . . . it's about Zara.'

'Is she giving the staff problems already? She's under strict orders not to fire anyone for any reason while I'm gone.'

'That's not –'

'Vanessa. There you are.'

The blood draining from my face, I turned around to see Raina standing behind me, holding a long white sundress. 'Mrs – Miss – Marchand. Sorry for disappearing. I actually remembered that I was going to borrow a book from Paige. I've been reading a lot, it

232

being summer vacation and all, and Paige told me she had a really great book that I *had* to read.'

'Which one?' Raina asked.

'*The Complete History of Winter Harbor*,' Paige said. 'It's on the top shelf, to the right.'

I froze at the title, then managed to shoot her a grateful look over my shoulder. When I turned back, Raina tucked the dress under one arm and held the book toward me. 'Thank you,' I said, taking the book.

'I assume Paige shared the good news.'

'Don't be mad,' Paige said. 'I was just so excited to tell someone, and Vanessa's a great friend. She won't say anything.'

'I hope that's true.' She looked at me, and her smile was gone. 'This is a very important time for Paige and our family. An important, personal, *private* time. You can understand a mother wanting to protect her daughter. *Your* mother would do the same for her daughters, wouldn't she?'

'Of course.' My face burned as I looked down.

'People will obviously find out in time,' Paige added, 'but we want to keep it quiet for a while. It would take all of three minutes for news like this to spread through Winter Harbor. Plus, Jonathan doesn't know yet, and I don't really know how to tell him.'

'Paige, sweetie, we talked about this.'

I looked from Paige to Raina. The stern disapproval in

her voice was gone; she sounded loving, almost motherly.

'Jonathan doesn't need to know anything.' Raina crossed the room and sat on the bed. 'You two have such a wonderful relationship right now. Why let something like this get in the way?'

'Something like this *wouldn't* get in the way,' Paige insisted, pulling away when Raina tried to take her hand.

'What about when he leaves for college in a few months?' Raina asked. 'And every year for the next four years? He's not going to give up everything to stay in Winter Harbor and be a young father.'

'He wouldn't be giving up everything,' Paige said, her voice wavering. 'He could take night classes somewhere. And besides, he wouldn't think about it like that. He'd think that whatever he was giving up didn't compare to all that he was gaining.'

'Would his parents agree? You know his family isn't like our family.'

Paige stared at her mother, then pulled the blankets to her chin and turned toward the open window behind the bed. 'Just because Dad disappeared doesn't mean Jonathan will do the same.'

'You'll feel better after a nice bath,' Raina said, as if she hadn't heard Paige's jab. She looked at me. 'I trust you can show yourself out?'

I nodded.

'Thanks, Vanessa,' Paige said, offering a small smile. 'I'll call you later.'

My heart drummed in my ears as I stepped into the hallway and closed the door gently behind me.

Vanessa . . .

I hurried down the hall, ignoring Justine's voice above me. Now wasn't the time. I'd taken a chance. I'd tried to find out more about Zara from Paige. It didn't work, and now it was time to move on to Plan B, whatever that was.

'Vanessa?'

I stumbled forward. I probably shouldn't have been more alarmed by a living person saying my name than I was by my deceased sister saying my name, but Betty wasn't just any person.

Please, Nessa . . . she can help . . .

My chest tightened as I reached the stairs. I didn't know what Betty could say that wouldn't just raise more questions . . . but maybe the questions could lead to clues.

'Good morning, Vanessa,' she said when I was in her room with the door closed.

She rested her hands on the needlepoint in her lap and seemed to wait for me to speak. I, in turn, waited for Justine to speak. If I was supposed to help Betty help me, I didn't know where to start.

'Doing some reading?' she asked finally.

'What?'

'Paige gave you a book.'

'Oh.' I looked down at my hands, which gripped Paige's copy of *The Complete History of Winter Harbor*. 'Right. She did.'

'Paige is a good girl.' Betty said that as if she thought I doubted it. 'She's young. She'll make mistakes, just like her sister and her mother before her. But she doesn't mean anyone harm.'

I focused on keeping my breathing steady.

'She doesn't know about you.'

I tightened my hold on the book when it started to slip.

'She doesn't know about Justine.'

My eyes watched hers; they were aimed above my head, flicking back and forth.

'And she doesn't know about your mother.'

'My mother?' I whispered.

She lowered her eyes slowly until they locked on mine. A dim light glowed behind the clouds. 'But then, of course, neither do you.'

I held my breath, unable to move.

'Your mother and Paige's mother were once very close.'

I stepped back. My hip hit a small table, sending a jug of iced tea to the floor.

Betty paused before picking up her needlepoint.

'There are towels in the bathroom.'

I placed the book on a chair and hurried to the room behind her, grateful for the break. I yanked a towel from the shelf above the toilet and turned on the water in the sink. As I dunked and wrung out the towel, the smell of salt was so strong, I wanted to gag. It wasn't until the towel was damp but not dripping that I was able to turn back to the sink and see that the water from the tap wasn't clear.

It was a light, murky green. Kind of like the ocean.

'That's a very good book,' Betty said as I came back into the room. She slid a needle in and out of her latest project, apparently done talking about Paige, me and our mothers. 'An old friend of mine wrote it. I read it once, a long time ago.'

Anxious to get out of there, I dropped to my knees and started scrubbing the carpet. 'What book?' I asked, hoping my voice sounded casual.

'The one you borrowed from Paige. *The Complete History of Winter Harbor.*'

'Betty . . .' I stopped scrubbing and glanced over my shoulder. The book still sat on the chair, untouched. I turned back to her. 'Can you see?'

'I haven't seen anything in seven hundred and thirty-three days.'

'Then how did you know what book Paige gave me? Or that I even had a book at all?'

She shifted the project in her lap and started on an-other corner. 'Page forty-seven.'

I looked at her, then stood up and took the book from the chair. It was old and had obviously been read many times. The brown cover was worn and frayed at both ends, and the pages were yellowing – some had even pulled away from the spine and slid out as I flipped through. Pages thirty-three through thirty-eight drifted to the floor, bringing with them a small handwritten note.

> For my beautiful Bettina. May Winter Harbor's brightness always drown out the darkness.
> Eternally yours, Oliver.

'Is it there?'

I looked away from the note and turned to page forty-seven . . . where there was a single lily, preserved perfectly in the crease.

'Can you smell it?'

The dead flower had lost its scent long ago, but I lifted the book and held my nose to the pages anyway. It smelled stale, like the Winter Harbor library. 'No,' I said.

'Well.' She looked at me, her eyes clearer than I'd ever seen them. 'I can.'

CHAPTER 17

'Oliver Savage?' Caleb said as we drove toward town ten minutes later. 'That cranky old man is the love of Betty Marchand's life?'

'I thought Betty was sick?' Simon said. 'And too weak to talk?'

'That's just what Raina wants everyone to believe to avoid questions,' I said. 'Betty's not completely well, but she's well enough to talk to me every time I see her.'

'How many times is that?' Caleb said.

I didn't answer. My head – and stomach – reeled from everything I'd just learned, and it took all my energy to stay focused. As we pulled into the library parking lot, I grabbed the canvas tote of books that Oliver had wanted – and that I hadn't had a chance to look at since borrowing them – and opened the door before Simon put the car in park.

'No offence,' Caleb said, 'but do we really have time for this?'

I looked at him through open space between the two front seats. 'We agree that somehow, some way,

239

Zara had something to do with Justine's death.'

His face flushed. 'Yes.'

'And that a lot of people have died, and many more might follow if we don't do something to save them.'

He didn't say anything.

'We need to find out as much as we can about the Marchands without them knowing. If Oliver is the love of Betty's life, he knows her better than anyone else does.'

Behind me, the wipers shot across the windscreen. I could hardly hear their quick rhythm over the rain pelting the roof. The sky had darkened and the clouds thickened during our drive, and it was only a matter of time before the lightning show started.

'She's right, Caleb,' Simon said. 'And if we're doing this, we have to do it now.'

I was ready to leave him in the car, but Caleb finally sat up and brushed his eyes.

'Let's go,' he said.

The rain pummelled us as we sprinted for the library entrance. By the time we entered the lobby ten seconds later, we looked like we'd just jumped in the harbour fully dressed.

We found Oliver in the library's designated reading area. He sat in an armchair by a fireplace, surrounded by open books. They were everywhere – on the table next to him, on the window seat behind him, on the

240

mantel, on the floor, propped against potted plants. But he wasn't reading.

He was looking right at me.

'Oliver?' Simon said when Oliver didn't speak or look away. 'I don't know if you remember us, but I'm Simon Carmichael, and this is my brother, Caleb. Our family lives on Lake Kanasacka?'

The rain grew louder overhead. A log shifted in the fireplace, sending sparks through the metal screen.

'I don't think he can hear you.' Caleb didn't bother whispering as he tilted his chin toward the table by Oliver's chair. A small brown hearing aid sat on top of the stack of open books.

'I know who you are,' Oliver said, his voice gruff but calm. 'And I can hear you. I heard you when you were in the parking lot.'

I felt Simon tense next to me.

'Vanessa Sands,' Oliver said, 'I believe you have something of mine.'

I blinked, suddenly remembering I hugged Paige's copy of *The Complete History of Winter Harbor* to my chest. I started to hand the book to him . . . but stopped when his eyes dropped to the canvas bag draped over my shoulder.

'This morning, per library policy, I brought back other books I needed so that I could borrow those. Mary informed me that someone else had taken them out.' His eyes shifted back to mine. 'For some strange reason, out of the thousands of volumes in the library, young Vanessa Sands wanted the same five books I did. What are the odds?'

'Slim.' I shrugged the bag off my shoulder and placed it on the floor near his other books. 'The odds are slim.'

He looked down at the bag, surprised I'd given up so easily.

'Oliver . . . we need your help.'

His eyes softened when he raised them to mine. I guessed it had been a while since anyone had asked cranky Oliver Savage for anything.

'Terrible things are happening in Winter Harbor. And you know some very important information that no one else knows.' I held out the book he'd written. He sat back and covered his mouth with one shaky hand. After a moment, he reached forward to take the book. 'It's still there. Page forty-seven.'

He removed the lily and stared at it, awed, like it was still vibrant and alive after so much time. 'Where did you get this?' he asked, slowly twirling the thin stem between his index finger and thumb.

'Paige loaned it to me.'

'Oliver,' Simon said, 'if there's anything at all you can tell us about Betty or the Marchands that might help stop what's been going on, we'd really appreciate it.'

Oliver replaced the lily, then turned to the back of the book. After a moment, he started reading aloud.

'"Winter Harbor's waters teem with life, and countless restaurateurs have tried to turn this natural bounty into financial gain over the years. However, none has been nearly as successful as Bettina Marchand, a Canadian transplant who opened the immediately popular Betty's Chowder House in 1965. A chef and businesswoman at just twenty-four years old, Miss Marchand admits to having had 'less than the proper training' for such a venture but, through hard work and her 'deeply rooted understanding of and respect for the sea', has managed to create and sustain what is already a Winter Harbor institution.'"

'That's it?' Caleb asked. 'No offence, but you didn't just tell us anything we couldn't have learned from a Winter Harbor visitor brochure.'

'Exactly.' Oliver patted the book. 'What's in here is all Betty was willing to share. The restaurant was already a local legend while I was working on this history, and as such, I thought it deserved an entire chapter. But – one paragraph. That's all she'd let me write.'

'Why?' Simon asked. 'Was she uncomfortable with her unexpected success?'

'Oh, she was uncomfortable, but her success had nothing to do with it.'

My head shot up as lightning struck the ground

nearby, making the lights flicker overhead. When I lowered my eyes, they locked on Oliver's.

'Out of respect for her, I've told no one what I'm about to tell you. And I tell you now only because I know you know things, too.' He shifted his gaze to Simon, then Caleb. 'Even if you don't quite realise or understand it, you all know things Betty didn't want anyone ever to find out.'

Simon and I sat on a couch opposite Oliver's chair. Behind us, Caleb leaned against a bookshelf and crossed his arms, willing to listen.

When Oliver spoke again, his voice was lighter. 'When I first met Bettina Marchand, she was doing what she loved to do more than anything: swimming. She was doing the backstroke in a purple swimsuit, and smiling as though she could hear someone dear to her whispering about just how lovely she looked. It was obvious that she wasn't swimming for exercise or sport, but simply because it felt good.

'It was July 1965. She was twenty-four, new to town, and getting lots of attention from the local boys. I was twenty-six, Winter Harbor born and raised, and among those taken by her. She'd been in town a few months by that point, but we hadn't officially met. If she'd had her way, we wouldn't have met the way we did, either.' He smiled. 'But it wasn't like I was stalking her, or hiding so she couldn't see me watching her. I was there to swim, too. I tried to leave when I saw her there, to give her privacy . . . but I couldn't. She was too beautiful.'

'Was she mad when she saw you?' Caleb asked.

'For Betty to have been mad, she would've had to have first been aware that I was admiring her. But she wasn't. She never invited or wanted any of the attention she received.'

'She found out eventually though, right?' I asked. 'That you admired her?'

'The only way she *wouldn't* have found out was if she'd left town. Fortunately, she was very committed to the restaurant, and that kept her here when she might've otherwise fled. The restaurant also made it easy to find her. I started going there on my lunch break every day, hoping for the chance to talk to her. When it was slow, she would sit with me. I did most of the talking, unfortunately – any time I tried to ask her questions about anything other than the restaurant, she always changed the topic. And she loved listening to stories about Winter Harbor – she called it the home she'd always wanted – so I told her everything I knew, because it made her happy. When I ran out of material, I dug up more.'

'Is that why you didn't talk about any of the unexplained deaths in your books?' I asked, handing him his note about Winter Harbor's brightness drowning out the darkness. 'Because you wanted the stories only to make her happy?'

Oliver stared at the note, and then placed one hand on the front cover without answering. 'After a few months, she finally agreed to go on a real date with me. By that time, it was almost winter, and the lakes had frozen over. We went skating on Lake Kanasacka, and afterward, I made her dinner.' He paused. 'That was the first night that she told me things about herself and her life that she said she hadn't told anyone . . .'

'Like what?' I asked, my heart racing as his smile faded.

'She said she was raised by her mother and aunts in an "unconventional" environment. And that she'd left without telling them why or where she was going because she didn't approve of their lifestyle, and never wanted to be found and made to go back.' He looked at the fire, as if preparing to say what he was about to say next. 'She told me, with tears in her eyes, that she spent so much time swimming not just because she liked to, but because she needed to. She physically *needed* to immerse herself in salt water several times a day.'

I looked at Simon without turning my head. He was watching Oliver closely.

'She said if she didn't . . . eventually, she wouldn't be able to breathe.'

'Why not?' Simon asked after a pause.

'She wouldn't explain. And she started acting differently as soon as she said that much – distant, even more guarded. She said she was embarrassed, but I knew it was more than that. She was afraid.'

The lightning was closer now; the ground rumbled, making the couch vibrate beneath me.

'I continued to see her every day and share stories about Winter Harbor, if for no other reason than to distract her from her fears. Her trust in me grew, and she seemed to forget how terrible she felt after revealing such personal details of her life. After two years of this, when things seemed almost normal, I asked her to be my bride.'

My heart ached for him as his eyes turned down.

'She said we couldn't be together like that . . . that she loved me too much to risk anything happening to me.' The book shook as he squeezed it with both hands. 'In an attempt to convince her it would be okay, I wrote this for her. I wanted her to know that I would always be there for her, to talk to her, to distract her from her fears, if that's what she needed from me. But she never changed her mind.'

My eyes fluttered closed as Simon's hand pressed against my back.

'That wasn't the worst of it, though.' His voice was lower now. 'Just because she said we couldn't be together didn't mean she wanted it that way. And one late

August night many years later, when I was missing her so badly I couldn't see straight, I looked for her at the restaurant. She wasn't there, and on a whim I returned to where we'd first met. She was swimming, and when she saw me watching this time, she climbed out of the water and came toward me without a word.'

I was glad when the lights flickered off and stayed that way. My cheeks were burning as I listened to Oliver talk about his romantic rendezvous on the rocks, and I imagined Simon's lips against mine last night.

'Nine months later, she had Raina.'

My eyes widened. I knew she was Betty's daughter, and that she had to have a father . . . but it was hard to imagine that strange Raina was the result of such real, passionate, forbidden love.

'She stopped talking to me completely after that night on the rocks,' Oliver said sadly. 'I still went to the restaurant. I told her I wanted to show our daughter as much light and happiness as her mother had shown me. But she wouldn't listen. It was like she didn't hear me.'

'And that was it?' Caleb asked. 'She didn't give you another chance?'

'I'm afraid not. I wrote, I called, I sent flowers. I went to the restaurant just to be near her. I sent gifts on every special occasion – birthdays, holidays, any day I thought of her so much I had to physically *do* something about it. And I did the same for Raina –

until those gifts and cards started coming back to me.' He paused. 'Years later, after Betty's accident, I tried to visit her at home . . . but Raina wouldn't let me in. She said it would be too upsetting. I still go to the restaurant now, though, just to feel as close to her as I can.'

'Oliver,' I said, 'the place where you and Betty first met, where you met again a few years later . . . where was that, exactly?'

He frowned, then reached into a leather knapsack at his feet. He pulled out a large drawing pad and held it toward me. 'I'm not much of an artist, but doodling is quite therapeutic.'

I took the pad and handed it to Simon to open. I already knew what Oliver wanted me to see.

'The water at the bottom of Chione Cliffs has always been a good swimming spot,' Oliver said. 'I liked it because it was secluded. Betty liked it because it was the area's deepest natural pool. She said when she dived into it from the cliff, she could swim straight down for minutes and never reach sand.'

A log shifted in the fireplace just as my breath caught. Thankfully, no one seemed to notice my surprise.

'She could swim underwater for minutes?' Caleb asked. 'How?'

'I thought it was a skill she'd learned after years of practice – that, or it was just another seemingly impossible talent she was blessed with. But when she stopped talking to me so abruptly after our night there, I started gathering information. I wrote down the few personal details she'd granted me – including swimming for minutes without oxygen. I wanted to help her. I wanted to figure out what she was so afraid of so that I could help her deal with it. I thought if I could just help her not to be so scared, maybe we could be together.' He reached forward and lifted the canvas bag of books to his lap. 'I didn't figure it out in time for Betty and me . . . but maybe we can figure it out in time for Winter Harbor.'

I eyed the covers of the books as he placed them one by one on the floor by our feet. '*Greek Mythology*? *Untold Sailors' Tales*? *Mermaids*?'

The last time I saw Oliver in the library, he'd said history repeated itself, that the way to figure out and stop what was happening now was to revisit what had happened in the past. I'd expected books about crime, murder, death and destruction – non-fiction works that chronicled true, gruesome events throughout time. Kind of like the obituaries with the smiling victims in the back issues of the *Winter Harbor Herald*, but on a bigger, more terrifying scale.

'*Les Chanteuses de la mer*?' I read aloud as Oliver pulled out the last book. It had a faded red cover with an illustration of a woman reaching out of the water, toward the sky.

'Songstresses of the sea,' Caleb translated, his voice grim. 'French was the only subject I ever liked,' he added when Simon and I looked at him, surprised.

I turned to Simon, my rock of scientific theory. 'Really? You *really* think Betty's some kind of evil singing mermaid? With, what? Webbed feet and a spiked coconut bra?' I tried to joke because he wasn't laughing. He wasn't rolling his eyes, or immediately dismissing the idea.

I turned back to the book, which Oliver now held open. My eyes skipped over the French text and landed on the illustration. The only light in the room came from the flickering fire, so I couldn't make it out right away . . . but then another bolt of lightning struck nearby, and the image was as clear as if it were blown up on a movie screen.

A man lay on a rocky shore. His body was limp, his limbs splayed across the beach like strands of washed-up seaweed. From the neck down, the picture suggested his death had been painful, even torturous. He looked like a fisherman who'd been caught in a storm, snatched from his boat and then tossed about among the waves before being thrown to land.

But despite the unfortunate outcome, from the neck up, he looked like he wished he could do it again.

Because the dead fisherman was smiling.

CHAPTER 18

'This is crazy. You *know* this is crazy.'

'It *sounds* crazy,' Caleb said, 'but it makes perfect sense.'

Simon stared straight ahead as he drove, not agreeing with either of us.

'Raina might be strange and Zara might be capable of doing some terrible, unimaginable things, but . . . sirens? Like the beautiful, *fictional* creatures that lured sailors to their deaths?' I shook my head. 'This isn't *The Odyssey*. This is actually happening – here, in real life. If you want to call all of the Marchands serial killers, fine. But to say that they magically sing to guys for the thrill of the hunt is insane.'

'Vanessa, I can *hear* Zara.' Caleb sounded excited, as if relieved to have an explanation finally. 'Even when I don't see her, I hear her. That's why I can't focus on anything else whenever she's calling to me. I can't even think about how much I can't stand the thought of her, or how I wish she would go away and leave me alone. I can only listen to her, and picture her, and want to be near her, even though being

252

within a hundred miles of her is normally too close.'

An image of the two of them on the rocks in the woods flashed through my head. He'd seemed simultaneously eager and uncomfortable as she'd crawled toward him and pressed her body against his – but he'd just lost his girlfriend. And despite whatever lay underneath the pretty exterior, Zara was still stunning. He'd just been hurt, and lonely, and guilty for being attracted to another girl.

'And you heard what Oliver said – this was the past Betty tried to escape. It's why she left her family and came here, and why she and Oliver couldn't be together.'

'Because the other crazy, man-hunting women in her family would find out, lure him away from her, kill him and then take her back?' I looked at Caleb. 'Do you hear how that sounds?'

'What about the man who fathered Zara and Paige?' he asked. 'Have you ever heard them talk about their dad?'

'No,' I admitted, 'but maybe they're just a very private family. I don't know Paige's favourite colour or when Zara's birthday is, either.'

'You don't know about their dad – just like we never heard anything about their dad – because there probably wasn't just one. And Raina probably killed them both after each deed was done.'

'Um, Simon?' I looked at him, then at his knuckles

turning white as he clutched the steering wheel. 'A voice of reason would be helpful right about now.'

'Caleb should go in.'

It took me a second to realise the car was no longer moving. I followed Simon's gaze and tried to make out where we were through the rain streaming down the windscreen. 'The Lighthouse?'

Caleb sat back and peered through his window. 'What are we doing here?'

Simon continued to stare straight ahead. 'Betty stopped talking to Oliver after they spent the night together on Chione Cliffs. The night she became pregnant with Raina.'

'And . . . ?' I wasn't making the connection.

'According to Zara's scrapbook, she dropped each guy the second he said he loved her, and then they disappeared.'

'Zara has a scrapbook?' Caleb asked. 'I wouldn't have pegged her as the type.'

'And now,' Simon said, ignoring Caleb, 'Paige is pregnant.'

My stomach dropped. I'd been so intent on disbelieving everything Oliver had told us, I hadn't thought about what it might mean if it was actually true. 'Jonathan.'

'Jonathan,' Caleb repeated. 'Jonathan Marsh? What about him?'

I looked toward the Lighthouse docks. The fancy yachts, all abandoned, bobbed like toy boats in the choppy water. 'He's Paige's boyfriend.'

'Betty loved Oliver,' Simon said. 'She wanted to protect him, which was why when they finally gave in to each other, she cut him off. She could've killed him – and it sounds like if she hadn't been on her own way she was, she would've. Not because she wanted to, but because it was expected. Because they didn't want anyone else finding out what they really were.'

I stared out the window, wondering how these words were coming out of Simon's mouth. Where was the scientific scepticism? The automatic insistence that such things were humanly impossible? The demand for proof?

'We have to tell Jonathan. We have to warn him about Paige before something happens.' Caleb's voice was resigned.

I shook my head. 'I know Paige. Even if – hypothetically speaking, in some alternate universe – Betty's a descendant of murdering mermaids, Paige hasn't been swimming in that gene pool. Or if she has, she doesn't know it. She's too nice, too good. And I've seen her with Jonathan – she's crazy about him. She would never do anything to hurt him.'

Simon looked at me. 'What about Zara? Or Raina?'

My face flushed. He wasn't kidding.

'What do I say?' Caleb asked. 'How do you tell some-one . . . this?'

Simon turned toward him. 'You don't. We don't want to scare him or give him reason to ask Paige anything. We don't know what she might say to Raina. The last thing we need is for *them* to be suspicious of *us*.'

'Do you want me to just check on him? Make sure he's still standing – and hopefully not smiling?'

'Pretty much. And see if you can find out anything about Paige, or their relationship. You worked together, right? So it shouldn't seem strange?'

Caleb half laughed, half sighed. 'Right. It shouldn't seem strange at all.'

He was still for a minute, and I thought he might be reconsidering the realistic plausibility of what they both seemed to think was true, but then he opened the door and jumped out of the car. I watched him fid-dle with his iPod and the headphones in his ears as he sprinted through the rain.

'You're right.'

I looked down at Simon's hand on mine.

'It sounds completely insane,' he continued. 'All of it. And under normal circumstances, I would've thanked Oliver for his time and dismissed everything he said. But these aren't normal circumstances.' He leaned to-ward me. 'Think about it. Oliver aside, think about everything you've seen. Everything you've told me.'

'I've seen some strange things,' I admitted. 'But I don't buy it. I can't. The idea of sirens had to have been invented back when men couldn't predict or explain certain things. Like the weather – when they didn't know how the moon and the sun and the oceans all worked together to create crazy natural drama, and when some guys accidentally died as a result. Sirens were imaginary tools used to explain what man couldn't.' I squeezed his fingers. 'But *you* know better. You know about the weather. You can explain why these things are happening.'

'You've been with me when I've tried to understand it the last few weeks. What's been happening breaks traditional rules. It defies scientific reasoning.'

'What about Justine?' I asked. 'She was a *girl*. And she wasn't found smiling.'

'I think she was getting in the way. I think, for whatever reason, Zara zeroed in on Caleb, and when he didn't respond the way she wanted him to, she went after the obstacle.'

I stared at him, my frustration giving way to concern. As a lifelong chicken and firm believer in all that went bump in the night, I was more likely to accept illogical, irrational theories. Simon was Mr Science Guy. He was the walking, talking weather channel. How was I the sceptical one?

'You know something else.' I wasn't sure of it until

257

I said it aloud. I ducked my head to get him to look at me. 'Don't you? You know something I don't. That's why this makes sense to you.'

He looked away.

'Simon.' I squeezed his hand tighter when he tried to release mine. 'Tell me. Whatever it is you think I can't handle, I can handle.' I watched him as he stared at the rain.

'It was the other day,' he said finally.

'The other day . . . in Springfield?'

He nodded. 'In the woods. When we first saw them on the rocks.'

I looked down. I wasn't sure he referred to the same moment, but I had no problem recalling at least one – when he'd looked at Zara like he hadn't known what beautiful was until he saw her there. And when he'd seemed to forget I was standing right next to him.

'At first, all I could think about was Caleb. I worried we wouldn't find him, and about the state he'd be in if we did.' He paused. 'And then when I saw his sweatshirt hanging on that tree, like some sort of twisted clue, all my worries and thoughts exploded in my head. I was mad. Running toward them, I thought about what I would say to her – what I would *do* to her. By the time we reached the trees, I was ready to plough through and run right at her.'

I waited. 'So what happened?'

'I don't know. My body was fully charged, but my head . . .'

'It's okay, Simon,' I said. 'Your head . . . what?'

'Vanessa, please understand, I couldn't control it, I didn't know what was going on . . . I was only vaguely aware that it was happening.' He took a shallow, shaky breath. 'But when we saw them there, on the rocks, I didn't want to hurt her . . . I wanted to hurt *him*.'

My chest tightened. 'Your emotions were displaced. Everything collided at that moment, and you were overwhelmed.'

'I wasn't.'

He said this so seriously, so earnestly, I had no choice but to believe that *he* believed what he said. 'But why?' I asked. 'Why would you want to hurt Caleb?'

His face scrunched up as he tilted his head, already apologising for what he was about to say. 'Because I was jealous.'

I sat back.

'As soon as I saw her everything else went away. The woods, the search, everything that had happened in the past few weeks . . .'

'Me?' I guessed, looking through the windscreen.

'All I was aware of was her,' he said, his voice wavering. 'Vanessa, she tried. She tried to get me to react, to respond to her. And what they do – it's strong. It's not

259

just a sound, or a song – it's nothing like the legends we read growing up.'

I looked at him, my heart drumming in my ears. 'What is it?'

He paused. 'You know how when you're floating on your back in the lake, the water rises and falls against your ears? So that for half a second you can hear everything around you and then for the other half a second everything's muted? It almost feels like you're suspended between two worlds?'

I knew exactly what he was talking about. Even before the accident, the half second that I couldn't hear everything above the water always made me nervous.

'It's kind of like that – like floating on the surface and then slowly, gently, being pulled under. You feel yourself going deeper, but you can't stop it, and it's not unpleasant, so you don't even try. You just kind of give in and let the water pull you down until you can't hear anything else.'

'Did you see her? When that was happening to you?'

'Yes. But she looked different. Everything looked different – softer yet brighter. It was like we were surrounded by a million mirrors, and the sun's rays were ricocheting back and forth between them until the woods were filled with a white, shiny haze.'

'Well,' I said, attempting to sound like I was ready to help him move forward the way a good friend should, now that the truth was out, 'it's a crazy story. But I trust you, and trust that you know what you saw and heard. So if this really is what we're going on, then –'

'Vanessa.'

I closed my eyes. All I'd wanted was to know what had really happened to Justine, and what she'd really been doing in the months before her death. I'd just wanted some answers so I could understand why she jumped when she did, deal with it and move on. How had I gone from that to this?

'Vanessa,' he said again, lifting a stray strand of hair away from my face and smoothing it behind my ear.

'Simon . . . don't. Please. It's just a lot. It's a lot, but it's okay.'

'I got away. Don't you want to know how?'

I started to shake my head, but stopped when he touched my chin.

'You.'

I lifted my eyes to his.

'I snapped out of the initial hold long enough to tell you to go after Caleb and to run at her because I heard you. You spoke, and I was pulled right back. And then when it was just the two of us, and she was doing everything she could to get me to come to her, to go with her, I heard you again.'

'But I wasn't there. I was nowhere near you.'

'I know.' He brought his face closer to mine. When

261

he spoke again, his voice was soft. 'Vanessa, what happened last night . . . wasn't just about last night.'

I searched his face, torn between begging him to stop and wanting him to continue.

'For as long as your family's been coming to Winter Harbor, I couldn't wait to see you every summer. We could always talk for hours about books, movies, Justine and Caleb . . . or we could talk about nothing. It was always easy, always comfortable, you know?'

I nodded. I'd often thought the same thing.

'But a few years ago, something changed.' He looked at me. 'Do you remember what we were supposed to do the night of your accident?'

'Of course. It was Thursday. Drive-in movie and ice-cream night.'

'Right,' he said. 'Only you couldn't make it . . . because you were in the hospital.'

'Where you and Caleb came with your laptop and a pile of DVDs.'

He lowered his eyes. 'Do you remember what movie you watched that night?'

'*Sleepless in Seattle*. Caleb allowed a romantic comedy due to my fragile condition.'

'And I don't remember . . . because I never knew. I didn't look at the laptop once because I couldn't look away from you. You and Justine were on the bed, with the computer on her lap, Caleb sat in a chair next to Justine, and –'

'You were on the window seat,' I said. 'On the other side of the room. You said you were hot and wanted to be near the AC vent.'

'I wasn't hot. I was scared. I'd never been so scared in my life.'

I tried to picture him, watching me for two hours from across the room. I'd welcomed the distraction from my thoughts about what had just happened and had been too engrossed in the movie to notice. 'But I was fine . . . they only kept me a few days for observation.'

'Vanessa . . . you were in the water for thirty-four minutes. You shouldn't have made it. And that night, I realised how lost I'd have been if you hadn't.'

I reached up to brush away the tear that fell to his cheek. He took my hand and leaned closer. I wanted him to kiss me. I wanted to believe what he said now and that what had happened between us wasn't a mistake. For a second, I thought he would, and that I could . . . but then he pressed his lips to my forehead instead.

'I'm sorry,' he whispered. 'I'm so sorry Zara got to me. But that's what I knew that you didn't know. That's why I believe Oliver.' He pulled back to look at me. 'I'm not saying that's all there is to it. It doesn't explain the weather, or why they're doing what they're doing. And I'll do everything I can to find out more, until we know enough to stop them.'

The back door flung open before I could respond, letting in a gust of wind and rain.

'What is it?' Simon's expression hardened. 'What did Jonathan say?'

Caleb sat in the back seat, chest heaving. His hair was plastered to his head, his clothes clung to his skin, and water dripped down his face, but he didn't seem to notice.

'Jonathan didn't say anything. No one's seen or heard from him in three days.'

CHAPTER 19

'Do you like blueberries?'

I stood in the kitchen doorway and scanned the room. The table was covered with opened packages of bread, bacon and pancake batter, their contents spilling onto the newspapers underneath. A thin layer of flour coated the entire counter, which was cluttered with mixing bowls and utensils. Eggshells littered the floor, leaking clear liquid remains onto the linoleum.

'I can't remember,' Mom said when I didn't answer. 'I can't remember if you like blueberries and hate strawberries, or like strawberries and hate blueberries. Or if you like them both, or hate them both.' She looked around her, as if the answer lay hidden in a pile of flour. 'Why can't I remember?'

Probably because she hadn't made anything but coffee for breakfast in ten years. 'I like all berries,' I said, keeping my theory to myself.

She sighed. 'Thank goodness. I was starting to worry that you might have an allergy, and I couldn't forgive myself if I'd forgotten *that*.'

'Mom . . . what is all this?'

'What's all what?' She turned back to a mixing bowl. 'You didn't eat much last night. I thought you might be hungry.'

This wasn't normal Mom behaviour. Even if it had been ten years since she'd cracked an egg, the time off wouldn't have made her so tense, so frantic now. Plus, she was the neatest neat freak I'd ever known. If she'd really wanted to make breakfast just because she thought I might be hungry, she'd be cleaning up as she went.

Already guessing what was wrong and knowing I wouldn't get a straight answer if I asked, I went to the kitchen table and slid the *Winter Harbor Herald* out from under a loaf of bread.

I coughed to cover my gasp. I'd expected the news, but not the headline.

Four More Bodies Wash Up in Winter Harbor,
Town Declares State of Emergency

I scanned the article, finding some small relief in that none of the most recent male victims was Jonathan.

'Mom . . . what do you say we go out for breakfast instead?'

She turned to me. 'Out?'

'You've been cooped up here for days. A change of scenery would do you good.'

She beamed like I'd suggested we hightail it back to

Boston, and I ignored the slight guilt I felt for deceiving her. For two days I'd been trying to figure out how to learn more about her connection to Raina without simply asking if and how they knew each other. I didn't want to risk upsetting Mom any more than she already had been, or give her reason to throw me in the back of the BMW and whisk me away. Short of just throwing out Raina's name and seeing how Mom reacted, I'd had no idea how to find out what I needed to naturally . . . until now.

'We could go to Betty's,' I said, watching her expression. 'The chowder house on the pier?'

'What a lovely idea. We haven't been to Betty's in ages.' She kissed my cheek as she passed through the kitchen doorway. 'Thank you for suggesting it.'

During the drive to town, I thought about how I never would've done this even a few days ago. Because Mom and I didn't *do* things like this. We barely even talked. She and Justine could always discuss clothes or make-up, and even took monthly mall and spa trips together. Not sharing the interest, I always opted out of those excursions, choosing to read or watch movies with Dad instead. Breakfast at Betty's would be the first time we'd been anywhere, just the two of us.

Normally, I would've been afraid of long silences and awkward conversations. But I wasn't afraid now. I'd felt stronger, more confident, since the night Simon and I spent together, and the feeling had only grown after he confessed his feelings in the car outside the Lighthouse. I'd even slept without the TV on the night before. It was as if Simon had become my night-light; even when he wasn't with me, he was illuminating the world so that I no longer feared it.

And when he and Caleb returned from Bates, where they were researching sirens and ways to stop them, I would make sure he knew how grateful I was.

'Not very busy, are they?' Mom commented as we pulled into the quarter-filled parking lot ten minutes later.

I swivelled in my seat and scanned the property. Garrett wasn't asking for reservations at his usual post. The latest deaths had either run more people out of town or kept them locked in their summer homes and away from danger.

I sneaked glances at Mom as we crossed the parking lot and entered Betty's. I'd hoped going to Raina's family's restaurant would automatically trigger some kind of reaction, but if it did, Mom hid it.

'You're quite popular,' she said after we were seated – and the hostess, busboy and a waiter had said hello.

'I've become friendly with Paige Marchand,' I said, lifting my eyes from the menu to watch her face. 'Her family owns Betty's, so I've got to know a bunch of the staff.'

'Oh, sweetie.' She tilted her head and smiled. 'I'm so glad you made some friends. I can't tell you how much I hated the thought of you all alone up here.'

I nodded and looked back down at the menu, thinking I might have to throw Raina's name out there after all.

'You know, that's how your sister always coped with everything.'

I looked up again.

'She absolutely adored you but didn't always have an easy time of it. That's why she was so outgoing and had so many friends and boyfriends. She desperately needed people to like her – the more who did, the better she felt.'

I shook my head, temporarily forgetting our reason for being there. 'What do you mean, she desperately needed people to like her? What wasn't easy?'

'What can I get you today?'

I dropped the menu to the table and clutched my head. I'd hoped Zara would be working – she was another potential memory jog for Mom, and if she was at Betty's, that meant she wasn't doing things she shouldn't be elsewhere – but had been too distracted to look out for her. Now she stood right by our table, holding an order pad and smiling like we were ordinary customers and she was an ordinary waitress.

'Hi, Zara.' I forced my hands from my head to avoid alarming Mom.

'Vanessa,' she said evenly.

'Mom,' I managed, trying not to wince at the searing pain coursing between my ears, 'this is Zara Marchand, Paige's sister.'

'Oh!' Mom held out one hand for Zara to shake. 'It's so nice to meet you. I was just telling Vanessa how happy I was that she'd made some new friends. It's been a very difficult summer for our family, as you can imagine, and –'

'We'll have scrambled eggs, toast and coffee,' I said.

Mom looked at me, surprised.

'Coming right up,' Zara said, her silver eyes gleaming as she took our menus.

'Sorry,' I said once she was gone. 'I'm pretty hungry.'

Mom frowned but didn't press.

'Anyway, what were you saying? About Justine not having an easy time?' This, too, was something I wouldn't have done a few days ago. I wouldn't have thought there was anything Mom knew about Justine that I didn't, and would've immediately dismissed the conversation. Plus, if she talked long enough, maybe she'd relax and let something slip about Raina.

She crossed her arms on the table and leaned forward. 'Sweetie . . . *you* are an exceptionally beautiful girl.'

I started to shake my head.

'Yes, you are.' She put one hand on mine. 'I know

you don't realise it. You never have. That probably drove Justine crazier than the fact that everyone always noticed you before they noticed her.'

'Mom, no offence . . . but this is silly. Justine was gorgeous. Everyone loved her. She had more friends and boyfriends than most girls have in a lifetime.'

'And she worked really hard at that.'

I slid my hand out from under hers and sat back.

'When you girls were very little, every day I would put you in the double stroller and take you for a walk through the Common. And every day, I would get stopped by at least a dozen people who told me what beautiful daughters I had.'

'*Daughters*,' I repeated.

'Yes. Justine was beautiful, too.' She paused. 'But, Vanessa . . . they were always looking at you.'

'So I was a cute baby,' I said, trying to be patient. 'Justine was too young then to notice or care about the attention, and by the time she *was* old enough, it had turned to her.'

She seemed to choose her next words carefully. 'Do you remember when you were in sixth grade and Justine was in seventh, and you came home on Valentine's Day with a lunchbox filled with cards?'

'I guess,' I said, not really recalling.

'Do you know how many cards Justine got?'

'Ten? Twenty?'

271

'Thirty-three.'

'See?' I felt strangely triumphant. 'There was no way I could've fitted that many cards in my lunchbox.'

'Only twelve of them were for her,' Mom said. 'Those were from her girlfriends.'

'And?' I said, when she looked at me like I should know what she was talking about.

'And some of the boys in her grade saw you when we dropped both of you off at school together. They had little crushes and gave her cards to give to you.'

'I don't remember that.'

'I know you don't. You didn't think anything of it – then, or in similar situations in the years following. You didn't notice when boys tried to ask you out, or hung out with Justine in hopes of talking to you.'

'But I've never even been on a date.' That was still true, despite what had happened with Simon.

'If you haven't been on a date, it's not because no one wanted to take you.'

'Mom,' I said calmly, 'Justine went white-water rafting, and sneaked out late at night, and kissed a *lot* of boys. She wasn't afraid of anything. That's what everyone loved about her. That's what *I* loved about her.'

'Yes, she did do all of those things – because she thought that as your sister, she had to try that hard to get people to notice her. She didn't talk about it to your father and me quite as much as she got older, but we knew that's what she was doing. And we did our best to reassure her and make her feel as loved as possible.'

'If that's true,' I said, not buying it for a second, 'then why did she go out of her way to protect me? To take care of me, to try to help me feel less afraid of everything that scared me? If being my sister made her work so hard, wouldn't she have been bitter? And resentful? Wouldn't we have been enemies instead of best friends?'

'You were so innocent, so unassuming. She knew you had no idea what everyone else saw.' She looked down. Her glossed lips parted again, as though she was going to elaborate . . . but then she remained silent.

'What are you saying?' I struggled to keep my voice steady. 'What does this have to do with anything?'

'Vanessa, Justine was beautiful. She was funny, and smart, and daring, and exciting.' She looked at me, her eyes watering. 'But she was also the most insecure person I've ever known. And I think that's why she did what she did. I think that's why she jumped, in the middle of the night, in very dangerous conditions.'

I stared at her. If what she claimed was true, then Zara had nothing to do with Justine's death.

I did.

'Anyway,' she said with a sigh. 'I don't want all of that to ruin our lovely breakfast. It's just we hadn't really talked about what happened, and –'

She stopped when I put the piece of paper on the table before her. I watched her eyes travel from the green Post-It note at the bottom to the nine words in the centre.

'What is this?' she asked, the pink gloss on her lips growing brighter as the colour faded from her face.

'Justine's personal essay,' I said, my heart racing. I'd been carrying it around in my purse since taking it off her bulletin board. 'About who she was, and who she wanted to become.'

She glanced at me. 'What are you . . . how did you . . . ?'

'She wasn't going to Dartmouth. She didn't even apply.'

My stomach turned when her eyes filled with fresh tears, and for just a second, I almost regretted telling her what would've been the worst possible thing she could've heard before Justine's death. But she'd basically just accused me of making Justine's entire life difficult before sending her over the edge for good. I wanted her to know that she didn't know Justine as well as she thought.

'I don't understand,' she said, her eyes locked on the middle of the page. 'She said she was accepted. She wore the sweatshirt. She carried the umbrella. We opened a college savings account in her name when she turned eighteen, and she sent in the deposit right after that.'

'Did you actually ever see a bank statement?' I asked gently. 'Or a returned cheque made out to Dartmouth?'

'I must have . . . or maybe I didn't. It seems so long ago now, I can't remember. But I know I was very busy at work at the time, and she was so excited, so I just assumed . . .' She shook her head, then looked up. 'Why would she lie?'

I frowned as the tears slowly spilled onto the tops of her cheeks. 'I'm not sure.' I debated telling her that finding out was the real reason I'd come back to Winter Harbor in the first place, but then decided against it. I didn't want to get into a heated discussion about Caleb, or field questions I couldn't answer. Plus, she hadn't looked so devastated since the police had delivered their terrible news at the lake house a few weeks before, and despite my intentions a few seconds earlier, I didn't want to say anything that would make her feel worse.

I looked across the room, surprised when a table of middle-aged men erupted in loud laughter. I'd been so distracted by our bizarre conversation I'd forgotten where we were, and why.

'Here you are – scrambled eggs, toast and two cups of coffee.'

I turned back, noting as I did that my head felt fine.

'Can I get you girls anything else?'

Raina. She stood by our table, talking to both of us

but looking only at me. She wore a short green sun-dress that showed off her tan – and curves.

'Hi, Mrs – Miss – Marchand,' I said, my eyes dart-ing to Mom. She was so thrown by Justine's blank essay she didn't notice the steaming plate before her. 'What are you doing here?'

'It *is* my restaurant,' she said, her fake smile growing wider. 'Why wouldn't I be here?'

'Right. Sorry.' Feeling like lasers were shooting at me from her silver eyes, I looked away. When I did, I saw that the table of middle-aged men across the room had stopped laughing and were watching Raina, transfixed.

'How's Paige?' I asked.

'Never better.'

I glanced at Mom. She didn't seem to be aware of Raina's presence. 'Mom,' I said loudly, as if her hearing was the problem, 'this is Paige's mother, *Raina*.'

I held my breath as she lifted her head.

'I'm glad our daughters found each other,' she said, before returning her gaze to the essay.

Raina was still smiling at me when I looked at her again. 'Will that be all?'

My face burned as I nodded.

'I'll be sure to give Paige your best,' Raina called over her shoulder as she started back across the room. 'Oh, and be sure to visit our booth at the first annual

276

Lighthouse Resort and Spa Northern Lights Festival! It's going to be *quite* a time.'

'Mom,' I whispered once Raina disappeared into the kitchen. 'That was Raina Marchand.'

Nothing.

'*Mom*,' I tried again, putting one hand over the piece of paper so she couldn't see Justine's words.

She raised her eyes.

'Raina Marchand,' I repeated. 'Mother of Paige and Zara, daughter of Betty – *the* Betty, who founded this restaurant more than fifty years ago.'

'And?'

'Don't you know her?' I could hear my heart hammering in my ears as I waited for her response.

'I'm sorry, Vanessa,' she said finally, sounding exhausted, 'but I've never seen that woman in my life.'

CHAPTER 20

'The Winter Harbor Chamber of Commerce?' Caleb asked later that night.

I read the sign above the front door of Winter Harbor High School, then looked around. The parking lot was packed.

'Who knew Raina was so civic-minded?' Simon said.

'She's not,' Caleb said. 'According to Monty, Betty never missed a meeting before her accident. After, when she couldn't leave the house, everyone assumed Raina would attend in her place. But that never happened.'

'Maybe she's keeping up appearances,' I said. 'To deflect attention.'

'Or maybe she's surveying the entire town for her next victim.' Caleb shrugged when Simon shot him a look. 'Kidding. Sort of.'

I grabbed the door handle. Simon put one hand on my knee. 'These meetings can last hours,' he said. 'Why don't we head back to our house and do some more research? We can come back later to see where she goes next.'

'You heard Caleb. Raina's here for a reason. I want to know what it is.'

I climbed out of the car before he could say anything else. I felt bad for disagreeing, but we'd sat slouched in our seats for two hours, waiting for Raina to leave Betty's. She'd driven to the high school so fast, we'd had a hard time keeping her SUV in sight while staying far enough behind that she wouldn't notice us. After her strange behaviour in the restaurant earlier, and after Mom had had no idea who she was, I was determined to learn whatever I could.

I hurried into the school, looking over my shoulder once to see Simon and Caleb jogging after me. Guided by the buzz of voices, I found the meeting easily. It was standing room only, so I weaved through the crowd until I had a clear view of the podium up front.

'What's Mark doing here?' Simon asked, squeezing next to me.

I followed his nod. Caleb's surfer friend sat in the front row, next to the only empty chair in the room.

'Good evening, everyone.'

Raina stood at the podium. She'd changed before leaving Betty's and wore a silky, sleeveless white dress that showed off her toned, tanned arms. Her hair was pulled back in a loose ponytail, and her light make-up made her eyes shine. The effect wasn't lost on the crowd, which fell silent as soon as she spoke.

'Thank you for coming on such short notice to discuss the first annual Lighthouse Resort and Spa Northern Lights Festival. I know it's difficult to celebrate, given the recent tragedies that have befallen Winter Harbor – including the untimely death of Paul Carsons, the Lighthouse's primary investor and a firm festival supporter.'

She paused. I glanced at Simon and followed his gaze to the front row, where Caleb sat, whispering to Mark.

'But because of these tragedies,' Raina continued, 'it's more important now than ever that we come together as a community. Our visitors need help getting through this dark time.'

'What visitors?' a woman called out from across the room.

'My business is down eighty per cent,' another added. 'Most people have left, and those who haven't are too scared to come out of their houses.'

'It's up to us to change that,' Raina said. 'That's why we're here tonight. The festival committee has been hard at work, brainstorming ways to bring people back to town. In addition to exciting entertainment and activities, there are many incentives that you, as business owners, can offer. I'd like each of you to meet with a committee member and discuss these options. Everything from raffles to free samples can increase attendance.'

'Be right back,' Simon whispered.

I reached for his hand, but he was already gone. I stood on my toes to see where he was going, but the crowd was too thick.

'I'd also like you to estimate how many guests your booths usually entertain,' Raina continued, 'and give the names of ten people you will be personally responsible for bringing.'

'What if we don't know that many people who will come?' asked the woman whose business was down eighty per cent.

Raina's silver eyes narrowed before she smiled. 'You do.'

Chairs scraped against linoleum as people stood and divided into small groups. I took advantage of the activity to move through the crowd. I'd lost Simon, and now I'd lost Caleb and Mark, too. By the time I reached the front row, their seats were empty. Making sure Raina was distracted by the group gathered around her, I stepped onto a chair and half stood for a better view.

The pain blinded me instantly. It wrapped around my head and pulled until my skull felt like it caved inward. My knees gave, and I grabbed for the back of the chair to keep from falling.

'Henry, Alan and Clifton: see Dominique.'

Zara.

'Thomas, Greg and Malcolm: see Sabine.'

I stumbled to the back of the room and leaned against the wall. I waited until the pain was dull enough that I could open my eyes without doubling over, and then scanned the crowd. Simon, Caleb and Mark were still nowhere to be seen. But since Zara milled about, directing people, listening to their conversations and writing in a notebook, the boys were safer wherever they were.

Careful to remain out of Zara's direct line of sight, I stayed against the wall and made my way toward Raina. She stood with the meeting's few female members, who seemed to have more questions and concerns than the men. After spending so many summers in Winter Harbor, I recognised almost everyone – except for the other committee members. They were women of various ages. Some were tall, others petite. Some were blonde, others brunette. None were as striking as Raina, but all held the attention of the men gathered around them.

'I understand your concerns,' Raina said to the cluster of local women as I neared. 'What's happened this summer is just . . . unthinkable. But we have to band together. We have to be strong.' She lowered her voice. 'And let's be honest – it's up to us. If we left it to our husbands, we'd all just hunker down and hide out until the storm passed. That's no way to heal a community.'

Raina didn't have a husband. And given her previous comments about marriage, she didn't want one. But these women didn't seem to care. They liked the idea of being strong. They liked being needed.

I stepped to the left and ducked behind Malcolm, the owner of Squeezed, as Zara looked up from her notebook. She surveyed the room, then leaned down to speak to Sabine, a blonde committee member. Malcolm shifted in his chair, blocking my view; when he shifted back, Zara was gone.

I started to shove through the crowd after her, but then spotted her notebook. She'd given it to Sabine, and as Sabine turned a page, I got a quick glance at the cover.

The white leather cover. With *La Vie en rose* written in small script.

I took my cell phone from my jeans pocket and changed direction, moving toward the refreshment table. I tried Simon, then Caleb, then Simon again. When the calls went to voicemail, I texted Simon.

Z here. Get C. Meet me @ car in 2 minutes.

I filled a cup with coffee, grabbed a handful of napkins and hurried back to Sabine's group. The pounding in my head grew stronger with each step. As I skirted between chairs and stood before Malcolm, who sat two feet away from Sabine, I forced a smile.

'Malcolm?' I asked, hoping I sounded excited and not nervous. 'Malcolm Donohue?'

He tried to peer around me, but I leaned to one side, then the other.

'You own Squeezed, right?'

'Yes,' he said reluctantly, leaning back in his chair. 'Can I help you?'

'You can – and you do. All the time. Your watermelon guava smoothie is the best I've ever had.'

'That's nice. Thank you. Now, if you don't mind –'

'You guys know what I'm talking about, right?' I nodded to Thomas and Greg, owners of Tommy's Tunes and Harbor Pets. 'Best breakfast on the East Coast.'

'Excuse me,' a soft voice said behind me.

I spun around. My right foot landed on a leather purse on the floor, sending me off balance – and the cup of hot coffee I held into Sabine's lap.

'I'm so sorry!' I gasped as she shrieked and jumped up. 'What a klutz – let me get that for you.'

'That's all right,' Malcolm said, nudging me aside as I tried to pat Sabine's wet knee. 'Let's get some cold water on that. You don't want to ruin your lovely dress.'

It was a lovely dress. It was yellow with a long ruffled skirt that floated behind her as Malcolm led her away.

It was also more important to Sabine than Zara's journal, which now sat where it was dropped, in a dark-brown pool on the floor.

As Tommy and Greg hurried after them, I crouched

down, shook off the journal, slid it in the waistband of my jeans under my sweatshirt and mopped up the coffee with napkins. 'I'll get some paper towels from the bathroom,' I called out, in case my intentional accident had alerted Raina.

I darted into the hallway and ran.

The pain worsened. Tiny white dots flickered like sparklers in front of my eyes, making it hard to see where I was going. After dead-ending at three locked classrooms, I finally found the main entrance and threw open the door. We'd parked in the back of the lot; if Simon and Caleb were already in the car, they would've driven to me to expedite our exit. That they didn't made me move through the darkness even faster.

'I missed you.'

I slowed to a stop behind a minivan. The Subaru was two rows away, and I couldn't see it from my hiding spot . . . but I could hear her as if she stood right next to me.

'Town wasn't the same without you. *I* wasn't the same without you.'

The pain in my head shot toward my chest. She'd found him. She'd found Caleb. I searched the parking lot, praying to see Simon running toward me, or hiding behind another car, waiting for the right time to intervene.

'I missed your smile . . . your laugh . . .'

A fresh shock gripped my skull. I lowered to a squat and pressed my forehead to my knees.

'. . . the way your glasses slip down your nose when you're reading.'

My breath caught.

Caleb didn't wear glasses.

I jumped up, ignoring the pain between my ears. I crept alongside the minivan and peered around the back.

'You probably don't know this . . . but I've been watching you.'

They stood in the glow of a dim streetlight. Zara leaned against the Subaru, her arms crossed behind her back. She tilted her head and gazed up at Simon, who stood before her, his arms limp at his sides.

'I've been waiting for you,' she said. 'And hoping that one day, you'd notice me.'

'I noticed you,' Simon said, his voice strained. He stepped toward her, his feet moving slowly, awkwardly, like they were weighted down. She remained still until he stopped, their bodies separated by inches, and then she reached for him, taking the front of his fleece with one hand and pulling him closer.

'Don't,' I breathed. 'Please . . . don't.'

'You don't know how happy that makes me,' she said, gently taking his hands and putting them on her hips.

His head snapped up as their chests pressed together. His fingers tightened around her, which made her smile.

'You don't have a girlfriend, do you?' she asked, her mouth near his ear. 'I wouldn't want to get in the way . . .'

'Vanessa!'

I was only vaguely aware of the voice behind me.

'Do something!'

Her lips grazed his neck. He gasped.

I fell back behind the minivan like I'd been punched in the stomach. My eyes landed on Caleb in the next row. He crouched next to an old station wagon, gripping his iPod and shaking.

'Please,' he hissed, tears running down his face. 'Please make her stop.'

I felt like crying, too, but didn't know if it was because of the pain in my head or the sudden aching in my chest.

Vanessa . . . remember the woods . . .

I squeezed my eyes shut against the images Justine's suggestion prompted. I remembered the woods. I remembered how easily Simon had been transfixed by Zara, even as I stood right next to him.

Talk to him . . .

'Why don't we go for a ride?'

My eyes snapped open. I heard footsteps, doors open and close, a car start.

287

'Simon!' I yelled, scrambling to my feet. I rounded the back of the van and sprinted toward the car. '*Simon!*'

The Subaru pulled out of its space and started for the parking-lot entrance. It sped up as I ran faster. Knowing I couldn't catch up if I followed them, I darted left and shot across the lawn separating the lot from the street.

When my feet hit pavement, I lunged forward, toward the double yellow line. I closed my eyes, shielded my face with my arms, and braced for impact . . . but the Subaru skidded to a stop, its front bumper inches from my shins.

'Simon!' I banged the hood with my hand as I ran to the driver's-side door. I yanked the handle, but the door was locked. 'Hey!' I forced a smile as he looked at me through the closed window, confused. 'You almost left without me.'

Zara leaned across the middle console, put one hand on his thigh and whispered in his ear.

'*Simon.*' I rapped on the window. 'Please open the door.'

He turned toward her. It was like he couldn't hear me.

I pounded the window with my fist. When he ignored me again, I spun around and bolted for the side of the road. I grabbed as many rocks as my hands could hold, ran to the car and hurled them at the back window. The glass cracked on the fourth. On the fifth, a hunk no bigger than an ice cube popped out.

'Simon!' I shouted through the small opening. 'It's Vanessa.'

He froze. 'Get out of here.'

My heart sank. 'Simon, please –'

'Get *out*.'

I stepped back as he shoved Zara off him. He threw open the door, strode to the passenger's side and yanked her out.

'Baby, what are you –?'

'They need you inside, Zara,' I said loudly, so Simon could hear me over her. 'You should go.'

She turned toward me, her short pink skirt rippling in the light breeze. 'Vanessa,' she said, her voice entering my ears like switchblades.

I didn't respond. It took everything I had to keep my eyes on hers.

'Your boyfriend's cute,' she said, stepping away from Simon. 'Not terribly loyal . . . but cute.'

I held my ground as she neared the back of the car. Standing so close I could smell her vanilla-scented perfume, she leaned toward me, smiled, and whispered a single word.

'Boo.'

Simon's arms were around me before I could hit the ground.

'Caleb,' I said when she started across the lawn. 'He's still back there.'

Simon jumped into the Subaru and moved it to the side of the road, then got out and took my hand. We hurried after her, keeping her in sight while staying a safe distance behind. She stopped once and tilted her head, like she was listening. After several seconds she continued walking and disappeared into the school.

'I tried to warn him.'

Simon and I spun around. Caleb stood behind us, still gripping his iPod. His face shone and his shirt was dark with sweat.

'I told him what she is,' he said. 'I told him what she does.'

Simon looked at me, then stepped toward him. 'Who, Caleb? Who'd you tell?'

His face crumpled, and fresh tears rolled down his face. 'Mark,' he whispered. 'He said he loved her last night.'

CHAPTER 21

'No answer.' Caleb snapped his cell phone shut and tossed it on the table.

'There's nothing on the Internet,' Simon said, closing his laptop.

'The sky hasn't been so blue all summer.' I nodded toward the window. 'Maybe he listened to you and got away.'

Frowning, Caleb returned to Zara's journal, which I'd learned he'd been translating with the help of a French dictionary in between calls to Mark since returning home the night before. I'd gone right to my family's house instead of hanging out with them, happy to use Mom waiting for me as an excuse to leave; I understood that Simon couldn't control his reaction to Zara, but I'd had a hard time controlling my reaction to his. I'd been uncomfortable the rest of the night and welcomed the chance to take a break and process what I'd seen.

By the time I awoke this morning, the only conclusion I'd come to was that I missed him. It was all I could do to down a bowl of cereal and shower before running next door.

'She doesn't talk about him in here,' Caleb said, flipping pages. 'His name's not mentioned once.'

'Who does she talk about?' I ask.

'Me, actually. Her feelings were apparently real – or at least she believed they were. She didn't even want to use her powers . . . or whatever you want to call them . . . but when I didn't give in right away, she thought she didn't have a choice.' He glanced at his notebook. 'Besides me, there's a whole lot of women: Betty, Raina, Brigitte, Marie, Eugenie, Isabelle, Josephine, Dominique, Sabine.'

'Dominique and Sabine were at the meeting last night,' I said. 'They're on the Northern Lights Festival committee.'

Caleb wrote that down. 'There's also a ton about Paige. I haven't gotten very far, but her name appears more than anyone's.'

'What was Zara writing in there yesterday?' I asked. 'During the meeting?'

Caleb flipped forward a few pages. 'It looks like some kind of roster. It's a list of everyone who was there, and some more people I've never heard of. Men, though – not women.'

'Raina asked everyone to give the names of ten people they'd be personally responsible for bringing to the festival. She said it was up to them to bring the community together during these dark times.'

Caleb looked at Simon. 'We should call the police.'

'And say what?' Simon said. 'That we're pretty sure a large group of murderesses plans to destroy the whole town during the first annual Lighthouse Resort and Spa Northern Lights Festival?'

'Yes,' Caleb said.

'We have no proof,' Simon said. 'I'm not saying they're not up to something, but we can't do anything until we know for sure what it is.'

A cell phone buzzed. Caleb snatched his from the table, and then dropped it again.

'Be right back,' Simon said, opening his phone and heading for the living room.

As Caleb returned to the journal, I got up, poured a glass of orange juice and sat back down. I slid last week's *Herald* across the table toward me and pretended to read.

'You know you have nothing to worry about,' Caleb said without looking up.

I bit my lip and turned the page. I wasn't worried. Curious, maybe. But not worried.

'Justine always said you two would be perfect together,' he said a minute later.

I stared at a headline without seeing it. She did? When? And why didn't she say so to *me*? 'I miss her,' I said softly.

He paused. 'I know. Me too.'

'Good news,' Simon said, coming back into the kitchen. 'Beaker's ready to roll.'

'Beaker?' I said.

'Professor Beakman, my professor and advisor. He usually travels during the summer, but decided to stay put once things started happening. I ran into him when we went to Bates a few days ago.'

'The guy won a Nobel Prize about a million years ago,' Caleb said. 'Something about molecular fusion.'

'He won a Nobel Prize and teaches lowerclassmen at Bates?' I asked.

'After teaching at Princeton for twenty years. We're like his pre-retirement.' Simon unfolded a large map and spread it across the table.

'Are you going to tell him what we know?' Caleb asked. 'About the Marchands?'

'No. I'm going to tell him what we know about the victims.' Simon's finger traced a thin line broken up by red dots on the map. 'Here's where their bodies were found. All onshore, near water.'

'Pretty close together,' I said.

'Very close together. There are twenty miles of coastline running alongside Winter Harbor, but all of the victims were found within a mile of one another. According to police reports, the ones found further south were submerged longer. Considering tides and currents, this suggests a common northern origin.'

'Chione Cliffs,' I said, my eyes fixed on Justine's red dot.

'The same current always follows the storms we've been having,' Simon said. 'It's strongest right outside the pool at the base of the cliff, heads south and fades about a mile and a half down the coast.'

'So you're saying they all died in the same place?' Caleb asked. 'At the base of the cliff?'

'I'm not positive . . . but yes. That's my theory.'

'And Oliver said that Betty loved to swim there because the water was so deep,' I reminded them. 'Maybe there was another reason.'

'Right,' Simon said. 'Anyway, Beaker said to come over any time, so we should go now. The festival's in forty-eight hours, so if the Marchands do have something planned, we don't have much time.'

'Actually,' I said, my heart beating faster, 'I think I'll hang back with Mom. She's been pretty rattled since I told her about Justine not applying to college, so I should probably spend some time with her to keep her calm.'

Simon turned to me. 'Vanessa, we should stay together.'

'I'll be on the porch,' Caleb said after a pause. He gathered Zara's journal, his notebook and his iPod from the table and headed outside.

I looked down at the map, strangely nervous. 'I'm sorry, I just –'

'Is this about last night?' he asked, his voice concerned. 'We didn't get to talk afterwards, and to be honest, I don't even know what happened. One minute I'm running through the school, looking for Caleb and Mark, and the next I'm in the car pushing Zara away from me.'

'It's not about last night,' I said, still unable to look at him. 'You know how my mom gets. I just want to make sure I stay long enough to finish what we started.'

The silence that followed was thick, as if filled with everything we'd say if only we knew how. When he finally spoke, he sounded hurt.

'I'm sorry,' he said. 'I'm so sorry for whatever I said or did. But please know that that wasn't me. I couldn't hurt you, Vanessa.'

'I know.' I wanted to ask why he couldn't snap out of her trance by thinking of me and hearing my voice, the way he had in the woods, but didn't.

Stepping toward me, he placed one hand against my neck and gently lifted my face until our eyes met. My heart raced, but my body relaxed. The second his lips pressed against mine, last night started to fade like a bad dream.

Until he reached for my hips. And his fingers tightened around me. And I saw his hands on her pink skirt.

I pulled away. 'You should go.'

His arms hung in the air, still reaching for me. 'Vanessa, what –'

'We don't have much time. Like you said. And my mom's probably up and wondering where I am.' I backed toward the door, my fingers to my lips. 'But please text me your teacher's address so I know where you are. And call when you get there.'

'Later, Vanessa!' Caleb yelled after me as I hurried down the porch steps.

Back in my house, I stood to the side of the kitchen door and peered through the small space between the curtain and glass. I held my breath as Simon and Caleb climbed in the Subaru and started down the driveway. When the car turned onto the street and disappeared from view, I scribbled a note to Mom, who was still asleep, and went outside.

Fifteen minutes later, I stood on the Marchands' porch holding a laundry basket of disposable nappies, dummies and babygrows that I'd picked up at the pharmacy in town. It was a little early for an impromptu baby shower for Paige, but it was the only excuse for returning to their house I could come up with.

I checked my phone, reassured by Simon's texts. He and Caleb were with his old teacher. They were safe. I debated texting him back to say where I was, just in case, but then slid the phone back into my jeans. He'd leave and come after me, and we didn't have time for that. He needed to do what he needed to do, and so did I.

I rang the doorbell and waited.

Nothing. No one answered, and no footsteps hurried toward the door. I tried to peer in the windows near the door, but they were covered by thick blue drapes. I walked back to the edge of the porch and saw Raina's and Zara's cars parked nearby.

I rang and knocked again. When there was still no response, I took the knob and slowly turned it.

The living room was dark. It had started to rain on my way over, and the lingering daylight was blocked out by the heavy drapes pulled across the tall windows. The only light came from the wall of lit sconces lining the staircase.

Stepping into the room, I grabbed a babygrow from the laundry basket and held it over my mouth and nose. The air was thick with the smell of salt. And seaweed. And something unpleasant that made me think of empty crab shells, rotting jellyfish and sick whales washed up on the beach.

As the air wrapped around me, pulling at my clothes and crawling against my skin, I hurried toward the stairs. The smell grew stronger the further I climbed, and by the time I reached the landing, my head throbbed and stomach turned.

I continued down the hallway. I didn't slow down until I neared Paige's closed door and heard muffled noises coming from the other side.

Keeping the babygrow to my face, I placed the laundry basket on the floor and leaned toward Paige's closed door. I listened without breathing, unable to decipher the noise I was hearing. Its pitch rose and fell as its volume grew louder and softer. It seemed to be coming from more than one source, but didn't exactly sound like music, or people talking.

I tapped on the door. When no one answered, I cracked open the door and peered inside.

The curtains were drawn here, too, and the air was even thicker with salt. The blankets Paige had been bundled up in the last time I saw her were piled on the floor by the bed. The strange sounds came from the bathroom and grew louder.

I walked across the room, careful to stay to the side of the bathroom doorway and out of sight of whoever was in there. When I was close enough to peek inside, I kept my chest pressed against the adjacent wall and craned my neck until my left eye had an unobstructed view.

The bathroom was filled with grey, salty steam. Small clouds of light came from candles placed throughout the room – on the sink, the floor, the glass shelves hanging on the wall. One corner of the room, the one with the bathtub, glowed brighter than the others, even though it was the only corner not illuminated by candlelight.

Raina and Zara sat on the edge of the tub, their backs to me. Raina held a thin, ivory hand in her lap. The hand shook, as if the body it was attached to was immersed in an electrified pool of water.

I wanted to look away but couldn't. My gaze travelled from the ivory hand, along a smooth, bare arm, toward Paige's face.

She lay naked in the tub. Her body shook so hard, her head knocked against the tile wall and water splashed onto the floor. Strange, inhuman noises flew from her lips. Her belly poked out above the surface of the water, already swollen with the life inside.

Despite all that, she'd never looked more beautiful.

Her creamy skin glistened, and her face was flushed. Her wet hair was almost black, and trailed across her bare shoulders onto her chest. Her silver-blue eyes burned white and seemed to be frozen open, shining a cool, ethereal light across the room. She didn't look like herself – she barely looked human – but she was the kind of stunning that makes all the surrounding darkness disappear.

My eyes locked on hers, which were raised up, toward the ceiling. I felt my body being pulled toward her, wanting to be near her, and I grabbed the edge of the doorway to hold myself back. My head pulsated, but I wasn't aware of the pain.

I snapped out of it when my phone vibrated in the pocket of my jeans. I took one more look at Paige, feeling almost like I'd never seen her before, and then backed away from the bathroom doorway.

Outside the bedroom, I grabbed the laundry basket and read Simon's text as I dashed down the hallway.

> C was right about the festival.
> Z wrote all about it. Call me
> when you can.

I closed the phone, torn between fleeing the house and trying to find out what could help stop everything from the one person who might know for sure.

Deciding a few more minutes really wasn't much to risk at this point, I flew past the stairs and headed for Betty's bedroom. I paused outside the door and glanced down the hallway. Paige's bedroom door was still closed. Temporarily reassured, I knocked lightly on Betty's door before going inside.

'Betty?' I whispered, closing the door behind me. 'I'm sorry to bother you, but –'

I stopped when I saw the empty chaise longue. The fireplace, which had burned brightly each time I'd been in the room, was dark. Here, just as in the living room and Paige's room, the curtains were pulled tightly across the windows.

The room was so dark I almost didn't see her. She was lying in the bed on the other side of the room, her tiny body still. Despite her supersensory abilities, she either hadn't heard me enter the room or was too tired to respond.

'Betty?' I whispered again, walking toward her.

She looked like she'd aged decades in a matter of days. Her thick, grey hair had thinned, leaving loose clumps on the pillow around her head. The folds of her skin had deepened, and the skin itself had dried to a brownish grey; large flakes were scattered across her blanket and purple bathrobe like confetti. If her chest hadn't struggled to rise every few seconds, I would've thought she was dead.

I sank into a stuffed chair pulled up next to the bed. I shifted when I landed on something hard and saw that the chair's last occupant had been reading to Betty either to distract her from the pain – or to worsen it.

There were a dozen copies of the *Winter Harbor Herald* – recent ones, featuring Paul Carsons, Charles Spinnaker and other victims, as well as older ones dating as far back as 1985. I recognised some of those from the day Simon and I had looked through back issues at the library.

Underneath the stack of newspapers was another

book – a scrapbook. It looked similar to Zara's – though it was thicker and obviously older, given its faded cloth cover and yellowing lace.

I lifted it to my lap and glanced at the bedroom door. When it remained closed, I opened the scrapbook, which was divided into sections, each chronicling the pursuits and accomplishments of a different siren. The group extended far beyond the Marchand family – and Winter Harbor. I flipped through decades of women, all striking, and all with the same silver-blue eyes that somehow shone just as brightly in black-and-white photos as they did in more recent, colour photos. They ranged in age, with the youngest looking not much older than Paige. The book didn't contain physical mementoes like Zara's did, but it tracked progress through photos and newspaper clippings, some of which came from other Maine towns, and as far away as Canada.

Knowing I could sit there for hours, I flipped faster. I'd just grabbed a thick stack of pages to fast-forward several years when five grey fingers reached for the book.

I stared at Betty's hand. Small flakes of dead skin drifted onto the open page.

I looked up when a puff of rancid, salty air shot toward my face. She'd turned her head, and her eyes were small slits as she faced me. Through the narrow openings, I could see the clouds had grown darker.

'What, Betty?' I asked quietly. 'What is it?'

She opened her brittle lips to speak, but nothing came out except more nauseating air. It smelled like the inside of her body was failing, just like the outside.

She told me . . . she spent so much time swimming not just because she liked to, but because she needed to.

I inhaled sharply as I recalled Oliver's words.

She physically needed to immerse herself in salt water several times a day . . . if she didn't, eventually, she wouldn't be able to breathe.

I looked at Betty, at her dry skin and thin hair. She was dying. She was dying because she couldn't breathe.

I placed the scrapbook on the bed next to her and ran for the bathroom. I turned on the bathtub and threw open closets and cabinets, looking for something to fill with water. I yanked towels from shelves and tossed them into the tub. The smell of salt and fish made me gag, but I worked through it. I rolled up my sleeves and pushed the towels deeper, holding them underwater until they were saturated.

Her eyes were closed again by the time I returned. I held the wet towels to my chest, hardly feeling the cold water soak through. I gently took the edge of the blanket tucked under her chin, pulled the blanket away and let it fall to the floor. The purple velvet robe seemed too big on her now. I loosened its belt and pulled it open.

Betty's frail limbs stuck out of her favourite purple swimsuit.

Her ribs lifted the swimsuit as she tried to inhale. I draped the wet towels across her entire body, starting at her feet and working toward her chest. Reaching her shoulders, I slid the robe down her arms and covered her to the top of her neck. When only her face remained exposed, I sank back to the chair and waited.

Her colour started to return first. Her cheeks went from ash, to white, to light pink. Her wrinkles smoothed, and her lips grew fuller. After a few minutes, her chest managed to rise for a complete second before falling again.

As she slowly regained strength, I picked up the scrapbook and turned to the back. Obituaries were displayed like wedding photos, and I flipped past those for Charles Spinnaker, Aaron Newberg, William O'Dell, Donald Jeffries and Tom Connelly. When I reached the group of four who had made that morning's *Herald* headlines, I turned back a few pages. Raina's scrapbook was thorough, but two recent victims were missing. I wasn't surprised that Justine wasn't included – she was Zara's target, after all – but I *was* surprised that one of the men was noticeably absent. His story was in one of the papers I'd just moved, and he was the first one found after Justine. I had no idea how this twisted form of scrapbooking worked, but assumed that the first of a string of targets warranted extra attention – maybe a few pages, or glitter, or stickers, or something.

But Paul Carsons didn't get glitter. He didn't get anything.

I flipped all the way to the back, my stomach clenching at the sight of the empty white pages awaiting their subjects. Perhaps Raina hadn't decided how to memorialise Paul Carsons. Maybe she was still collecting articles and photos, and would make a separate book just for him. Maybe –

I was glad for the reason to look away when Betty moaned softly.

'Betty,' I said, hugging the book to my chest as I leaned toward her, 'it's Vanessa. Was there something you wanted me to know?'

Her head turned toward me. When she spoke, her voice was barely a whisper. 'Nineteen . . . ninety . . . three.' Her fingers slid out from under a towel and grazed the top of the scrapbook.

I turned pages quickly, skipping over entire decades of death and seduction. When I reached 1993, my eyes froze on a picture of a smiling, dark-haired woman in a long red skirt and white peasant blouse. I couldn't recall ever meeting her, but she looked strangely familiar.

'"Charlotte Bleu,"' I read the photo's caption out loud. '"Thirty-four, originally of the Canadian Nenuphars, died during childbirth on November seventeenth, 1993."'

I stared at the date before making my eyes move down the page. When they reached the photo in the bottom-right corner, the one of Charlotte clinging to some happy, unsuspecting man, I slammed the book shut and threw it to the floor. My heart thundered in my chest as I looked at it lying there, half expecting it to open by itself, flip open to 1993 and force me to see it again.

I had no idea who Charlotte Bleu was. But there was no mistaking the slouched frame or frizzy hair of the happy, unsuspecting man with her.

Big Poppa.

CHAPTER 22

I couldn't hear anything. I couldn't hear the rain pelting the roof, or the wipers sliding across the windscreen. I couldn't hear the tyres flying across tarmac, or the wind rushing past. I couldn't hear the radio, or the cell phone buzzing on the passenger seat. I couldn't hear my heart drumming in my ears, or my breath coming in short, fast gasps. I couldn't hear any of the millions of thoughts and questions spiralling through my head.

I couldn't hear anything, because I was listening for Justine.

The phone buzzed again, but I ignored it. I didn't know how long I'd been driving, but I knew it was either Mom or Simon on the other end, wanting to know if I was okay. And I couldn't tell them I wasn't. If what I'd just seen was true, if Big Poppa wasn't who I'd always thought he was, if *I* wasn't who I'd always thought I was, then I'd never be okay again – and neither would they.

'Say it,' I whispered, clutching the steering wheel so tightly my fingernails dug into my palms. '*Say it.*'

But she wouldn't. She wouldn't tell me what I wanted – what I *needed* – to hear.

I punched the gas. The illuminated doors and windows of Winter Harbor's shops and restaurants glowed dimly through the darkness, and I drove faster, not wanting to see the charcoal sky swallow what little light remained. I didn't think about where to go, or which direction to head in. As soon as I'd landed in the driver's seat and started the car, my hands and feet had moved on their own.

'Please,' I begged quietly as the car turned onto Burton Drive. 'It's not true. Tell me it's *not true*.'

I waited in the driveway, watching the lake house go in and out of focus as the wipers shoved aside the water. When Justine remained silent, I turned off the car and climbed out. I walked across the front yard, along the side of the house and down the back yard. The rain fell so hard my hair and clothes clung to my skin, but I didn't feel it. The only thing I managed to note was that the BMW was missing, which meant Mom was out.

My hands were on the red rowing boat before I realised where my feet had led me. I dragged it from the shed and across the slick grass. Reaching the lake's edge, I shoved it into the water. I followed behind it as I pushed it out, not feeling the coldness soak through my sneakers, grab my ankles and travel up my legs. This was the deepest I'd gone in any water in two years, and I didn't know what I was doing there now when

I should've been driving away from Winter Harbor, away from the coast, the lakes and the ocean, away from the truth that I didn't want to believe but couldn't deny.

When the water reached my thighs I waded to the side of the boat and pulled myself in. I rowed slowly at first, but once my hands got a good grip on the oars, I pushed the water forward like it was air. I steered the boat away from shore, not looking at our house or the Carmichaels' house as I moved further out onto the lake. Justine had always preferred floating just above the water's deepest point; that was where we'd been when Big Poppa had taken the picture she'd hung on the centre of her bulletin board.

Nearing the centre of the lake, I stopped rowing. I pulled the oars into the boat, peeled off my drenched sweatshirt and rolled up the bottoms of my jeans. My skin was already chilled, but I could feel the drops growing cooler and the air temperature dropping. I was the only person out, but I sat there in my tank top, rolled-up jeans and flip-flops like it was a sunny summer day.

I tilted my head toward the sky, welcoming the frigid rain streaming across my face.

'I'm sorry,' I said. Not hearing myself over the rain slamming into the water, I tried again, louder. 'I'm sorry! Okay? I'm sorry that you're there and I'm here and that we can't be together, but I still need you. I still need you to tell me that this isn't happening, that I can just pretend everything will be fine.'

I was shouting, but she didn't seem to hear me. Or maybe she did, and just didn't know what to say. Maybe she'd been watching and listening when I saw the photo of Big Poppa with Charlotte Bleu, and maybe she thought it'd been for nothing. Maybe she thought that she'd wasted a lifetime watching out for and protecting me, and was relieved that she didn't have to any more, since we weren't really the sisters we'd always thought we were.

'Please,' I said, only slightly aware of the warmth on my face as tears joined the rain. 'Please, Justine. I can't do this by myself. I'm not strong like you. I thought I was – for just a few days I thought I could be – but I was wrong.'

After Simon and I had been together, I'd actually started to believe I was strong. I'd started to believe that I was capable of more than I'd always thought. I didn't have to be afraid of the dark. I could stand up to Mom. I could even go in the water again and not fear going below the surface, where the light turned black, voices faded to whispers . . . and I was more comfortable than I was on land.

'Justine,' I said, lowering my head. 'Please.'

How could I pretend now? I didn't want to believe that Big Poppa – *my* Big Poppa – could do such a thing, but it explained everything. It explained why Mom and I looked and acted nothing alike, and why she cared about things like fancy dresses and garden parties while I preferred jeans and books. It explained Paige's and my natural, almost instantaneous connection, and had to have something to do with the blinding pain I felt every time I was near Zara. It explained why Simon thought he felt what he did for me, since someone so smart would never be attracted to someone with so many issues. It explained why I could hear Justine after she died. And if what Mom and Dad had said about her feeling like she had to fight harder to draw attention away from me and toward her was true, it explained that, too.

And it explained what happened, what I hadn't wanted to think about but couldn't forget, the day the other sirens sounded two years ago.

The sky darkened as clouds dropped toward the water. My body took over again and I moved without thinking, slowly sliding from the narrow rowing boat bench and lowering myself to my knees. I rested both hands on the edge of the boat and leaned forward, looking at the water only inches below. The surface rippled and popped from the rain, but I could still see them as if the sun shone brightly overhead, and the water was as smooth as ice.

My eyes. To me, they'd always looked not quite

green, and not quite blue. Now, either because I hadn't paid close enough attention or because circumstances made me see them differently, they shone silver.

I leaned closer to my shifting reflection. I reached down with one hand, and then the other. I closed my eyes as my fingertips dipped below the surface, and my tears fell faster as the water covered my knuckles, my palms, my wrists.

'I'm sorry,' I whispered as the water reached my elbows, my biceps, my shoulders. 'I'm so sorry.'

'*Vanessa!*'

I froze.

'*Vanessa!*'

I sat up and squinted through the rain. Another boat came toward me — fast, as if it were racing an invisible clock. I turned back and grabbed the oars from the bottom of the boat.

'Stay there!'

I was too startled to handle the slick wood. I dropped the oars in and out of the water, my arms moving faster than they had when I was rowing out. But thanks to the Bates crew team, I moved five feet for their every ten. Soon, they were pulling up next to me.

'Stop!' I brought in the oars and scrambled toward the back of the boat. 'Just stay there. Please.'

'It's okay, Vanessa.' Caleb reached over the side of their boat for mine. 'You're okay.'

I reached into the water behind me, trying to paddle out of his hold even as the boat bobbed up and down. 'Don't come in here, Caleb.' Fresh tears stung my eyes. 'Please . . . just stay where you are.'

I cried out when two strong arms circled my waist and pulled me back. I grabbed Simon's hands and tried to pry his fingers from my body. 'Simon,' I whimpered. 'Please. Let me go.'

He pulled me so close my back pressed against his chest. I closed my eyes, desperately wanting to give into my body's urge to melt next to his and accept the warmth and safety of his arms, and hating that I couldn't.

'She was scared.'

I looked up. Caleb held on to the edge of my boat with both hands so that it knocked against theirs.

'Justine,' he continued, speaking loudly to be heard over the rain. 'That's why she didn't apply to Dartmouth. That's why she didn't apply anywhere else. She was too scared.'

I shook my head.

'Before I say anything else,' Caleb said, 'you need to know that she loved you. She loved you more than anything or anyone, and she would've done anything for you – including letting you believe she was fearless so that you'd continue to depend on her. She didn't want me to tell you any of this . . . but you need to know. You deserve to know. It will help you understand.'

I wasn't sure how to feel now that I was finally about to find out what I'd wanted to know when I came back to Winter Harbor. 'What was she so afraid of?' I finally asked.

He looked at Simon, who nodded. 'The day you had your accident . . . do you remember why you went in the ocean?'

'She dared me.' Just like my body had been operating on its own, the words were out before I could think about saying them aloud.

'Justine dared you,' he repeated, like he wanted me to really think about that.

'The accident was *my* fault,' I said quickly, my heart racing. 'It was a joke. She was kidding. She never really thought I'd go in.'

'She might've said it jokingly, but part of her wasn't kidding.'

I tried to sit up, but Simon's arms pulled me back. 'You don't know what you're talking about. Justine looked out for me. She protected me. She would never have pushed me into a dangerous situation.'

'Vanessa,' Caleb said gently, 'what I'm telling you now she told me herself.'

His eyes were steady on mine, and I reminded myself that she'd loved him. In the months – and possibly the years – leading to her death, she'd confided in him more than she'd confided in anyone. 'Go ahead.'

Caleb lowered his eyes and took a deep breath. 'Justine loved you, but she was also very, very jealous of you.'

I bit my lip to keep from protesting. He was the third person in a matter of weeks to tell me that Justine envied me, and if I was to believe anyone, it should be him. Plus, this information was easier to accept knowing what I now did about who . . . what . . . I really was.

'For as long as she could remember, everyone wanted to know you. Relatives, neighbours, teachers, class-mates. You were completely unaware, and that's why she never mentioned it to you, but it drove her crazy. In order to deal, she did whatever she could for atten-tion. She played sports. She joined a thousand clubs. She got straight As. She tried to be everyone's friend. When she was old enough, she dated a *lot* of guys.'

I lifted my eyes to his and frowned.

'Yes, I knew about the guys. And I knew why. I didn't care for me – I know she didn't feel for them what she felt for me – but I did care for her. I hated that she felt she had to go to such extremes just to feel . . . important.'

Justine didn't have to kiss a thousand guys or sky-dive out of airplanes to be important. She just *was*.

'She did what she did not to make you feel bad, but to make her feel better. Like I said, she would've done anything for you. She never wanted to hurt you.'

'So then what part of her wasn't kidding the day of the accident?' I asked.

He paused. 'Do you remember whose idea it was to have a picnic on the beach?'

'No,' I said honestly. 'I don't remember much about that day,' I added, not as honestly.

'According to Justine, she wanted to go to the movies. You wanted to have a picnic. As soon as you suggested the idea, your mom made sandwiches and your dad packed board games. And when Justine pushed the movie, they ignored her.'

'If they did, it wasn't preferential treatment,' I said. 'Justine was always closer to Mom than I was . . . and Dad was crazy about her, too.'

'In any case, Justine wasn't happy about it. She knew it wasn't your fault, but she was resentful. When she dared you to go swimming, she knew how dangerous it was . . . which was why she couldn't forgive herself when you took the dare and disappeared.'

'But I came back,' I insisted, like I could still convince her that it wasn't her fault. 'I was pulled under, but I was fine.'

'Vanessa . . . you were under for thirty-four minutes before divers reached you.'

I leaned back.

'It's a miracle you made it out alive.'

That was one way of putting it.

317

'It stayed with her,' Caleb continued, 'the fact that you almost drowned because of one moment of weakness on her part. She kicked her outgoing, adventurous, protective, overachieving behaviour into high gear. She still did it for attention – which she needed more than ever after the accident – but she also did it to be the best sister, daughter, student and friend she could be. She always blamed herself for almost taking you away from everyone who adored you.'

I tried to imagine Justine doing everything she did out of guilt and for the purpose of pleasing other people. 'So when it came time to apply to colleges . . . ?'

'Dartmouth,' he said. 'Harvard, Yale, Stanford, Brown. All the Ivies, all for your mom.'

'And the personal essay?' I said.

'She couldn't do it. After working so hard for so long to impress people, she had no idea who she was, or what *she* wanted to do.'

I tilted my head and looked at him. 'With one exception?' I guessed.

His gaze dropped to the water.

'She wanted to be with you.' It wasn't a question.

He nodded and looked up. 'And I wanted to be with her. More than anything.'

I didn't try to pull away when Simon took my hand.

'But old habits are hard to break, and she knew your mom would've flipped if she suddenly said she was putting off college to hang out with some Winter Harbor local.'

'She was lucky to have you, Caleb.'

'I don't know . . . but I was trying to be better. I didn't want to lose her, so did everything I could to make your mom happy. I left Monty's for the Lighthouse,' he said, glancing at Simon, 'so that I could make more money and keep company with CEOs instead of fishermen. That was probably one of the hardest things I'd ever done – it was so hard I couldn't even tell Monty in person. I knew he'd try to talk me out of it, and I didn't want him to.' He paused before continuing. 'Eventually, when school started again, I started studying more and worked on improving my grades.'

'What about lunch with the Lighthouse people?' Simon asked. 'Mark said you met with them to try to talk them out of invading town.'

'That was before I started working there, when I still thought Justine and I might be able to live here together one day. You know I love this place. I was fighting to keep things the way they were.' He sighed. 'Anyway, as graduation got closer, she started looking into other options.'

'Options?' I repeated.

'For September. She had to go somewhere, and she obviously wasn't going to school. She looked into

California, Washington, Oregon, Vancouver. She thought we needed to go far away so that she couldn't just drive back to Boston whenever she felt guilty.'

'So putting thousands of miles between us was easier than just telling the truth about you and college?' I asked.

He looked at me like I should get it. 'She was afraid.'

I *should* get it. I was used to being that scared. I knew there probably weren't monsters hiding in the shadows when I went to sleep, but that hadn't kept me from worrying they'd attack as soon as the lights went out. And running away supported Justine's belief that the best way to deal with your fear of something was to pretend it wasn't happening. She couldn't be afraid of disappointing us if she pretended we no longer existed.

'She made me promise not to tell anyone,' he said. 'She thought people would think we were crazy, or doing the wrong thing, and she didn't want to hear it. She didn't want anything to change our minds.'

'But if she had a plan,' I said, fast-forwarding to a few weeks ago, 'why'd she jump off Chione Cliffs in the middle of the night?'

'I didn't know at first,' Caleb said. 'She was pretty fired up after that dinner, when your mom was talking about school and responsibility, and when she found out that other people knew about me.'

I was glad the rain was still falling when my face

started to burn. No wonder she'd been so mad – after she'd spent so many years trying to protect me, I'd revealed her biggest secret.

'We went back to Boston first. She thought we could just hang out there for a while, until we decided where to go next.'

That explained the red beach towel I'd found stuffed behind her bedroom door the day of the funeral.

'But as soon as we got there, she wanted to turn around and go back to Winter Harbor. She wouldn't – or couldn't – explain why, but she was obsessed. It was already late, and I suggested we leave the next morning, but she insisted on going that night.' He watched the water lapping against the bottoms of the boats. 'So we did. And once we got back, she wanted to go right to Chione Cliffs.' He looked at me. 'I didn't understand it then. I thought she was just trying to prove a point, or wanted to get out some built-up anger. But I understand it now.'

I followed his eyes to Simon. 'What?'

Simon shifted slightly so that he faced me. 'Do you remember that day, when Justine and Caleb did their backflips? And Justine cut her leg?'

I nodded.

'According to Zara's journal, the water at the base of Chione Cliffs is basically the lion's den. It isn't like this water, or even the water in the ocean. It's filled with them – it's where they meet, swim, give birth, and live, in some cases. It's where they lure their victims. It's where they control the weather. And when Justine's leg was cut – whether they did it on purpose or she accidentally hit it on a rock – once that water entered her bloodstream . . .'

'It was already too late,' I finished.

'They called her back,' Simon said. 'Somehow, once that water was under her skin, they had her.'

'That's why she jumped,' Caleb said gently. 'Not because she wanted to get back at you, or your family. But because she had no choice.'

And there was my answer. It was everything I'd wanted to know.

I looked away, toward our house. All of the windows facing the lake were dark. It looked so empty, so lonely.

'We do have some good news,' Caleb said, tentatively, after a minute.

I turned back just as Caleb pulled a small metal vial from Simon's backpack. He unscrewed the top and a thin cloud of steam swirled toward the sky. He exchanged looks with Simon before holding the vial over the edge of the boat, tilting it and releasing a thin stream of clear liquid.

I grabbed Simon as the rowing boat rocked sharply, then stopped. The rain continued to pound the lake, sending small waves rippling toward shore. But our boat didn't move. Neither did Caleb's. My feet, resting on the thin wooden floor, grew colder. Holding my breath and keeping Simon's arms around me, I leaned forward and peered over the boat's edge.

'Ice,' I exhaled, my breath forming a small white cloud. Seconds before, our boats had knocked together as they bobbed in the water. Now, they were locked in place by a solid white patch.

'We have to beat them at their own game,' Simon said, his voice level. 'We have to do what even Mother Nature can't do in the middle of winter.'

I turned to him, already knowing what was coming.

'We have to freeze Winter Harbor.'

CHAPTER 23

'"The bodies of Jonathan Marsh, seventeen, and Mark Hamilton, sixteen, were found on the southern jetty of Beacon Beach. So far, twelve people have died since a series of sudden, erratic storms struck Winter Harbor four weeks ago."' Caleb lowered the paper and looked out the window.

'I'm sorry, Cal,' Simon said after a pause. 'You did everything you could.'

'Think of all the lives you saved,' I said, my eyes watering for both boys – and for Paige. 'Zara's targeting you kept her from focusing on anyone else for weeks.'

Caleb didn't say anything. I looked at the clock, then at Simon. The sun still shone overhead, but it was only a matter of time before the clouds rolled in.

'You don't have to do this,' Simon said. 'We can figure out another way.'

'There isn't another way,' Caleb said. After a minute, he tossed the *Herald* on the seat and climbed out of the car.

'Hey,' Simon said as I reached for the door handle. 'You okay?'

I looked at his hand on my arm. What was one more lie now? 'I will be.'

We ran after Caleb, who was already jogging up the Marchands' porch steps. My chest tightened even though I knew Raina and Zara were gone; we'd waited across the street from Betty's until they'd arrived, then flew to their house.

Inside, the curtains were still pulled across the windows. The sconces lining the staircase were dark. The only light came from the beam shining through the front door. I was encouraged by the air; it was still thick with moisture, but smelled only of salt – not decay.

I led them through the living room. Simon reached for my hand as we started upstairs, but I pretended not to notice and quickened my pace. Today would likely be the last day we spent together. I didn't want to make things harder than they were.

'This way,' I said, heading toward Paige's room at the end of the hall. I paused outside her door and listened.

Silence.

I shook my head against the sudden image of her shaking in the bathtub and opened the door.

'Wow,' Caleb said.

'Are you sure this is the right room?' Simon asked.

I turned slowly as I stepped inside. Paige's stuff – her

325

bed, clothes, books and picture frames – was gone. Her walls had been painted pink. The white curtains had been replaced with pink shades.

In the middle of the room, under a mobile of stuffed starfish, was a small crib.

This time, I let Simon take my hand. I wouldn't have moved otherwise.

'She probably just switched rooms,' Caleb said back in the hallway. 'Remember, she wasn't part of tonight's plan.'

That was according to Zara's journal. But her last entry was three days ago – the day I'd stolen the journal at the Chamber of Commerce meeting. What if the plan had changed? There was someone who might know.

Standing before Betty's bedroom door, I held my breath and raised my fist.

'Come in, Vanessa.'

I glanced at Simon, then opened the door.

The last time I saw Betty she'd been lying in bed, gasping for life. I hadn't known what to expect now, and was relieved to find her not only alive but dressed and sitting up.

'I've been waiting,' she said, standing from the chaise longue. She walked across the room, stepping easily around tables and chairs.

'You know what's happening?' I asked gently.

'I didn't,' Betty said, standing before us. 'I do now. Raina tried to keep it from me for a while. She was very careful with her thoughts when I was stronger, and made sure I stayed in the dark. But she relaxed as I weakened, trusting that I couldn't hear. Fortunately, with your help, I regained enough strength to listen.'

'What did you hear?' Simon asked.

'A lot of what you already know. That they're going to kill tonight, that they won't stop unless stopped . . . and that you need me.'

'How did you . . . ?' Caleb's voice trailed off.

'I'll do whatever you need me to do,' Betty said.

'Are you sure you're strong enough?' I asked. 'The last time I saw you –'

'I'm stronger now. I'll be even stronger in the water.'

I looked at Simon. He looked at me, concerned. Clearly, Betty's physical condition was worse than he'd imagined.

'I don't need to see,' she said suddenly, her cloudy eyes aimed at Caleb. 'My other senses make sight unnecessary.'

'I didn't say anything,' he said quickly. His face reddened as he looked at us for confirmation.

'Betty,' I said as she started for the door. 'Do you know where Paige is? We wanted to take her with us, but she's not in her room.'

She stopped in the doorway, her back to us. 'She's

very ill. This pregnancy may kill her if we don't take care of her.'

'*L'épuration du sang*,' Betty said as we drove back to town.

'What's that?' I asked.

'Purification of blood,' Caleb translated, looking to Betty, who sat next to him in the back seat, for explanation.

'A siren's ability exists at birth, but lies dormant for the first part of her life. As she matures, and is able to have children, she's taken below the surface for purification. During this process, the regular water in every human cell is replaced with salt water, which then makes swimming in, bathing in and drinking salt water necessary. Raina, Zara and I would dry out and die if we didn't constantly replenish.'

'That's what was happening to you a few days ago?' I asked.

'Yes. For two years Raina's given me just enough to survive one day to the next. I was physically weak, which limited and sometimes confused my sensory capabilities. It worked so well I didn't even realise I was severely dehydrated until you helped me. I've been listening to their thoughts ever since.'

I felt Simon's eyes on me. I'd told him about my trip to the Marchands' to check on Paige, and my accidental

328

run-in with Betty ... but I hadn't told him everything I'd learned.

'Why would Raina do that?' Caleb asked.

'My daughter has always been intrigued by her potential power. She knew I changed my life to protect the lives of others, but she was still curious. I thought it was because she'd never witnessed the resulting devastation first hand ... but now that she has, I don't know what to think.' She paused. 'In any case, when I had my accident, Raina took advantage of my changed physical state and kept me weak so that she could explore her powers without interference.'

'What about Paige?' I asked. 'She doesn't swim every day, and she's fine.'

'Sirens don't need constant replenishment until after purification. Zara's happened shortly after my accident. Raina wanted to focus on her – to teach her how to use her beauty, which is enhanced post-purification, and to help build her power before moving on to Paige. Paige's would have happened this summer ... but unfortunately, she became pregnant first. That's why she's suffering. Her body isn't fully equipped to give her baby what it needs. That's why she's been so sick.'

'We're getting close,' Caleb said suddenly, sliding down the seat and plugging his ears.

I felt Zara's presence, but didn't show it. 'Zara had a thing for Caleb,' I explained to Betty as we turned onto a narrow road that ran parallel to Main Street. 'She went after him, but he –'

'Loved Justine,' Betty finished, her voice soft. 'I know.'

We parked behind a row of trees at the far end of the chowder house parking lot. Several yards away, Louis and other employees served soup to a large crowd gathered around their booth.

'Paige is inside,' Betty said, her head tilted toward the restaurant. 'She's alone. She doesn't know what they plan to do. She'll have questions, but show her your proof. Tell her what I just told you. And if you must, tell her about Jonathan.'

'Maybe Betty should come,' Caleb said. 'Paige would believe her grandmother, wouldn't she?'

'I can't,' Betty said. 'They don't know I'm here because they're not listening for me. They think I'm still in my room, too weak to move. If they see me – or if anyone else does and brings attention to me – they'll know something's wrong.'

'Are we sure she's up to this?' Caleb asked once we'd started across the parking lot.

'At this point, we don't have much of a choice,' Simon said. 'Beaker said the solution needs to detonate at the core of their atmospheric manipulation for maximum reactivity. Who else do you know who can swim a mile underwater without coming up for air?'

He knew at least one other person, but I didn't say so out loud.

We continued walking and spent the next forty-five minutes avoiding the Marchands and wandering the quaint streets with other visitors. Each year the Northern Lights Festival brought in from all over New England vendors who sold homemade everything – food, furniture, jewellery, quilts. People shopped and ate all day, and at night, there was live music and a fireworks display over the water. The best part came just after sunset. As a tribute to Winter Harbor's early fishing days, all of the lights – in the stores and restaurants along Main Street, in the boats on the water – went out at the same time and were replaced by hundreds of candles and lanterns. The warm glow softened the entire town and made the harbour look like the starry night-time sky.

'I should go,' Caleb said once we reached the pier. The sky was grey with dusk, and the clouds had grown thicker, heavier, as they sank toward the water. 'I'll keep her moving. I have my phone if I need you, or vice versa.'

I understood why Justine had felt so strongly about Caleb the more time I spent with him, and my heart ached for both of them as I watched him prepare to go. He seemed so focused, so determined, so glad to be able to do at least this one thing in retaliation for all that had been taken from him and Justine. I wished

Mom were there to see him. Even she would've had a hard time not being impressed.

'Betty's diving at eleven fifty,' Simon said, 'so Zara should be in there by –'

'Eleven forty,' Caleb finished. He plugged his ears, covered them with thick padded headphones and turned on the iPod so loud I could hear it three feet away.

I grabbed his hand as he started to walk away, and pulled him into a tight hug. 'Thank you,' I whispered into his shoulder. 'Thank you for doing this, and for being there for her when she needed you, and –'

'It's okay,' he said, hugging me back. 'When you love someone as much as I loved your sister, there's nothing you wouldn't do.'

Your sister. The words swirled through my head as he let me go, and then he disappeared into the crowd without looking back.

'He'll be okay, right?' I asked, watching him go.

'I don't think we could stop him now if we tried,' Simon said.

I nodded, not sure if that was true but knowing it was too late. Overhead, the sky was turning from grey to black, and the first drops were starting to fall.

'He's right, you know.'

I didn't feel the light rain on my face as I turned to him.

'When you love someone that much,' he said, putting his arms around my waist and gently pulling me to him, 'you would do anything to keep her safe. You would do everything to make sure she's happy.'

I looked down as he brought his face closer to mine. This was wrong. It was wrong, and it was only going to make the inevitable harder.

'Vanessa,' he whispered, his breath warm on my lips, 'before anything else happens tonight, I want you to know . . . I *need* you to know that I –'

'Sorry,' I said, pulling away. I reached for my cell phone in the pocket of my jeans, relieved to have heard the ringing over the thumping in my chest. Thankful that we'd been interrupted before Simon said something he'd only regret later, I answered the phone without checking the caller ID.

'Vanessa? Oh, thank goodness.'

'Dad. Hi.' I closed my eyes at the sound of his voice. We hadn't talked since I'd seen him with Charlotte in Raina's scrapbook.

'Is everything okay there? Your mother's been worried about you, and she didn't sound like herself the last time we spoke, so now I'm worried about both of you.'

'Everything's fine,' I said, hoping my voice didn't betray my bitter confusion. 'We're both still adjusting . . . but we're fine.'

He hesitated. 'I'm sorry I haven't been more attentive. I should've been, but I wanted to give you your space. I wanted you to have time to heal.'

'I appreciate that,' I said, turning away from Simon. It was so dark I didn't think he could see my face burning, but I wanted to avoid questions, just in case. 'I'm kind of in the middle of something, though. Can we talk later?'

'Sure. Of course. We'll talk tomorrow. I'm taking a train up and will be there in time for lunch.'

I tried to imagine where I'd be, how life would be, at lunchtime tomorrow, but couldn't. 'Sounds good. Have a safe trip.'

'Oh, and Vanessa?' he said quickly. 'I love you. Please remember that.'

I blinked back tears, wishing I could say it back. 'See you soon.'

I'd expected to feel hurt, confused and even angry the first time I spoke to Big Poppa after knowing what I now did. But I hadn't expected those feelings to be overwhelmed by an even bigger one: sadness.

'We should go,' Simon said gently after I'd hung up.

I nodded and took his hand. I held on tightly as we weaved through clusters of kids and families. I would have to let go eventually, but I wasn't ready yet.

Just being near Simon was calming, and I quickly refocused on the task at hand. When we reached Betty's, Louis and most of the staff were still busy serving a long line of customers. They didn't notice Simon and me pass behind the booth and slip through the restaurant's back door.

We found Paige in the dining room. She sat in a chair, facing the windows. Her back was to us, and when we reached her, I saw that her eyes were closed.

'Paige?' I said quietly.

She opened her eyes and sat up, clutching her stomach with both hands. 'Vanessa. What are you doing here?'

I tried to keep the concern from my face. Even in the dim light I could see that her eyes were flecked with white, her skin glistened with perspiration and her hands shook. When I saw her in the bathtub she hadn't looked well, but she'd still been stunning. Now, just two days later, she looked like she was about to pass out from the exertion of trying to stay awake.

'I haven't seen or heard from you in a while,' I said. 'I wanted to make sure you were okay.'

'I know, I'm sorry,' she said, glancing behind her, toward the entrance. 'It's been a tough few days.'

I looked at Simon. He nodded. Releasing his hand, I sat in the empty chair next to her. 'How are you feeling?'

She sat back and offered a shaky smile. 'Awful.'

I paused, not wanting to ask my next question. 'Has Jonathan been by to see you?'

'Not lately,' she said, looking down. 'Raina told him

I wasn't feeling up for phone calls or company.'

She didn't know. 'Paige,' I said gently, 'how far along are you?'

She tried to smile. 'Five weeks. And I know – I'm enormous. Raina says it's from all the salt water I've been drinking. She was the same way –'

'When she was pregnant?' I eyed her stomach, which was as round as a cantaloupe. 'Have you been to a doctor?'

'No. Raina had us at home with Betty's help, and I'll have my baby at home with her help.'

'But you're five weeks pregnant and look five months pregnant. Don't you think it's strange that your mother hasn't taken you to make sure everything's okay?'

'A little,' she admitted. 'I'd take myself if I could, but Raina and Zara have had me under house arrest. And I'm so tired. I can't even walk downstairs by myself to use the phone.'

I was tempted to snatch her up and take her to the hospital immediately but forced myself to sit there. 'Will you please look at these?'

Her hand shook as she took the papers I'd pulled from my purse. 'What is all this?' she asked, turning slowly through the pages of photos and newspaper articles.

'Xavier Cooper, Max Hawkins, John Martinson,' I recited as she turned past pictures of each one.

She looked up. 'Zara's boyfriends.'

'Not exactly,' I said, pulling out another stack of papers.

She took them and flipped through photos of and articles about the men in Raina's scrapbook. 'I don't know any of these people.'

'No, but your mom did. Friends of hers did.'

As she continued flipping, I looked over my shoulder at the front windows. The rain was falling faster, and people huddled under coats and umbrellas. Some were already beginning to hurry back to their cars, most likely nervous to be so close to water with the weather getting worse.

'Paige,' I said, turning back, 'I know it's hard to hear, and you certainly have enough to worry about . . . but you're going to have way more to worry about if I don't tell you everything now. We all are.' Through the window facing the harbour, I could see the sky turning black, the water growing rough. Tiny gold pockets bounced around like lightning bugs in a glass jar as boats moved toward their docks.

Her breaths were coming faster. 'Whatever you have to tell me, tell me fast. Z'll be back any minute.'

'Paige . . . Zara's not coming back. She's with Caleb Carmichael.'

'What?' She shook her head. 'But she told me –'

'There are a lot of things Raina and Zara have told

you that aren't true, and a lot of things they haven't told you at all.'

The first bolt of lightning shot down from the sky. She grabbed her stomach and winced.

'After Betty had her accident,' I said, talking quickly, 'your mom kept Betty locked up because she didn't want her to recover. Not fully. She wanted her weak so Betty wouldn't try to stop her.'

'Stop her?' she said, gripping her stomach and wincing. 'From what?'

'From Xavier Cooper. Max Hawkins. Alex Smith.'

She opened her mouth to protest.

'You said Zara started "dating" two years ago,' I said quickly. 'Betty's accident was two years ago. I bet Betty's accident happened first.'

She closed her mouth without disagreeing.

'They had to wait for Betty to be out of the picture. After the accident, when she was no longer strong enough to care for herself, they could control her and finally do what they were . . . born . . . to do.'

'What they were born to do? Like, run a restaurant and wait on tourists? Because that's what they do.'

'They also make men love them. Or make men *think* they love them.'

'Vanessa,' she said, taking a shaky breath, 'I know Z's had a lot of boyfriends, but she's gorgeous. Of course men love her.'

'It's not just about what she looks like. It's about who – what – she is. About what they are.' I paused. 'About what *you* are.'

She looked at me. 'I should find Raina,' she said, starting to stand.

'They're sirens,' I said, my voice rising. 'Like the ones we read about in school – but real. They get inside their targets' heads until the guys can't think straight, and then they drag them out to sea to kill them. That's what happened to all of Zara's boyfriends – they didn't just leave Winter Harbor for home after having their hearts broken. That's what happened to all of the men who died this summer. And that's what will happen again tonight, if we don't stop them.'

'Vanessa, Z might be mean, but that doesn't make her a –'

'It sounds crazy – insane, actually – but think about it.' I glanced behind me as thunder rattled the glass vases on the tables. 'Before the accident, Betty went swimming for hours every day. Raina's in the water several times a day. In the past two years, Zara's been swimming more and more. You all bathe in salt water.'

'You've been to our house. It's old and practically sits in the ocean. That's just how the ancient plumbing works.'

I leaned toward her. 'In the past few weeks, whenever

you didn't feel well, Raina made you drink ocean water. And it helped, right? You felt better afterward?'

She hesitated, then nodded.

'There's a process that sirens go through at a certain point – usually once they reach child-bearing age. It happened later with Zara because of Betty.'

'What about me?' she asked, lowering her eyes to her stomach.

'You got pregnant,' I said. 'Your body isn't completely ready for that. That's why you're sick.'

She looked at me, then toward the harbour.

I chose my next words carefully. 'There's one more thing you should know.'

Her white-flecked eyes met mine, then fell to the newspaper I held toward her. 'Jonathan?' she whispered, reading the headline.

'I'm so sorry, Paige,' I said gently.

'Don't be,' she said, her voice louder, firmer. 'It's not him. That's not my Jonathan.'

I paused. 'Yes, it is. Raina knew how strongly you felt about him, and she didn't want those feelings getting in the way of –'

'Vanessa, stop it!' she exclaimed, her voice cracking. She shoved the paper away and clutched her stomach. 'Okay? Just stop it. Please. I can't hear any more.'

My heart lunged against my chest as she started to cry softly. I looked up at Simon, who nodded once.

Knowing we had to keep moving, I leaned forward, placed one hand over hers, and tried again. 'I'm sorry. Really. I know it's hard to believe, but it's all true. Between Betty and Zara's diary –'

'Zara's diary?' Her eyes flashed as her head snapped toward me. 'What are you doing –'

'Paige, Justine Sands was my sister.'

Her face fell. She knew who I was talking about.

'She died because she dived in the wrong place at the wrong time. She died because the sirens eventually dragged her under. So, yes – I took Zara's diary to try to learn more.' I took it from my purse and held it toward her. 'My sister didn't get to tell me everything she might've wanted to before she no longer could. Everything your sister *should* tell you – and would, if she really cared about you – is in here.'

She took the book. It was thicker than the last time she'd seen it, as it now held Caleb's translated pages.

She'd just started to turn the cover when the dining room went dark.

I spun toward Simon but couldn't see him. I couldn't see anything. In years past, this was when electric lights throughout town were replaced by candles and lanterns. But now, the sky remained black.

'It's okay,' he whispered, putting his hands on my shoulders. 'I'm here.'

Rain and wind rattled the glass in the windows

around us. The window behind Paige cracked as a large hailstone flew into it.

The rain was turning to hail. And we were running out of time.

I reached down and fumbled for my purse on the floor. My fingers shook as they searched through the main pocket, and the cell phone slipped from my grasp twice before I finally pulled it out and snapped it open.

It provided just enough light for me to see Paige standing in front of the windows facing the harbour, standing perfectly still.

I didn't say anything as I stood next to her.

Bolts of lightning burst through the darkness like fireworks. Silver shards of light separated the sky into tall, black columns. Unlike the lightning, the silver shards didn't fire down from the clouds above.

They shot up from the water.

The shimmering pillars began to take shape. Feeling the warmth of Simon's body standing just behind mine, I was calmer than I should've been as the female figures emerged and more beams of light broke through the harbour's choppy surface. There were eight of them now. Judging by the patches of light growing brighter underwater, more would follow.

Christabel.

My breath caught. The voice inside my head wasn't Justine's.

'Christabel.'

Paige's head snapped toward me. 'What did you say?'

I looked at her. 'Christabel.'

Her face was white. 'I didn't tell anyone my baby's name. Not one person.'

'You didn't have to.' I gave her a small, sad smile. 'Betty heard it in your thoughts.'

CHAPTER 24

A half-hour later, we were driving in the mountains outside town.

I looked at Simon, who was leaning so close to the windscreen his chin reached past the steering wheel, then at the speedometer needle. The Volvo was pushing seventy and vibrating from the exertion. 'Maybe we should slow down a little,' I suggested. 'Visibility's terrible and the roads are slippery.'

'It's fine,' Simon said. 'It's just like driving in the winter.'

'Except it's *summer*,' Paige reminded us from the back seat. 'It's the middle of summer, and it's hailing.'

I peered between the seats. Paige couldn't seem to inhale and exhale fast enough. Between breaths, Betty held an open bottle of murky ocean water to her trembling lips.

'I don't understand,' Paige gasped lightly a moment later. 'Why now? If everything you're saying is true, why is this happening now? Why not a year ago, or two years, or five years?'

As we'd been driving, Betty had told Paige everything she'd told us earlier. But Paige's question was one we hadn't had a chance to ask, and I listened anxiously for Betty's response.

'Your mother's heart is colder than most,' Betty said, stroking Paige's forehead, 'but it's not immune to warmth. She was at the restaurant the first time Paul Carsons stopped by and was immediately taken by him.'

'Paul Carsons?' Paige said. 'The first man who died? What happened?'

'He didn't return her feelings. He was married with small children. He was still drawn to her – no man she sets her sights on isn't – but he loved his family more.' Betty turned toward the front seat. 'Please forgive my bluntness, but I'm afraid there's no other way of putting it.'

'Putting what?' Paige breathed.

Betty turned back to Paige and lightly rubbed her belly as if to calm the turmoil inside. 'When Raina couldn't have Paul Carsons . . . she made sure no one else ever could.'

Paige groaned, but it was hard to tell if it was because of Betty's story, or her growing physical pain. 'But what about the others? After he was gone, why did more men have to die?'

'Just as your mother's heart isn't immune to warmth, it isn't immune to what follows when it's broken. She was hurt. And angry. She wanted to teach other men like Paul Carsons – handsome, wealthy, successful men – a lesson they wouldn't forget.'

I looked away from the side-view mirror as Betty kissed Paige's cheek and held her close. I couldn't help but wonder who would soothe me whenever I was scared, or hurt, or confused after tomorrow.

'So what are we doing?' Paige whimpered after a few minutes. 'How are we stopping them?'

Betty looked toward me, and I looked at Simon. When he didn't respond, I lifted the duffel bag from the floor by my feet.

Paige's eyes widened at the sight of the silver tank.

'It's a highly potent combination of dry ice, liquid nitrogen and chemical catalysts,' I said. 'Kind of like a winterised bomb. One of Simon's professors has been experimenting with a similar prototype as part of his global-warming research, and when Simon explained what was happening and asked for help, Dr Beakman built this. According to his calculations, once we get it where it needs to go, Simon will activate it . . . and Winter Harbor will freeze for the first time, locking in place everything – and everyone – beneath its surface.'

She looked at me. 'But will Raina and Zara be . . . ?'

I opened my mouth to explain why it was necessary that they both be in the water when the bomb

346

went off. But then she shot back, and her shoulders slammed hard against the seat.

I grabbed another plastic bottle of murky ocean water from the duffel bag and handed it to Betty. Paige had already gone through five bottles. The water seemed to ease the pain, but for a shorter amount of time with each one she consumed. We'd thought ten would last her until after everything was done and we took her to the hospital, but we had only five left. At this rate, we needed to get to the ocean as fast as possible, if only to keep her drinking – and alive.

'It's okay,' I said when Simon let up on the gas. 'You're right – we need to move as fast as possible. Don't slow down.'

'I'm not.'

I followed his eyes to the speedometer. The needle was falling even as he pushed the gas pedal to the floor and the engine groaned.

'It's the hail,' he said. 'It's falling so fast it's sticking to the road. The tyres can't get traction.'

My heart raced as I watched the speedometer needle fall from forty, to twenty, and all the way to zero.

Less than two miles from the trail leading to the top of Chione Cliffs, the Volvo let loose one final squeal before rolling backward. Simon guided her to a stop at the side of the road.

'Can we walk it?' I asked.

He didn't answer. Because of course we couldn't walk it – it was already after eleven. Climbing two miles up the steep road on foot would take at least thirty minutes in perfect weather. And once we reached the trail, we still had to hike the mountain.

'What about Caleb?' I asked. 'The Subaru has four-wheel drive. Maybe he can leave her for a few minutes and –'

He grabbed his cell phone from the cup holder and dialled. After a few seconds, he hung up. 'No answer.'

'Oliver? Beaker?'

He tried both, unsuccessfully.

'Oh no . . . oh, God . . .' Paige fell back against the seat.

Like any geezer in good health, she gets tired – especially on hills.

'Can I try?' I asked suddenly, my stomach flip-flopping at the sound of Big Poppa's voice in my head. 'Driving, I mean?'

'Why?' Simon asked. 'The hail's falling even faster now. There's no way –'

'I have an idea. Something Dad told me about the car before leaving Boston. It might not work, but it's worth a shot.'

Simon looked at me, his expression a combination of confused, frustrated and concerned. I thought he might protest, but then he grabbed the handle and pushed open the door. I climbed over the centre console and landed in the seat just as he opened the passenger-side door. I waited for him to buckle his seat belt, then started the car and put it into drive.

'Backward,' Paige gasped. 'We're rolling backward.'

I hit the brake. The car skidded to a stop.

'Vanessa,' Simon said tentatively, 'are you sure – ?'

I punched the gas once and the car lunged forward, its tyres crunching through the road's icy coating. Almost immediately, the car started rolling backward.

She'll get you where you need to go. . . .

I tightened my grip on the steering wheel and resisted the urge to slam on the brakes. I let the car roll for a few seconds, then punched the gas again – lighter this time. The tyres swerved slightly before inching forward. As soon as they slowed, I tapped the gas again. Already moving in the right direction, the tyres rolled ahead several inches. Any time they began to lose momentum, I tapped the gas.

It was this way – inch by inch, with Dad's voice re-assuring me the whole time – that we made it to the Chione Cliffs trailhead.

'Paige, dear, you must wait for us here,' Betty said once we were parked.

'Wait for you?' Paige gasped. 'What do you mean? Where are you going?'

'They're gathering on the ocean floor,' Betty explained

gently. 'The tank won't sink that far that fast on its own. Someone needs to take it. I'd planned for you to come with us, to wait with Simon by the water, but your condition is worse than I feared. You'll be okay, but you need to stay in the car and continue drinking. I'll come for you as soon as I can. I promise.'

'Grandma.' Paige's voice was stern through her fast breaths. 'You can't be serious. Do I have to remind you that you can't *see*? How are you even going to find them?'

As Betty spoke softly near her ear, I looked at Simon. He stared through the icy windscreen, his jaw clenched and his lips pressed tightly together.

'I don't want you to go,' he said a moment later.

My chest tightened. He was referring to tonight, but I was thinking of tomorrow. 'We agreed someone should go with Betty. And Caleb's with Zara, and you have to monitor conditions at the base.'

'I know that's what we agreed . . . but Vanessa, if anything happens to you –'

'Here.' I reached into my coat pocket and pulled out a small tape recorder.

He looked at me, then at the recorder.

'It's my dad's. I found it in the lake house and taped myself saying your name about a thousand times. I thought it wouldn't hurt to have . . . just in case.'

He frowned but took it.

We didn't speak again. He gathered our stuff while I bundled Paige in blankets, placed the bag of salt-water bottles within easy reach, and said goodbye. We started down the trail silently, and as we climbed, the only sounds were of our feet crunching across the ground and hail clattering against the canopy of leaves overhead.

Twenty minutes after leaving the main road, we reached the trail's fork. I wanted to keep walking, to casually wave over my shoulder as Betty and I veered left, toward the top of the cliff, and Simon veered right, toward the pool at the bottom, but I couldn't. My brain kept going, but my feet stood still. Behind me, Simon stopped, too.

'I'm going to rest my legs,' Betty said gently, squeezing my hand. She'd been walking in front of us like night was day, and her eyes and muscles were fine. I knew was she resting now not because she needed to, but because she thought Simon and I needed her to.

She perched on a rock several feet away, and I waited for Simon to say something. When he didn't, I turned around. My chest warmed at the sight of him standing there, shivering in his Bates fleece and looking at me like it was all he could do to keep from throwing his arms around me and shielding me from the cold and the wind, the rain and the hail, the past and the future.

'Whenever you're ready.'

My eyes filled immediately.

'Whenever you're ready . . . or never at all . . . is totally fine.'

I nodded, the hot tears thawing my skin as they ran down my face. It was what he'd said the last time we were on top of the cliff together, when I couldn't make myself jump. Even now, after everything, if I chose to head back down the mountain instead of continuing, he would support me.

I suddenly wanted to tell him what I'd learned – about Big Poppa, my mother, myself. I wanted to tell him that I didn't care, that it didn't matter, because what I felt wasn't about power, or control, or ego. It was just about him. And me. And the way he helped me think of the darkness not as something to fear, but something that made the light that much brighter.

But he spoke before I could find the right words.

'I love you, Vanessa. I'll be waiting for you.'

My eyes were steady on his. I walked to him and tilted my face so close to his I could feel his warm breath on my lips. 'Be careful,' I whispered.

I wanted to kiss him, to feel the comfort of his lips against mine, but resisted. I simply took the duffel bag when he handed it to me and continued up the trail.

For the first few minutes, I could hear the hail that blanketed the other path give under his boots. But his footsteps faded as the distance between us grew, and soon Betty and I were completely alone, in the middle of the woods, in the middle of the night. My one comfort was that I didn't have to worry about monsters or ghosts following behind us, waiting for the right moment to snatch us off the trail.

Because I knew where the monsters were. And we were heading right for them.

CHAPTER 25

I felt her before I saw her. Now I knew why my head felt like it was about to shatter into a million pieces any time she was near. And that was because, somehow, Zara Marchand and I were connected.

I'd turned off the flashlight before reaching the mouth of the trail, but could see her with Caleb in the silver light beaming up from the water below. They faced each other near the edge of the cliff. She wore only a long red sundress, which was soaked through and clinging to her skin. Her long dark hair hung loose down her back, and she gazed up at him adoringly.

She said something, and he smiled. She shivered, and he rubbed his hands against her bare arms to warm them, just as he'd done for Justine so many times. He pulled her to him, circled his arms around her waist and lowered his face to her hair as she rested her head against his chest. They looked like any couple so consumed by each other that they tuned out the world around them.

The plan was to convince her that he finally returned her feelings so that she'd go to the top of the cliffs when he asked, and it seemed to be working. I just hoped

Caleb hadn't really tuned out the world in the process.

I glanced at my watch. Eleven thirty-six. Four minutes to go.

'She doesn't hear us,' Betty whispered next to me. 'She doesn't know we're here.'

My head throbbed as I watched them, but the pain was different, less severe. I couldn't be sure but guessed that was because, this time, we were here intentionally. We were the pursuers.

Eleven thirty-eight.

They were inches away from the edge now.

I stopped breathing when Zara turned away and looked back at the trail. The silver light shooting up from the water didn't reach the tall bush we hid behind . . . but her eyes seemed to find mine.

'It's okay, Zara.'

I ducked back in the shadows as Betty stepped onto the cliff.

Zara glanced at Caleb, then turned back. 'Grandma? What are you – ? I thought you were –'

'Too weak to walk?' The white sundress whipped around Betty's bare ankles as she ventured further onto the rock. 'I was.'

Zara inched backward as Betty neared her.

'You love him, don't you?'

Zara stopped. Behind her, Caleb stood still, watching them.

I checked my watch. Eleven thirty-nine.

'He loves you, too.'

My head snapped up as Betty looked toward Caleb. 'Don't you, Caleb? You would do anything for Zara, wouldn't you?'

His eyes darted toward the trail. Could he see me? Did he need my help? Or was he just hoping I wouldn't be upset when he said what Betty wanted him to?

'I . . .' His voice trailed off as he stepped closer to Zara. 'You know I . . .'

My heart lunged toward my throat. He couldn't do it. He couldn't say those three words to anyone but Justine.

'It's okay,' Betty said, improvising quickly as Zara stared at Caleb, hurt dulling the light in her eyes. 'You can still love him. You don't have to hurt him.'

Zara opened her mouth as if to disagree, but then closed it without speaking.

'You don't have to live Raina's life.' Betty stood only a few inches from her now. 'You can live, and love, without hurting anyone.'

'I'm sorry, Grandma,' Zara said, her voice wavering. 'I love you . . . and I'm sorry.'

I held my breath as Betty walked toward them, then bolted from the trail when I realised what was about to happen.

But it was too late. Betty hurled herself at Zara when

Zara lunged for Caleb . . . and then Zara dived off the cliff, taking her grandmother with her.

'Vanessa,' Caleb said when I reached him. His entire body trembled as he looked toward the cliff's edge. 'I'm so sorry – I couldn't do it. I wanted to say it because I knew it was what she wanted to hear, but –'

'It's okay.' I dropped the duffel bag to the ground and started taking off my jacket. 'You have nothing to be sorry for.'

'But Betty was supposed to take the tank, and it's already so late, and how are we going to – ?' He stopped. 'What are you doing?'

I yanked off my sweatshirt and kicked off my sneakers. Down to jeans and a T-shirt, I opened the duffel bag and lifted out the tank.

'Vanessa, stop. You can't –'

'Caleb, you heard Simon and Dr Beakman. The bomb needs to detonate at the centre of the atmospheric activity, and it won't get there on its own. Someone has to take it.'

'Right – someone with extremely strange, unnatural abilities.'

I didn't respond as I slid the tank's thick straps on my shoulders and snapped the belt around my waist.

'Vanessa,' he said, stepping toward me, 'I'll go. I'll take the tank as far as I can, and then release it. That's the best we can do now.'

'Caleb, no offence, but you won't last ten seconds in those waves.'

'And what makes you think you will?'

I looked at him. 'Thirty-four minutes.'

He started to protest, but I continued before he could.

'Two years ago, I was underwater for thirty-four minutes. And I was fine.'

'But –'

'I have to do it, Caleb,' I said, my voice gentle but firm. 'After everything she did for me, I have to at least try.'

He shook his head but didn't say anything else.

'Paige is in the car,' I said, giving him a quick hug. 'She's very sick and needs to get to a hospital. Will you – ?'

'Of course.' He squeezed me tightly before letting me go. 'Please be careful.'

I watched him go, then stepped toward the rocky ledge. The light was so bright I couldn't see the base below.

Doesn't Simon look different this year? Older? Cuter?

As the salty spray from water slamming into rock a hundred feet below reached my face, I closed my eyes and saw Justine. I didn't pretend she was right there with me, whispering encouraging words. I didn't pretend anything. I just saw her as I remembered her – constructing a fort of pillows and stuffed animals around me in my bed when we were little. Drinking eggnog and huddling under the duvet on the back stairs at home. Fishing in the red rowing boat. Leaping off the cliff. I saw her smile, her blue eyes. I just saw her, my Justine, exactly as I'd always known her.

Feeling strangely calm, like this moment was what every moment of the past two years had been leading up to, I took a deep breath . . . and jumped.

I slammed into the water. Waves shoved against me and currents rushed like subways past my ears. The light was as bright above me as it was under me, making it impossible to know which way to go. My arms and legs flailed through the water, and I stopped moving only when I realised that I was holding my breath, and that my lungs threatened to explode. The currents swirled, tugging me from side to side. After almost a minute, I hadn't moved more than a few feet – and my lungs were about to give.

It was time.

The pressure in my chest pushed up my throat. The air I'd been holding shoved against my clamped lips until they gave, releasing a small pocket of air. Water rushed into my nose, making my entire face burn. My throat tightened, reflexively trying to keep air in my lungs.

I watched the surface grow further away. I thought of Mom, Big Poppa and Justine. I thought of Caleb and Paige. I thought of Betty, Raina and Zara. I thought of

Simon and hoped that he continued to believe that whatever he felt for me was real, and that he held on to it, no matter what happened next.

I relaxed my lips. Water poured into my mouth, and my body shot back from the force. I pressed both hands to my burning chest and prayed for death to come, for the dark – or the light – to stop the pain and wash everything else away. Because it was too much. It was lasting too long. I just wanted it to be over – for *all* of it finally to be over.

And then, it was. My lungs relented. Soon, the inside of my body was colder than the outside. The pain disappeared.

I opened my eyes and looked down. My chest still rose and fell. Underneath my palms, my heart still beat.

I was still alive . . . and just as I had done two years ago, I was breathing underwater.

I looked at my watch. Eleven fifty.

I dived deeper, away from the surface. The currents still tugged, but my arms and legs sliced through them easily now. My muscles felt stronger, my body recharged. The only thing making the swim more physically challenging than a walk in the park was the light; it surrounded me and shone brighter the deeper I went. Closing my eyes against it didn't make a difference.

I was beginning to worry that I wouldn't know I'd reached the bottom until my hands hit sand . . . when the water started to change around me. It seemed to thin, to gently drift away . . . and then it stopped moving. I stopped moving, too, and my body stayed still. It was as if I was floating on the calm surface of Lake Kanasacka. I tried to open my eyes to see if I could tell why – and immediately closed them and spun around.

I'd reached some kind of barrier. The light just below me glowed white and was concentrated in what appeared to be a long, thick wall. Looking into it was like staring directly into the sun.

Keeping my eyes closed, I inhaled deeply and reached my arms toward the light. My eyes shot open when my fingertips touched the wall – it was like I'd grabbed a lighting bolt with both hands. The energy was simultaneously exhilarating and paralysing, and I couldn't do anything but stare, powerless, as the light pulled me in.

I should've been terrified. I should've been fighting it, and twisting around, and trying to claw my way back. And I probably would've been – if not for Simon. He was everywhere. Crouching next to me on top of the cliff. Rowing toward me. Standing on the beach, waiting for me to climb down the rocks. Holding me in his lap on the kitchen floor. Hugging me, kissing me, touching me. I could feel him as if he were right there, and it felt so good – almost as good as the real thing – that I thought if this was it, if the end meant being suspended in the light between these worlds, then it was okay. I would be okay.

Eventually, the light faded. The water was still illuminated, but the light was dim enough that I could see my surroundings. I'd left the wall and now floated toward the sandy floor, where dozens of shimmering figures were gathered in a circle. Tall clusters of rocks enclosed the circle, and I quickly shifted direction and darted behind one.

When I was sure they couldn't see me, I reached behind me for the tank. Simon had told Captain Monty that he was researching the recent strange weather and asked if Captain Monty would be willing to take him out on the water tonight. Once the water reached zero degrees, Simon would press a button from his position on the *Barbara Ann* that would make the tank vibrate. It hadn't shaken yet, but I wanted to check the attached external thermometer to see how close to freezing the temperature was. We knew what their schedule was, and ours had to match.

I froze when my arm pushed through the water behind me. The tank wasn't there. It must've fallen – or been sucked off – as I passed through the illuminated barrier.

Trying not to panic, I glanced at my watch. Eleven fifty-four. I had six minutes to find and activate the tank and swim a mile back to the surface.

I scanned the ground, spotting Betty and Zara standing in the circle as if they'd planned to participate all along. The sirens seemed to be waiting; their glittering eyes kept shifting up toward the wall of light.

The men. They were waiting for their next victims.

A high-pitched note sounded from the circle. It started softly but grew louder, as if someone was standing nearby, turning the volume knob. My heart raced as a single siren emerged. I couldn't see her face, but recognised her immediately.

Raina. Her mouth was closed, but she was emitting a steady, high note that caused the other sirens to lower their eyes and the water to shift around them.

The sirens started singing without opening their mouths, the soft notes blending together in a pleasant, soothing harmony.

I looked at my watch. Eleven fifty-six.

I waited until they were all focused on the centre of the circle, and then darted to the next boulder. My eyes scanned the rocky towers for a silver spark or flash of light glinting inside the dark openings and crevices.

Nothing. The only light came from the wall floating above the circle, and from the circle itself.

There, Nessa . . .

My eyes widened at the sound of Justine's voice.

Look up . . .

They could hear her, too – they stopped singing as soon as she spoke.

I shot out from behind the rock. The tank was slipping through the wall, and Raina was already rising up to meet it. I kicked and pulled at the water as fast as my arms and legs would allow. A siren below noticed me and released a shrill alarm that slammed into my head like an axe. The pain was a million times worse than any I'd felt around Zara – my legs froze immediately, and I had to stop paddling to grab my head. I tried to kick, but the alarm grew louder and the pain even greater as another siren joined in. I managed to lift my eyes as I started drifting down, and I saw Raina nearing the tank just as the entire length of light began to shift.

They were coming. They were coming, and I couldn't even move.

The noise swelled. I drifted into the circle head first, barely noticing the light dimming. By the time I landed softly in the sand, it was completely dark.

The lights were out, and the monsters were coming.

I was trying to stand when something tugged sharply at my hand. I was lifted off the ground and spiralled through the water. We moved so fast, so quickly, I had no idea which way was up.

But I didn't struggle, or try to pull away. It wouldn't matter. I just hoped Justine would speak to me, would help me.

Stay here.

My head swirled as my feet stood still. The sirens had stopped sounding their alarm and were now singing. A gentle glow came from the circle as their eyes burned like night-lights. It was bright enough for me to see that I stood on a rock high above the circle, and that more sirens were floating down from above, trailing happily confused men in shorts and T-shirts.

The men were a mile below the surface, but they weren't dead – yet.

The water swirled suddenly around me. My arms lifted, and a dull heaviness travelled across them before landing on my shoulders and back.

I tried to see the face of the siren before me, but unlike the others, her silver eyes were dull. I couldn't make out anything until another siren came rushing toward us; her eyes cut through the water like a lighthouse beam cuts through the black night sky.

My eyes widened as the light of the approaching siren grew brighter. It was Zara. She looked different – sad instead of angry, scared instead of sinister – but it was her.

By the time I looked back up, she was gone. She flew at the siren heading for me, and then toward the circle. The glaring light shifted as the second siren darted after her.

I reached both hands behind me when my back vibrated.

The tank. Zara had brought me the winterised bomb. Beakman said the control panel attached to its side would buzz when the water was cold enough for detonation.

I looked down at the circle to see the sirens transfixed by the men drifting toward them. My heart fell as the men embraced the women who'd brought them there.

The tank vibrated again. I closed my eyes, pictured Simon waiting for us somewhere above the surface of the water . . . and pushed off the rock.

I stayed high above the circle as I swam toward its centre. When I trod directly over the men, I reached behind me. My fingers fumbled before finding the latch that would release the tank from my back. The men's smiles grew as the sirens continued to sing to them, and I pictured their faces freezing like that – similar to the way other victims had been found, but for a very different reason.

Sing, Vanessa . . .

I shot back as if punched. Looking down, I saw every siren focused on a man . . . every siren, that is, but one.

You must sing . . .

Betty. The others didn't seem to hear her – or notice that she was watching me floating above them – but her voice was clear inside my head.

What did she mean, sing? What? How? What would it do now besides attract unwanted attention?

You can still save them . . .

And then I heard it. A soft, light note that swelled then exploded into a million smaller notes. Some were loud, others soft. Some short, others long. Some high, others low. They bounced off rocks, ricocheted off sand and enveloped everyone beneath the water's surface. They sounded like they were sung by many sources, an entire symphony of sirens . . . but in fact, only one siren was singing.

Me.

And as the men, freed from their holds, shot up, and the sirens swarmed toward me, I pushed the button that would freeze Winter Harbor for the first time ever.

The silver light shot up. I kicked once, out of the spotlight, and then up. The tank floated somewhere below, but I didn't look to see where it would land. I didn't look to see if the sirens were still chasing me.

Later, after we'd been picked up and were recovering in the hospital, I would try to tell Simon what it was like. I would tell him how the singing grew louder before it died. I would tell him how the ice spread like wildfire, and how I could actually hear the water crystallise. I would tell him how I swam as fast as I could, until it reached my legs and I could no longer kick.

But right then, as the tank exploded and a silver,

frosty cloud billowed toward us, I was only aware of one thing: I was smiling. Winter Harbor was freezing in the middle of July . . . but I was smiling.

CHAPTER 26

'Don't be scared,' Dad said, holding both of Mom's hands.

'I'm not scared.'

'You're shaking.'

'Well, of course I'm shaking. I'm seconds away from breaking an arm, a leg, my back, my neck, my –'

'Lovely.'

She stopped complaining long enough to smile at Dad.

'You're my lovely.'

I looked away as he leaned down to kiss her for the fourth time since they'd stepped onto the ice. I'd been out of the hospital and recovering at the lake house for a week, and whenever they weren't checking on me, serving me tea or bringing me yet another blanket, they were hugging, kissing or smiling at each other. Losing Justine had driven them apart, but losing Justine and *almost* losing me had apparently rekindled something between them I didn't recall ever having seen. It was nice . . . but I also wasn't sure how to feel about it now.

'I've got you,' Dad said, moving his hands to her waist. 'I won't let you go.'

'Vanessa,' Mom called over her shoulder, 'I'll scream as soon as I go down, but if for some reason the lifeguard doesn't hear me –'

'I'll send the emergency sled,' I said.

'You'll be okay, kiddo?' Dad asked. 'You'll yell if you need anything?'

I nodded, even though there was nothing I needed. Simon was already walking down the pier toward me.

I watched them move further onto the ice. Dad was steady, but Mom's ankles bent like noodles in her ice skates. I was glad the lifeguard had hung around even after the harbour had frozen over – he still sat in his stand overlooking the ice, though now he wore sweat-pants, a down jacket, gloves and a fuzzy hat instead of swimming trunks and a Winter Harbor Recreation T-shirt.

He wasn't the only one dressed for snow. There hadn't been a cloud in the sky in two weeks – since the day after I dived off Chione Cliffs – but temperatures still hadn't risen above four degrees. Simon's chemical bomb combined with the sirens' atmospheric manipulation had finally made Winter Harbor live up to its name – even in the height of summer. The air was slowly warming, but Simon said the ice probably wouldn't melt until early fall. So while residents and visitors in other towns lining the Maine coast continued swimming and boating, everyone in Winter Harbor had unpacked their cold-weather gear and taken to the ice.

I hadn't taken to the ice yet and didn't think I would, but it was nice sitting by it and watching people skate, play hockey and try – unsuccessfully – to ice-fish. And personally, I thought if the harbour never thawed, if the town stayed stuck in a perpetual state of winter, that that wasn't such a bad thing. There was no way whatever was frozen beneath the surface would still be alive when the ice finally melted, but I was still comforted every time I looked out at the water and saw a solid, impenetrable surface.

'I know you've been through a lot and don't want to freak you out,' Simon said, sitting next to me on the bench. 'But I think your mom is actually smiling.'

I laughed. 'Yet another example of the impossible suddenly becoming possible. She's taking the rest of the summer off from work, too.'

He held out a foil-wrapped sandwich and a paper cup. 'In honour of your first day out – eggs, sausage and cheese on a kaiser roll, and Harbor Homefries' newly famous hot chocolate. I thought it was still a little cold for a watermelon guava smoothie.'

'This is perfect,' I said, taking the breakfast. 'Thank you.'

We ate without talking for a few minutes. Unlike the

first time we'd eaten breakfast together that summer – in the Subaru, on our way to try to find Caleb – the silence wasn't uncomfortable. After being through so much together, being able to just sit quietly was a pleasant change.

'I was at the hospital this morning,' he said finally.

I nodded. He'd been visiting the victims every day and giving me updates when he stopped by the lake house for quick, chaperoned visits every night.

'The men are doing well. Still sleeping a ton, but the doctors said they've been communicating when they're awake.'

I looked at him. 'And they still haven't said anything about what happened . . . ?'

He shook his head. 'Apparently they don't remember. The doctors are blaming it on the crazy weather, just like they are with everyone else.'

I turned to the harbour. 'You'd think that explanation would fall a little short.'

'I think it's easier to blame the weather than it is to raise more questions they don't know how to answer.'

'And no one thinks it's strange that after weeks of non-stop rain and thunderstorms, the sky has cleared for good?'

'It ended as abruptly as it started. Scientists and meteorologists are chalking it up to an inexplicable natural fluke. Maybe once enough time has passed they'll dig a little deeper.'

'Like when Simon Carmichael, boy genius, brings it to their attention?' I smiled at him.

'I think I'm shelving the test tubes for now. I might even change my major – to theatre, or English, or some other non-science track – when I go back to Bates.'

I raised my eyebrows. I didn't buy that for a second.

'In any case,' he continued gently, 'they were extremely lucky – the doctors estimated that they were underwater less than two minutes before the harbour froze. They'll still need to be monitored for a while, but they're getting stronger every day.'

'That's good news.' I'd been stunned to learn that every man who had been lured all the way down to the circle of sirens had been found in the ice, not far below the surface. When Captain Monty started drilling, he'd actually found three of them before he found me. He'd said we were all found at different depths, but that our frozen smiles were identical.

I was the first one released from the hospital. The doctors and nurses called me their 'miracle patient', as even though we'd all endured the same physical challenges, my recovery was much faster. Even Simon couldn't explain it.

I could. But I hadn't yet.

'Paige is also hanging in there,' he said. 'She's still devastated from losing Jonathan and the baby, but she's improving.'

My stomach turned at the thought of Paige. We hadn't spoken since that night, so I didn't know how she was really doing. Simon said the doctors had done everything they could, but no medically trained doctor could have known that the only way to keep the baby alive was to infuse its tiny body with salt water. And by that point, the stresses on Paige's body had taken their toll; she was unconscious before Mom flew up to the emergency-room entrance, and, for better or worse, couldn't tell the doctors what to do.

'And Betty's doing okay?' I asked after a few minutes.

'She says she hasn't felt this physically strong in years. She hasn't left Paige's side, and Oliver's with her more than he's not.'

'I'm glad they have each other. Paige will need them.'

He nodded and looked at me. 'I still don't know how you did it.'

I focused on the steam rising from the hot chocolate.

'I mean, that you made it without a wet suit, or an oxygen tank . . . and the fact that you were even able to jump at all, after everything that happened and everything you knew.'

I held my breath and waited for him to make the connection, just like I always did whenever he'd brought it up during the past two weeks. Logically, scientifically, I shouldn't have survived. But either his emotions were clouding reason or my power over him was strong enough to keep him in the dark, because he hadn't put it together yet. And I was more relieved every day that he didn't.

'I had to jump,' I said, just like I always did. 'Fortunately, letting the tank fall on its own to the ocean floor was more effective than we'd thought. And Betty told you that she heard the water crystallising before the other sirens realised what was happening, and immediately started swimming toward the surface. We were lucky.'

I looked out to the harbour when he didn't say anything. I was so afraid of his knowing the truth I hadn't even prepared a response for when he finally did.

'How are you feeling today?' he asked softly.

'Great,' I said, my voice too bright. 'I'm out of the house, so that's a good thing, right?'

He waited for me to say something else.

'I get tired,' I offered. 'I sleep more than I'd like, my chest aches so much that I sometimes gasp for air, and I wake up with headaches. But every day's easier than the one before.'

He glanced at the harbour. Seeing Mom and Dad wobbling across the ice several yards away, he moved toward me on the bench.

My breath caught in my throat. This was the closest we'd been since we stood together at the fork in the trail leading up Chione Cliffs. My muscles ached to be even closer – I wanted to put my arms around him and kiss him and feel his body warm against mine. I'd been imagining how it would feel to be that close to him ever since I'd opened my eyes after waking up for the first time in the hospital. But I *couldn't* be that close. It wasn't right.

'Vanessa . . . I'm still here. I know things are strange right now, but I need you to know that I'm still here. And I want to be with you, whenever you're ready.'

I turned to him. 'Or never at all?'

He paused. 'If that's what you think is best, yes. But that's not what I want.'

I searched his face. It wasn't what I wanted. I wished I could pretend it was, but even suggesting it out loud was a struggle.

Surprisingly, finally jumping off the cliff and making it out alive hadn't instantly made me fearless. I was still pretending things weren't like they really were – probably more than I ever had. I hadn't brought up Charlotte Bleu with Dad yet, and I was pretending he was still my beloved Big Poppa, who could do no wrong. I was pretending that Mom was my real mother. I was pretending our family would be okay, even though we'd lost Justine. I was pretending that sitting on this bench with Simon was a perfectly acceptable thing to do, and eventually, when we were *really* alone together and not just alone together on a public bench with my parents a few yards away, I would pretend that that was acceptable, too. I was pretending I was still me. I was pretending I was still boring, ordinary Vanessa Sands instead of accepting who – and what – I really was.

Because after jumping off Chione Cliffs and facing my greatest fear, I was still scared. My body hadn't been the same since that night, and I was scared of what it now needed to function. I was scared of what Simon and I had done three weeks before, and what that might mean now.

Most of all, I was scared I'd lose him if he knew the truth.

I placed the cup of hot chocolate on the bench between us, reached into my coat pocket and pulled out a small packet of white powder.

'Vitamin supplement,' I said, pretending for a few minutes more as I watched the salt fall into the hot chocolate like rain on an iceless harbour. 'It helps me breathe.'